# THE
# DAR LUMBRE
# CHRONICLES

By Don Johnston

# COPYRIGHT

## THE DAR LUMBRE CHRONICLES

Copyright 2018 by Don Johnston

ISBN-10: 0692086161
ISBN-13: 978-0692086162

The Dar Lumbre Chronicles is science fiction laced with political satire.

## DEDICATION & SPECIAL THANKS

The Dar Lumbre Chronicles is dedicated to everyone who reads it, especially those who buy it rather than borrowing a copy from a friend. In addition, it is dedicated to my family-- whether they read it or not.

My special thanks to Janice Stewart for encouraging me to write this novel, and for her help in proofreading and editing.

Prologue

Oct. 21, 2086--A black sedan coasted to a stop in front of the Anaheim Lofts on La Palma Avenue. Four burly NatGov Special Agents dressed in black uniforms jumped out and charged through the front door of the building. Bypassing the elevator, they bolted upstairs to the second floor and stopped in front of Unit 6.

The lead agent, Lieutenant Garza, rang the doorbell, waited five seconds, and rang it again.

There was no answer.

After ringing the bell for a third time, Garza pulled a thumb-sized megaphone from his utility belt and spoke into it, "Attention, Dar Lumbre. Special Agents have your unit surrounded. Please open the door immediately."

Still, no answer.

Garza turned toward the agent at his right. "Sergeant Bly, open the door."

Bly stepped forward, took a sonic vibrator from his belt, and knelt down in front of the doorknob. He tapped at the screen of the hand-held device, gradually increasing the frequency until it duplicated the code programmed into the lock. The door clicked and swung open.

With his team at his heels, Garza stepped inside and shouted, "Dar Lumbre, we have a warrant for your arrest."

Silence.

Garza walked to the middle of the living-dining area, and by hand signals, instructed his assistants to check the bedroom, bathroom, and closet beside the entrance.

No one was in either of the rooms.

"He got away again," Garza said, as the team regrouped near the front door.

"I'm glad," Bly said, sighing.

"What do you mean?" Garza asked.

"Dar Lumbre is a great American."

"We're officers of the state. We have duties to perform."

Bly took off his badge and extended it toward Garza. "I can't do this anymore. I quit."

# Chapter 1

Oct. 21, 2135--Crane Hopkins left his office and stepped into the hallway of CellTech Limited. He joined the throng of white-clad scientists surging toward the exit at quitting time, but didn't make a serious attempt to slip into weekend mode. As he passed the side door of the cytogenetics lab, Annie Lee popped out and fell in step with him. Like everybody else, she wore white scrubs, but her yellow headband and matching iTab case set her apart from the crowd. Crane shortened his stride, but said nothing.

"What's wrong, Protein Man?" Annie said.

"DL-666."

"Talk to me."

"That culture is acting strange."

Annie's eyebrows shot up. "The lag phase again?"

Crane nodded in mute affirmation.

"My tests showed the final culture to be typical before we sent it to the Production Department," Annie said. "Obviously, it returned to normal during the logarithmic growth phase."

"I still don't like it, and my job description requires me to worry about every detail, big or small."

"Then, I'll worry with you."

Crane smiled faintly. "We have to find out what's going on and fix it."

They walked on in silence.

Crane's concern was personal, as well as professional. Richard Hunter, a relative-by-marriage, was waiting for a heart transplant. Seemingly, NatGov had put Richard's life on freeze-frame while their red tape machine generated a digital mountain of redundant data. Problems with the cardiac tissue culture, DL-666, could lead to additional delays, and Crane was determined not to let such a thing happen on his watch.

At the security exit, the sensor plate of the retina scanner gave a cricket-like chirp and noted their exit from the building. They stepped out onto the sidewalk near the intersection of Dryden and Main Street, the busiest location in the Houston Mediplex at this time of day.

The sidewalk was teeming with people, most wearing hospital scrubs in a rainbow of colors. The quitting-time crowd drifted toward nearby Metro stops as the crisp October air vibrated with Friday shift change noises--whirring traffic, shoes scuffing on pavement, murmuring voices, and sirens approaching from every direction. Buses crept along Main Street, weaving in and out of a writhing swarm of bicycles and ever-present robo-cabs shaped like giant jellybeans.

Every time Crane saw this motorized melee, he was glad he no longer owned a vehicle of any kind. He'd sold his car a few months ago when the Houston Traffic Act of 2135 banned the driving of personal automobiles inside Loop 610 except on weekends, which by CityGov definition, began at six o'clock on Friday evening. He lived within walking distance of the Mediplex, but usually rode the Metro, as did Annie. Most people in their age group—the late twenties— no longer felt like they needed to own a personal car while living in a large city.

They stopped at the curb momentarily before sprinting through the traffic to the other side of the street.

Crane made an attempt to switch off his work-mode mindset, but couldn't do it. He had curatorial responsibility for DL-666, CellTech's flagship product, and it was always on his mind. If the tissue culture died off, or became unusable for any reason, NatGov would descend on CellTech like the proverbial *Locusta migratoria* swarm. A lot of people's jobs would be in jeopardy.

In the worst-case scenario, the Office of Financial Stability would take over the operation of CellTech and replace the Technical Director and other management personnel with a bevy of NatGov-appointed operatives. The distribution of funds, including the Human Resources budget, would be controlled by complex formulas that made little sense to anyone outside of the Washington beltway. Crane had always suspected that the OFS management system consisted of partisan politics, nepotism, paybacks, bribes, and other under-the-table scams.

He realized that he might be on the verge of finding out if his worst suspicions were true.

The thought sent a chill down his spine.

6

In addition to the obvious medical importance of DL-666, the product had political ramifications as well. Within the last two years, three Mid-Eastern heads of state had received life-saving transplants with CellTech's artificial organs. Crane had witnessed all three operations. The foreign dignitaries arrived at the Mediplex in Cryo-Units, dead by all appearances. But appearances were deceiving, and like Lazarus, the three rulers returned from the dead, called forth by the gods of medicine. Achmed come forth. Abdul come forth. Mohammed come forth.

Crane realized that no one would have much of an argument if NatGov declared CellTech to be an essential business which couldn't be allowed to fail.

To make matters worse, The Office of Financial Stability had reported a significant dip in the economy over the last quarter, and every economist was predicting worse numbers for the future. Republican operatives in the media were trying to turn the economy into a dead albatross to hang around the Democrats' neck, and some had revived the well-worn slogan, *It's the Economy, Stupid.* News banners scrolled across every public screen in sight, including the one atop the Metro stand that Crane and Annie were approaching. The headlines were glum:

RECESSION OR DEPRESSION?
BUDGET DEFICIT REACHES 500 TRILLION
PRESIDENT KEYNES PROPOSES A STIMULUS

Annie jabbed an elbow into Crane's ribs. "Don't read that nonsense. It'll cause you to come down with clinical depression."

"I'm just trying to stay actively engaged in the political process," Crane said, fearing the dire predictions might come true this time. Bipartisan reports suggested as much.

At first, only Republican-funded news organizations reported the economic downturn, the expected approach with a Democrat currently in the White House. But earlier in the week, several Democrat news outlets joined the fray. Even their standard bearer, *The NYT in the Cloud*, acknowledged the possibility that financial trouble might be imminent, although they blamed the previous president for the current problems.

"Hey, let it go," Annie said, as they reached the Metro stop. "Enjoy the weekend. Live a little."

Crane knew he owed it to his lab assistant and friend to talk about something other than work all the time and decided to make a valid effort to do so.

"Are you and Brad doing anything special this weekend?" he asked.

"We're going to Brazos Bend State Park tomorrow night to do some stargazing."

"How'd you get Brad interested in astronomy?"

"It wasn't anything I did," Annie said, with a shrug. "He got hooked by some nut job calling himself the Zodiac Prophet. The video went viral. Did you see it?"

"I saw the posting, but didn't play it. It looked like a waste of time."

"It was bizarre. The guy was wearing a disguise and claiming that a world-shaking event will occur next year on September 22, 2136, when a planetary conjunction forms near the constellation Serpens."

"September 22 is my birthday," Crane said, "so I'll be watching the skies." He was surprised that Brad had given a second thought to such an idea. It wasn't like his lifelong friend to be taken in by hucksterism.

"I told Brad that the serpent is a rather dim constellation," Annie said. "If he's disappointed with it, we can watch the last dregs of the Leonids, even though they're not up to par this year."

"Have you joined a stargazing club yet?"

Annie nodded vigorously. "Affirmative. We joined the Fort Bend Astronomy Club that meets in Brazos Bend State Park. It's fantastic. Houston annexed 5000 acres in the area, and the park boasts all city services, as well as plenty of open sky. I got caught up in this thing. Now it's my favorite hobby."

"I thought your hobby was classic movies."

"Can't a person have more than one hobby?" Annie asked. "You could use one yourself."

"I'm a biohacker. I have butterfly eggs and larva in my fridge at home--you know that."

Annie shook her head. "That's too much like your work. You need something completely different for a hobby."

"I read science fiction--the oldies written on real paper."

Annie cast a sideways glance at Crane. "I thought you just collected them."

"I read them."

"Still too much like your work."

Crane guided the conversation back to the subject of astronomy. "What about Brad? Is he into constellations, sky maps, that sort of thing?"

"Not too much," Annie said, "but he's willing to listen while I blather on about it. Come with us tomorrow? You'd like it. The serpent won't be much to see, and the meteor shower is fizzling out, but we'd still have fun."

"I don't want to come between my two best friends, especially when they're sharing a blanket on the ground."

"You sound like a prude," Annie said, rolling her eyes.

Crane shrugged, but didn't reply.

"Anyway, Brad and I are just friends. We'd enjoy your company."

"I don't have time to watch a meteor shower," Crane said. "Tomorrow is Dad's fiftieth birthday, and Mom is giving him a party. She'll decorate the condo and cook a big meal. Larry and Kim will be there."

Annie cringed in mock horror. "Uh-oh. The big family get-together again. Didn't you and Larry have a shouting match at your last family celebration?"

Crane shrugged. "It was my fault. Larry said he was thinking about changing his registration to the Democratic Party, and I opposed the idea."

"You let politics spoil the family's time together?"

"We're dyed-in-the-wool Republicans," Crane said. "My great grandfather was a cabinet member during Donald Trump's administration."

"Remember, I'm a Democrat."

"I knew it before I met you."

Annie scowled in fake anger. "That's ridiculous."

"Not really. I knew you were from Marin County and

9

graduated from UC Berkeley. I didn't have to be a mentalist to figure out that you were a Democrat."

Annie waved a hand in a dismissive gesture. "How'd we start talking about me? You were telling me about Larry's wavering political views?"

"Not just his political views. My brother is gullible about a lot of things."

"What things?"

"Any new idea—political...social...religious..."

"What about Kim?" Annie asked, arching her eyebrows. "Is she okay with his beliefs?"

Crane nodded. "Yeah, I guess. Actually, he settled down a lot when they got married."

"Why didn't Larry finish college? He seems plenty smart to me."

"He is. He carries a Mensa card to prove it."

"So do I. Don't you have one?"

"I never felt the need to prove anything by flashing a card. You don't either."

"I got mine when I was twelve," Annie said, as they took their place at the end of the line waiting for the Metro. "Maybe it's time to shred it."

"Probably."

"I know you love your brother. If you didn't, you wouldn't get so frustrated with him."

"We're incredibly different," Crane said, shaking his head. "Other than our parents, the only thing we have in common is that we both use Starbucks as an office."

"And you're both tall and skinny."

Crane nodded. "Yeah...that, too."

"It's a good thing NatGov declared Starbucks to be an essential business which can't be allowed to fail," Annie said. "That might help you and Larry keep your sibling connection intact."

The Bissonnet Metro approached. Annie moved closer to the curb along with a dozen other people jostling for position. Crane stood beside her to block out an eager Johnny-come-lately who edged toward the front of the line. As the crowd converged on the passenger loading area, Crane widened his stance and stuck out his pointy elbows.

"Whatever happened to queues?" he asked.

"They became obsolete when the sun set on the British Empire."

"Apparently."

"I'll see you on Monday," Annie said, "unless you decide to stargaze with us tomorrow night."

"I won't."

Crane's *to-do* list was already set and not subject to change. DNA was at the top, the birthday dinner was next, and stargazing wasn't on it.

Annie hopped on the bus, and Crane waved. He loved her high voltage enthusiasm. She had popped into his life a year ago as a transferee from CellTech's satellite lab in San Francisco. At their first meeting, she was sipping a bottle of Rojo Monster, the latest energy drink from Hi-Caff Beverages and looking like she stepped out of an Anime Manga game. In fact, her real name was *Anime*, but she preferred to be called *Annie*. Crane's life changed with her arrival. He was a semi-loner in the CellTech family; however, he and Annie shared the same wavelength from the outset. Time and again she set up the computer to process tests that he was merely thinking about running. She was his best lab assistant ever, and had become a good friend, as well.

A short time after Annie moved to Houston, Crane introduced her to Brad, and the trio hit the Saturday day-trip circuit. After a couple of months of seeing the sights together, Crane began to suspect that he was in the way of a budding romance and eased himself out of the triangle with a series of phony excuses. Six months later, Annie continued to invite him to go out with them, and he continued to decline. He concluded that his *boy-meet-girl* introductions always worked out better for those being introduced than they did for him. Most likely a corollary to one of Murphy's Laws, he surmised. Still, he was happy for Annie and Brad, and for Larry and Kim as well. Maybe he was destined to be the Lone Ranger, after all.

The Kirby Street Metro swung into the loading area and Crane stepped on, ducking to keep from bumping his head. It seemed that each successive model of the self-driving bus was slightly smaller than the previous model.

The bus was packed, as usual. A teenage girl dressed in Goth style and sporting spiked green hair scooted over to make room for him. Crane declined the seat because it faced backwards, a position that triggered his motion sickness instantly. He grasped the overhead handrail as the bus pulled away from the curb and eased into the traffic.

Crane looked back toward the Mediplex. Evening shadows swallowed the Methodist Hospital, but CellTech's glass block monolith glistened in the last rays of sunlight. The company's logo stood out in bold relief on the western face of the building. He remembered the first time he noticed it more than fifteen years ago. At the time, he thought it was a regular caduceus, but several years later, he realized that the winged staff was wound with strands of DNA, rather than snakes. The logo impressed him as a teenager. He still thought it was ingenious.

The bus lurched. Crane sucked in a deep breath and let it out slowly, attempting to shake off the uncertainty of things scientific, political, and personal.

His attempt failed.

## Chapter 2

"I don't like this," Kim Hopkins said, casting a disgruntled look toward her husband as they walked along the bustling sidewalk. "I totally hate filling out forms."

Larry sighed in frustration. He hoped Kim wasn't going to back out again. She would be twenty-seven next month, and still hadn't registered her political preference with NatGov. Her naiveté in the field of sociopolitical machinations defied logic. He had cajoled her with every trick he could think up, even promising her that she could get a pet, a weak-moment concession he already regretted.

"You need to register," he said. "For one thing, it'll help your dad move up on NatGov's surgery waiting list. There're other benefits, as well. We've discussed this a hundred times."

"The office will be closed before we get there."

"No, it won't. It's only five o'clock, and they stay open until six on Fridays. We have plenty of time. In fact, we've got enough time for a quick stop at Starbucks."

Kim ignored Larry's Starbucks invitation and continued her protest. "I still don't like it."

"What would you do if something happened to me?" Larry asked. "Housing and Urban Development would move you out of the city and treat you like an Outsider."

"What about my CityGov registration? Wouldn't that count with HUD?"

"It wouldn't count much. You'd be about like a foreigner with a green card."

Kim grimaced. "You're trying to scare me."

"No," Larry said. "I'm just trying to explain how NatGov operates. Republicans and Democrats take turns holding office. Right now, both are saying they'll cut back on Entitlement Points after the presidential election, so we need to grab as many points as we can right now."

"I'm not sure which party to choose."

"I've told you it doesn't make any difference," Larry said. "You'll get an E-Point bonus just for registering." He was registered as a Republican, but considered it to be temporary because he was third party at heart.

As the law currently stood, third parties were prohibited, but independent candidates could qualify as a write-in on either party's ballot--a law designed, as everybody knew, to make it impossible for anyone to get elected without vowing allegiance to one of the two approved parties. Still, Larry clung to the hope that the third-party prohibition would be overturned, even though ideologues in both parties marched in lock step to oppose any change which would alter the status quo. A suit challenging the two-party system was stalled in the lower courts, and the politicos in both parties were doing the *paso doble* with the appeals process. So far, they'd managed to keep the case from going to the Supreme Court.

Larry pointed to a Starbucks on the opposite side of the street. "My office away from home," he said, grabbing Kim by the hand and pulling her toward the curb. "Let's get a latte."

"Look!" Kim said, her voice rising. "There's a pet store next to Starbucks. Can we stop there?"

Larry sighed. "We'll look at pets after you register."

"You promised me a dog," Kim said petulantly. "Remember?"

Larry sighed again. "I remember."

"I want a Golden Retriever."

"Retrievers are too big for our mini-condo," Larry said. "HUD wouldn't allow it. You'll need to get a smaller dog--or a cat."

"What about a Shih Tzu?"

"I can't stand that breed," Larry said. "Mom had one while we were growing up. It was a pest...and incredibly dumb. It fell into the swimming pool and drowned."

"Did she get another dog?"

Larry nodded. "A Jack Russell Terrier?"

"A Jack Russell? They're such cute little dogs," Kim said. "That's what I want."

They cut across West Gray Street in front of the River Oaks Theater, an ancient Houston landmark protected by the Historical Society. A line of robo-cabs disgorged passengers in front of the theater, and the bicycle rack was maxed out. A steady stream of patrons filed into the entrance.

The art deco structure was showing its age, but was one of the few venues remaining that still featured classic movies. The marque indicated that *African Queen* was playing now. After more than a hundred years in the archives, the oldies had sprung to life again. Some of the long-deceased actors were more popular than ever, even out-drawing many of the current Hollywood idols.

Kim pointed at the faded poster of Humphrey Bogart and Katharine Hepburn. "Look," she said. "My friend at work thinks that's the best movie ever made. She's seen it four or five times. Could we come to see it on my day off next week?"

Larry was noncommittal. "TCM spoiled those old movies when they converted them to 3D."

Moments later, they entered the Starbucks and the tantalizing aroma of fresh-roasted coffee greeted them. They picked their way through the tables, over half of which were occupied, and approached the counter.

"Hey, Larry," the late-twenties barista said, casting a sidelong glance at Kim.

"Jim, meet my wife," Larry said, motioning in Kim's direction.

After the introduction, they ordered tall lattes and Larry touched his right thumb to the mini-screen atop the cash register. The screen blinked green, indicating acceptance of Larry's payment. They moved to the end of the bar and watched Jim prepare the drinks the old-fashioned barista way, a nice personal touch no robot server could match.

"Are you taking Kim to register?" Jim asked.

"Yeah, finally."

Thirty seconds later, Jim placed two steaming lattes on the counter and looked at Kim. "Do you really believe that solar flare back in the eighties erased all of NatGov's census data?" he asked abruptly.

Kim shrugged. "I don't have a clue."

Before Jim could reply, Larry said, "I've told you a million times that cyberterrorists did it using electromagnetic pulse strikes. It was probably Iran or North Korea. They'd tried to pull this off for several years, and finally succeeded. Nothing else makes sense."

"I think NatGov erased everything right after the solar flare," Jim said. "The flare provided the cover needed to erase everything they wanted to. That was their way of declaring bankruptcy--just wipe out everybody's records and start over. They saved a lot of entitlement money over the last fifty years."

Larry shook his head. "That doesn't make a bit of sense, Jim. Think of all the tax revenues NatGov missed during that time. Besides, they're constantly urging people to re-register, and have been ever since I can remember. Anybody who wants back in the system can get in immediately."

The two friends engaged in political banter every time Larry came into the coffee shop, which was nearly every day. The exercise might seem flippant to those within earshot, but it was based on their shared belief that NatGov had shredded the constitution. Solar flares, cyberterrorists, and NatGov conspiracies were their favorite topics.

Jim claimed to be a registered Democrat, but he was such a conspiracy theorist that Larry didn't believe either party would put up with him. And, even though he denied it, Larry shared many of Jim's off-the-wall political views, particularly those related to the Outsiders. He believed the country was on the verge of a quantum shift in the political arena. The status quo was no longer sustainable. Harbingers of change were in the air.

"NatGov collects a lot of taxes from Outsiders," Jim said. "Sales taxes on goods and services bought inside the city limits, VAT taxes, and the like."

"Not big taxes like income tax and social security," Larry said. "The government has to know who you are and where you live in order to tax you. That's why so many people stayed off the grid when they had the chance. The way they saw it, the loss of their census data and tax records gave them the opportunity to escape NatGov's clutches."

"You sound just like an Outsider."

"I could be one," Larry said, "except the big conglomerates can't buy my software programs unless I'm registered. That's the deal they have with NatGov, and there's no way to circumvent the system."

Jim wiped the bar with a damp cloth until it glistened. "Whatever the case, change is in the air. Dozens of customers come in here every day on their way to the NatGov annex down the street. I hear them talking. They're all going to register."

Larry was incredulous. "How many?"

Jim nodded. "At least two dozen a day—sometimes more."

"Are they total Outsiders? Or people already on CityGov rolls like Kim?"

"Mostly people living in the city," Jim said. "I don't think many Outsiders are registering right now, but I hear rumors that a big surge is expected in the near future." He moved back toward the center of the serving bar as three giggling teenage girls approached.

With coffee in hand, Larry and Kim left the Starbucks. Five minutes later, they crossed Shepherd Street and entered the NatGov office, a drab brown cube that looked completely out of place among the eclectic shops of the River Oaks area.

Government offices seemed to be ubiquitous. Shortly after the solar flare, NatGov had constructed annex buildings in virtually every neighborhood of most major cities. Politicians considered the abundance of the government facilities to be a big help to city residents, even though public opinion polls showed exactly the opposite.

Once inside, they located the building directory on the wall between the escalator and restrooms. A sign near the restrooms read: *Handicapped Restroom Upstairs— Please Take Escalator*. Larry eyed the sign with disdain, but didn't say anything, although it reminded him why he took an anti-NatGov stance on so many things.

They went to the directory and studied the floor plan of the building. Larry glanced at Kim. Her lips moved slightly as she read from the list of offices.

"Second floor," Larry said, motioning toward the moving staircase.

"I still wish we could do this online. This kind of thing makes me nervous. It's worse than going to the dentist."

Larry sighed again, but didn't reply.

He couldn't understand why Kim was so hard to convince. He'd told her numerous times why the process couldn't be completed online. National Security Agency rules prohibited the transmission of brainwave patterns on the internet for fear that terrorists might intercept them and use them to construct cephalotrophic drones. In this instance, he thought the NSA ruling made sense. DARPA was working on cephalotrophic weapons right now, so it was reasonable to assume that Islamic terrorists were doing the same thing in Iraq, or in the no-man's land between Afghanistan and Pakistan.

They found the NatGov registration office and went inside.

"You have to get a number over there," Larry said, pointing toward a group of wall-mounted monitors.

They went to the nearest screen, and after surveying the menu, Kim touched *Register To Vote*. A ticket popped out of a slot below the screen. She retrieved the ticket and showed it to Larry.

"Number 138," he said. "This may take a while."

"I wonder how many are ahead of me?" Kim said, as they moved toward the benches.

"Now serving Number 118 at Window 10," a digital voice announced, as if responding to Kim's query.

"Looks like we'll have to wait at least fifteen minutes," Larry said. "Let's sit down."

They looked around. There was no place to sit. The pew-style benches were packed with young adults, many wearing threadbare designer jeans and baggy sweatshirts like Larry and Kim wore. Everybody looked alike at first glance, but not after closer observation. Kim stood out with her auburn ponytail, and Larry was the tallest person in the room. Larry loved the differences. Fitting in was fine, but he didn't want to be a clone, or worse yet, a lemming going over the cliff because everybody else did. Sometimes it was necessary to change courses.

Numbers 119 and 120 were called; two people stood. Larry and Kim sat down in the vacated spaces and tried to get comfortable on the hard benches.

The number-calling process dragged on.

Twenty minutes later, with the time nearing six o'clock, the computer voice announced, "Now serving Number 138 at Window 12."

Larry and Kim jumped up and went to the window. Kim handed her ticket to the middle aged woman behind the counter.

"Name, please," the clerk intoned.

"Kim Hopkins."

"Identification, please."

Kim called up her CityGov documentation on her iTab and held it across the counter. The clerk read the screen with a hand-held scanner. A warning buzzed.

"Your identification says Kim Hunter," the clerk said.

"Hunter is my maiden name," Kim said. "This is my husband, Larry Hopkins. We've been married a year." She looked toward Larry and he edged closer.

The clerk tapped at the monitor in front of her. "Your marriage documents don't seem to be in the system. Did you record them?"

Kim cast a questioning glance toward Larry.

"Of course I did," he said, his voice rising. "Try again."

The clerk touched the monitor again and stared at it a few seconds. "Your marriage record is not coming up."

"This is nonsense," Larry said. "I'd like to speak to your supervisor."

"No need for that, Sir," the clerk snapped. "We'll try another way. What is your address, please?"

Larry recited the address of the West Gray Condos where he and Kim had lived since marrying. The clerk entered it and looked up at Larry. "May I have your identification, please?"

"What do you need my ID for? She's registering--not me."

"ID, please."

Not trying to hide his resentment, Larry held his iTab toward the clerk for scanning.

"This shows you live on Kirby Street," the clerk said.

"We moved to West Gray after we got married," Larry said. "The address change is registered with HUD. Can't you look it up?"

---

19

The clerk went through the screen-tapping process again and said, "I found the HUD registration."

"Okay," Larry said. "Do you have everything you need now?"

The clerk studied the screen intently. "I can't pull up your wife's address change. You need to get all of your records in order, then come back."

Larry leaned over the counter. "Call your supervisor."

"It's nearly six o'clock."

Larry glared at the woman. "We're not leaving until we speak to your supervisor."

"Are you threatening a government employee, Sir?"

"No, but I'm asking to speak with someone who has more authority than you have. We demand our rights. Please, call someone now. Otherwise, call the police and have me arrested."

Kim tugged at Larry's elbow and whispered, "Calm down."

To Larry's surprise, the clerk turned and motioned to a woman seated at a desk near the back of the office. The woman, a near-clone of the clerk at the window, got up and came forward. The clerk turned around and the two women spoke briefly.

"Mr. Hopkins, I am a Registration Supervisor," the woman said. "I apologize for the inconvenience. You have provided sufficient information for us to register Mrs. Hopkins, but your information is not in proper order. That being the case, the only thing we can do is issue her a Provisional Registration."

"What does that mean?" Larry asked.

"It's a temporary document pending full registration status," the supervisor said.

"How long will it be before she is completely registered?" Larry asked.

"Thirty to sixty days."

"What about E-Points?"

"She won't get those until full registration status is granted."

Larry grimaced. "She needs the points now. Is there any way to speed up the process?"

"Not unless you can correct your records in less than sixty days," the supervisor said with an air of finality. "That's how long it will take us, and I doubt you could do it any quicker."

Kim tugged at Larry's arm again and said, "Let's take the provisional registration and leave."

Larry let out a long sigh. "Go ahead with the provisional registration."

Ten minutes later, after completing the process, Larry and Kim left the NatGov building. Finally, Kim was in the system—or would be in sixty days. Larry had been trying to get her to register for months, but she kept putting it off with one excuse after another. After her father's sudden heart attack, he'd convinced her that belonging to one of the approved political parties would increase her NatGov benefits. He believed the E-Point bonus would be of help to Kim's father, but now they were on hold. The whole process seemed to be a game of charades the *politicos* had worked out to the *nth* degree.

Kim stopped in her tracks and grabbed Larry by the shoulder. "Look at that!" she said, pointing toward a huge news screen atop a roof adjacent to the NatGov office. The screen blinked the headline, again and again:

PREPARE FOR DAR LUMBRE'S RETURN

They stared at the headline as a small crowd gathered. Everyone stopped talking at the same time and stood transfixed before the news screen, eyes filled with wonder and jaws agape.

Kim broke the silence. "Many people believe that he'll come back. You believe it too, don't you?"

Larry gazed at the repeating headline. "Sort of."

More than fifty years earlier, the legendary scientist, Dr. Dar Lumbre, had performed miraculous healings by using genetic procedures banned by the government. After several years, his medical legerdemain began to morph into political power among average citizens. NatGov, fearing that the popular doctor  had the force of personality to create a nexus between science, religion, and  politics, drew up a list

21

of charges against him and swore out a warrant for his arrest. But, the warrant was never served, even though several attempts were made. While NatGov was fine tuning their trumped-up charges, a solar flare erased massive amounts of government data. In the midst of the chaos and confusion following the flare, Dar Lumbre disappeared like a will-o'-the-wisp, and hadn't been seen in fifty years.

Questions abounded. Did NatGov assassinate him? Did he change his identity and go into hiding? Did he ascend? Whatever the case, his most devout followers never lost hope that he would appear again.

Kim squeezed Larry's hand and asked, "What are you thinking about?"

"Something that happened last week--a hot mike incident that could be a harbinger of things to come."

"Tell me about it."

"An organization called the *Dar Lumbre Society* just opened an office in California. While I was working on my computer program, I picked up some of their conversations--very revealing private conversations about the society's plans."

"What does the society plan to do?"

Larry pointed toward the blinking headline. "They're preparing the world for the return of Dar Lumbre."

## Chapter 3

"Matilda visits every Monday--just stays until noon, period," Annie said, as she turned toward Brad.

Brad sat upright on the blanket. "What are you babbling about?"

Annie laughed softly. "It's a mnemonic device. The first letters of each word are the initials of the planets, Mercury, Venus, Earth, Mars, Jupiter...and so forth."

"You're nearly too smart."

It was eight o'clock Friday evening, and after moving their stargazing date ahead twenty-four hours, they were reclining on a blanket near the George Observatory. Brazos Bend State Park, home of the observatory, was a gathering place for astronomers and others who enjoyed nature. The night was clear and crisp, a perfect October evening, much appreciated after a smoldering hot summer on the Texas Gulf Coast. Having lived in California all her life, Annie still hadn't adjusted to the weather, but she loved everything else about the area. She was slowly morphing into a Texan.

Nearby, stargazers and other assorted outdoor adventurers milled to and fro throughout the park as they began to prepare for a celestial display. Some lay blankets on the ground, while others set up folding chairs. Serious stargazers began to probe the night sky with binoculars, telescopes, and cameras. Other groups laughed and talked constantly without ever looking up at the sky.

Above, in the canopy of space, stars and planets spread out like flawless diamonds displayed on black velvet. Several well-known constellations were visible, and the crescent moon was setting. The evening was perfect for stargazing, and the Friday night crowd was getting in the mood.

While gazing at the starry sky, Annie pondered her relationship with Crane and Brad, the two most important men in her life—almost the only two men, since her father died two years ago in a space station accident. When she arrived in Houston and started hanging out with Crane and Brad, she dubbed them *The Three Musketeers.* The bond between them seemed unbreakable, and she was surprised when Crane dropped out, apparently to leave space for her and Brad to develop a romance, if they wanted to. But, it hadn't happened. Their relationship remained platonic, even though her women friends, whom she referred to as her *double X amigas*, thought she was already playing house with Brad. He was a brown-eyed handsome man, like the old songs extolled, and a successful financial analyst, as well. What more could a woman want?

Brad, still sitting Native American style on the blanket, interrupted Annie's introspection, "I'm ready for an astronomy lesson. Show me Serpens...the serpent."

Annie studied the sky. "This isn't going to be easy. Maybe we should identify some brighter stars."

"But, I came to see the serpent."

"Okay," Annie said. "I'll try. Do you see that fairly bright red star about to set in the west?"

After a moment of searching, Brad said, "Yes, I see it."

"That's Antares in the scorpion constellation. Now, if you'll look slightly to the east, you'll see a line of pale stars— seven or eight of them making a right angle. That's Serpens."

A moment of silence passed. "I don't think I see the stars you're talking about," Brad said, "but, I see an irregular circle of stars in that area."

"That's Ophiuchus," Annie said, suppressing a chuckle.

"Ophi...what?"

"I'll say it slowly. It's *Off-e-YOU-kis*, the Serpent Keeper."

They both laughed, and Brad said, "Okay, you're right. The serpent is a dud, and so's his keeper. Tell me about some of the bright stars."

Annie pointed straight up. "That star is Steve Jobs."

Brad lay down and adjusted his binoculars. "Which one?"

"The bright one nearly straight overhead."

"I see a constellation shaped like a cross," he said. "Is it in that group?"

"Not exactly, but you're looking close to the right direction," Annie said. "That's the Northern Cross."

"The Northern Cross?"

"Yes, but that's not what I'm trying to show you. I want you to see that triangle of bright stars that sort of overlays the cross."

"Start over."

Annie sat up and reached for the thermos of hot chocolate. After pouring the steaming liquid into cups and handing one of them to Brad, she continued, "I think you lost your chain of thought. Look overhead. Do you see that triangle of stars around the cross?"

"I see it."

"That's the Great Summer Triangle," Annie said. "The star at the northwest corner of the triangle--the brightest of the three--is Steve Jobs. The other two will have new names in the near future."

"You've been studying a lot."

She tugged at the edge of the blanket to free it up. "I was busy looking up info while waiting for you to pick me up," she said, as she covered her legs.

"Why is that star called Steve Jobs? He's been dead for well over a century."

"NatGov did it," Annie explained. "They strong-armed the International Astronomical Union into changing the names of the three stars in the triangle. The old names were Deneb, Vega, and Altair. The IAU agreed to accept new names in order to get a financial bailout. The star that is now called Steve Jobs was originally named Vega."

"What about the other two stars in the triangle?" Brad asked. "Your star-naming story isn't finished, is it?"

"Not quite," Annie said. "Congress will come up with two new names shortly. One of them will be Marilyn Monroe—that's already been settled. There's a big argument about the final name. The candidates are James Dean and Elvis Presley."

Brad scoffed. "How can congress be concerned with something like this when there's a financial crisis unfolding?"

"You're the financial analyst--you tell me."

"Speaking of star names," Brad said, "somebody's been trying to scam me. As soon as I joined this club, I started getting texts from several star-naming companies.

---

25

They claim I can name one after myself for a fee."

"I got those texts, too," Annie said. "The names listed in these so-called star registries aren't recognized by the IAU, so they're totally bogus. I block every number that sends me garbage like that."

"I won't be sending them any money—that's for sure. Now, I have another question."

"What?"

"Where are the meteors?"

As if answering Brad's query, a meteor blazed across the sky, leaving a yellowish green streak in its wake.

"Make a wish," someone shouted.

Other observers voiced a spontaneous approval of *oohs* and *ahhs.* The stargazers fell silent in anticipation of another fireworks display, but the Leonids were reluctant. Five minutes after the opening salvo, two more small orange specs eked out a split-second appearance. Then, toward the east, a streak of light zipped upward from the horizon, announcing a rocket ship's departure from NASA on its way to the space station. It reminded Annie of her father.

After that, nothing for a long time.

"The show's supposed to be better after midnight," Annie said.

"Do you want to stay that long?" Brad asked. "It's up to you."

"Probably not."

With few meteors to hold her attention, Annie's thoughts drifted back to DL-666 and Crane's long face as they left work. Her cheerleading effort had been primarily for his benefit. She was the cheerleader for the team, the unofficial standard bearer for team morale, and considered it to be a part of her job description, even when she was worried too.

When she and Crane met, they'd bonded instantly. The idiosyncratic scientist was not nearly as handsome as Brad, and had some characteristics that women generally didn't seek in a man—he was a nerd, a worrier, a workaholic, and somewhat of a loner. In addition, he seemed haunted by memories of a past romance gone bad, although he'd never mentioned anything like that to her.

So much for negatives.

On the positive side, he was kind and easy-going. Also, brilliant--a quality Annie admired highly. Her IQ was over 150, in the same range as Crane's, she surmised. That was one factor that made them mesh together into such a formidable force. Maybe they weren't quite soul mates, but they were teammates with strong chemistry. Clearly, the captain of the team was worried, a fact that made her responsibility clear. Cheerleading wouldn't get the job done anymore. She had to step onto the court as a playmaker and bring her *A Game*. Nothing less would do.

The meager display of Leonids lost its appeal.

Time to go.

Chapter 4

On Saturday evening, Crane got off the Metro at the last station on the Sugar Land Loop. The bus stop was two blocks from the Brazos River Condos, a trendy high-rise where his parents had lived for fifteen years. Crane held fond memories of his years living in the condo. He and Larry had explored every inch of the Brazos River bank for more than five miles in each direction. The east side of the river was in the City of Houston, while the settlements on the west bank were in Outsider territory. Like many other small towns, Richmond-Rosenberg, had been unable to reproduce their census records after the solar flare, and were still unincorporated. A few parks and historic locations in the area were maintained by NatGov, but little else.

While living the life of teenage adventurers, Crane and his brother had crossed the Brazos River bridge frequently to go into the region west of the river. On most forays into the area, they observed a steady flow of traffic on the bridge, and eventually realized that Outsiders were ordinary people content to live without NatGov services in order to avoid the choking red tape which came with those services.

During this time, they also learned that NatGov maintained tight surveillance on Outsider areas, regardless of official statements to the contrary. One cool fall day, when Crane and Larry were in their mid-teens, they observed a trio of stealth drones prowling the skies high above Richmond-Rosenberg. The two brothers were taking in the Fort Bend County Fair, and for some inexplicable reason, they both looked up simultaneously. Three CIA drones were circling high over the crowded fairgrounds like a trio of vultures. Apparently, an unusual weather phenomenon had interfered with the stealth apparatus, thereby allowing the drones to become visible for a few seconds. When news organizations began to investigate the sightings, NatGov put out a video describing them as Amazon drones delivering pizza. A congressional investigation into the matter eventually died a natural death when the CIA Director and his top aides caught a severe case of *I don't recall syndrome*.

28

Crane took the public escalator up to the crosswalk arching across two ground level streets and connecting to the entrance of the Brazos River Condos. Crane admired the artistic flair of the crossover, which was originally designed to withstand flooding of the Brazos River, even though the PubWorks Administration had already built a series of water-level control dams several miles upstream.

The Brazos River Condos were housed in a rectangular tiered tower designed by two Iraqi architects participating in an engineering exchange program near the end of Gulf War Four. The project raised eyebrows, and some public demonstrations as well. The citizens of Texas objected to building a Tower of Babel in the Houston area; Texans understood Washington on the Brazos, but not Babylon on the Brazos. The rancor passed quickly, and now the building was one of the most famous landmarks in the area, as well as a highly desirable place to live. Hundreds of people filed HUD applications every month to get on the waiting list for one of the condos, and the wait was several years long.

He took the elevator to the sixth floor and touched the doorbell of his parents' unit. Betty Hopkins opened the door, with Andrew Hopkins close behind her. Crane entered and handed an archaic paper card to his father.

"Happy birthday, Dad," he said, as they exchanged hugs.

"Kim had to check on her dad," Betty said, "so they're going to be a little late."

"How do you like the fancy decorations?" Andrew asked, with a wave of his hand.

Crane looked around the room. A large black balloon hung near the ceiling in the living area. The words, *Fifty-- Over the Hill*, were written around its equator. A dozen small balloons circled around the black balloon in a slow-moving orbit, changing colors as they circled. Multicolored streamers decorated each end of the sofa and the cocktail table was covered with a red tablecloth with the words, *Happy Birthday*, emblazoned across it in flashing green letters.

"Mom must have bought out Party Town."

"Kim helped Betty pick out this stuff," Andrew said.

29

"Sit down and Dad will pour you a glass of wine," Betty said.

"What kind would you like?" Andrew asked. He motioned toward the sofa to indicate where they should sit.

"Maybe a French Chardonnay, if you have one," Crane said, taking the seat indicated. He didn't consider himself to be a wine expert, but knew that the finest French wines were no more expensive than American wines since NatGov had acquired stock in some of France's vineyards. The French were chagrined at having to take a financial bailout, but the outcome was good for both countries. Continued operation of France's best vineyards was assured, and excellent French wines were available in the United States at a modest price.

Andrew opened the refrigerator and stared inside for a moment. "We have Chardonnay and Pinot Grigio in here, and I think there's a bottle of Malbec in the pantry."

"Chardonnay."

"I'll have one myself. Would you like a glass, Betty?"

"I'll wait until dinner," Betty said, "and you need to stay out of my way. I don't want to run into you with a hot bowl."

Andrew moved to the opposite end of the counter where Betty was putting the finishing touches on dinner. He filled two glasses with wine, went over to the sofa where Crane sat, and handed one to him.

They lifted the glasses and clinked them together. *"Salud,"* Crane said.

Andrew sat down and lifted his glass a second time. "And to a happy family visit."

From the kitchen, Betty joined the conversation. "I'm cooking a new dish called Frisco Bay Snapper."

For twenty-five years, all meat products had been grown in tissue cultures and shaped on a 3D printer. The technique had advanced so much that no one talked about how good beef, pork, chicken, and fish tasted in the old days. Nowadays, most people preferred cultured meats, and had gotten over their initial outrage at the Supreme Court for ruling in favor of the SPCA in a suit banning the slaughter of animals for food.

"The snapper smells good," Crane said. "Didn't you cook it the last time I was here?"

Betty shook her head. "No, not this one. This is a new product from West Coast Gourmet Foods. Dad and I tried it last week, and we really liked it."

"What are you serving with it?" Crane asked.

"Soil-grown carrots and baby sweet peas from the Farmers' Market out on Highway 36. I got them at Adamcek's Produce. They always have good vegetables."

Crane chuckled softly. "Mom, you're preparing a culinary oxymoron—cultured fish served with soil-grown vegetables."

"Veggies raised in the ground taste better than those grown in NatGov-subsidized hydroponic farms," Betty said. "Everybody thinks so. The farmer's market is always busy."

After a few more minutes of small talk, the doorbell announced the arrival of Larry and Kim. Betty opened the door, and everyone exchanged greetings, hugs, and birthday wishes.

"How's Richard?" Betty asked.

"Good news," Kim said. "Dad's surgery was approved today—for this coming Monday, no less. They want us to bring him to the hospital tomorrow, even though it's Sunday."

"He's waited a long time," Betty said.

Kim nodded. "More than six months."

"Waiting on NatGov has become our hobby," Larry said.

"How long will he have to stay in the hospital?" Betty asked.

"Hopefully, no more than a week," Kim said.

While they were taking their places, Larry said, "I want to tell you something else. That is, Kim wants to tell you something. She finally registered as a Republican."

Betty wagged a finger in a *no-no* gesture. "You know *Mom's Rule*--no talking politics, religion, or work until dessert is served. And that goes double on Dad's birthday."

"Okay, Mom. Nothing but a rehash of the old stories while we're eating," Larry said, as he pulled back his chair and sat down next to Kim.

—

31

"Oh…I forgot the tea," Betty said. "Kim, would you fill everyone's glass, please? I'll serve the food."

Kim nodded. "Sure, no problem." She picked up the iced tea pitcher and went around the table, carefully filling each glass. When she stopped beside Crane, he looked toward her and their eyes met. Time rolled back fifteen years to their days together in middle school. Kim was shy and he was a nerd. They both needed friends and formed a strong bond which still existed. During Kim's senior year, her parents divorced, and Crane became her confidant. Their long history made Crane feel like a surrogate big brother to her. He hoped Larry knew how lucky he was to have her as his wife.

Betty plated the food with style and efficiency gained over many years of cooking and watching the Food Network Chanel. After sampling the Frisco Bay snapper, everyone agreed that it was one of the best seafood dishes they'd ever tasted.

As Crane expected, conversation drifted back to the time when he and Larry were growing up. Table talk was always the same at family get-togethers—a replay of oft-told tales. With Mom's Rule enforced at this stage of the meal, the old stories were the only topic permitted, no matter how many times they'd been repeated.

Betty's cheeks flushed with excitement. "Remember that day at the zoo when you boys found a green snake with a forked tail near the lake?"

Crane and Larry answered in unison, "We remember, Mom."

Crane was weary of the story and knew that Larry was as well. The snake saga was Betty's all-time favorite, and she mentioned it nearly every time the family got together. She once said the incident revealed the differences in her sons, and Crane tacitly agreed that her assessment was correct. He wanted to capture the odd creature so he could preserve it in formaldehyde solution and display it in a science fair, but Larry insisted on letting it go. While they argued, the snake resolved the conflict by slithering into the lake. Crane poked around the edge of the lake with a long stick for half an hour, but the odd reptile never reappeared.

Fifteen years had passed since the snake incident. During that time, Crane had heard reports of other bizarre animals being found near the Houston Zoo. Snakes with rudimentary legs, lizards with six or eight legs, and salamanders with two heads had been reported. No good explanations existed, but urban legends asserted that illegal animal experiments had been performed in the Mediplex years ago, although no records had surfaced to substantiate such claims.

When the main course ended, Betty leaned over and touched a button on the countertop. A coffee maker sprang to life with a comforting gurgle. She went into the kitchen and brought back a pitcher of soy cream and a bowl of Mexican sugar, a sweetener banned by NatGov, but readily available in shops west of the Brazos River.

Betty sat next to Crane and put her hand on his shoulder. "How's your social life? Do you have another girlfriend yet?"

Silence engulfed the room, and all eyes fell on Crane. He was slightly put out by the question, but hid his feelings behind a nervous chuckle. "I think all of the good ones are taken, Mom." He glanced toward Kim to see if she reacted to his tangential compliment. She smiled faintly.

Betty parried her son's non-answer with another question. "What about that lab technician you work with-- Anna Mae?

"She's a cytogeneticist, and her name is *Anime*--one word--but, everybody calls her Annie."

*"Anime?"* Betty pronounced the word slowly. "That's what I thought I said. Anyway, she's a real doll—cute as a bug, and not much bigger than one either."

"Mom!" Crane said. "She's my best friend. That's all."

Betty pressed on. "Remember that day I met her in the snack bar? She was wearing a pink headband with sparkles, and you were eating lunch together. I'd been to the doctor and stopped for a Coke. She was so nice to me. Remember?"

Crane nodded.

"She called you *Protein Man*," Betty said. "Why'd she do that?"

"It's a joke."

"What does it mean?"

"It's based on a memory device that some biology students use to remember the chemical elements in protein," Crane said. "The phrase is *C Hopkins Café, Mighty Good*, which helps biologists remember carbon, hydrogen, oxygen, phosphorus, potassium, iodine, nitrogen, sulfur, calcium, iron, and magnesium. My name reminded her of the memory aid."

Betty was totally oblivious to her son's science lesson. "I figured you might ask her out."

"She's going out with Brad," Crane said in a monotone.

"You let another good one get away," Betty said emphatically. This time she looked directly at Kim, who was beginning to seem a little uncomfortable.

"I'm only twenty-nine, Mom. I'm not over the hill yet."

Crane felt like his mother should be a little more diplomatic in affairs of the heart, but she had never shied away from the direct approach. Clearly, she thought it was time for him to find a replacement for Karol, his former fiancée who had returned her engagement ring and moved to New York to play guitar in a rock band called *Apocalyptic Madness*. Two years had passed since the breakup, apparently a time frame consistent with his mother's idea of how Cupid works to restart the process. She seemed intent on giving the winged cherub some help with his bow and arrows, whether he needed it or not.

Crane decided to make an attempt to squelch the girl-friend inquisition. "Are you and Dad still planning to take a trip over the Thanksgiving holidays?" he asked.

"Yes, we are," Betty answered. "We're going to Colonial Williamsburg. I love that place. Remember the time we went there when you boys were teenagers?"

Again, Crane and Larry nodded and answered in unison, "We remember, Mom."

"We had a great Thanksgiving dinner at Christiana Campbell's Tavern," Betty said, "the place that George Washington visited from time to time."

"It was really cold that day," Larry said. "We waited

outside over thirty minutes before they called our name. We nearly froze to death."

"Since we won't be together on Thanksgiving, I'm already planning Christmas dinner," Betty said. "I'm going to try out some new recipes."

"She's looking at of some exotic French recipes," Andrew said. "Stuffed lamb chops, with all the trimmings."

"Don't spoil it, Andy," Betty said. "I want to surprise them."

"Okay," Andrew said with a loud sigh, "if we can't talk about Christmas dinner, let's have dessert."

"I made a German chocolate cake," Betty said, as she pushed back from the table and stood. "Andy, would you get the dessert plates?"

Before Andrew Hopkins could move a muscle, Kim jumped up and said, "Let me help."

The two women retreated into the kitchen, leaving the men to make small talk while they waited. Three minutes later, Betty and Kim came back to the table with the cake and dessert plates. Betty set the cake in front of Andrew, and they sang Happy Birthday. Andrew blew out the single candle shaped like the number 50, and they all clapped.

Betty cut the cake and began to serve it. When the first dessert plate touched the table in front of Andrew, it was the signal that the restrictions on conversation topics had been lifted.

"Are you keeping up with the Dar Lumbre news?" Larry asked in Crane's direction.

"Headlines are on every news screen I pass," Crane said. "They're impossible to miss. Dar Lumbre sightings are like Elvis sightings in the last century."

"Without Dr. Lumbre, CellTech wouldn't exist," Larry said. "I thought you'd be excited about the news."

"I'd certainly be excited if I could believe it," Crane said, thinking how fantastic it would be to talk to Dr. Lumbre about the current DL-666 problem. Larry's assertion of Dar Lumbre's importance to CellTech was beyond a doubt. Shortly before his disappearance, the enigmatic doctor had assembled a group of entrepreneurs to launch a startup company called Cellular Technologies. The initial product offered by the company was DL-666, Dr. Lumbre's famous heart tissue.

"I believe he will come back soon," Larry said with strong conviction.

Crane scoffed. "These reappearance stories get recycled every ten years, or so. The last time one made the rounds, I was a freshman in college. It turned out to be a fabrication by the news media to detract from the president's monumental failures. This looks like *deja vu all over again*."

Larry's tone was passionate. "I believe it's going to be different this time."

"What makes you think so?"

"Something strange happened to me the other day."

"Go on," Crane said, eschewing the sarcasm that was on the tip of his tongue. He'd already heard reports of Dar Lumbre's image appearing on an apple fritter, and hoped his brother wasn't headed in that direction.

"I witnessed a harbinger," Larry stated.

"A *harbinger?*" Crane said. "That's a pretty strong word."

"No other word describes the incident," Larry said. "A few days ago, I was working on my new computer game and picked up a broadcast from California--one of those hot mike incidents that ended up on a wild satellite feed, or something like that. I'm certain the general public wasn't supposed to hear it. I acquired the signal because my computer is amped up for the program I'm developing."

"What did you hear?"

"A man named Elmore Larson was talking," Larry said. "He was working on a speech. My computer flashed a couple of blurred images of him and went blank, but I could hear his voice for several minutes. Some of it was loud and clear, and some was garbled."

"Who is this...Elmore Larson?" Crane asked.

"He's the leader of the Dar Lumbre Society, an organization which has been underground for fifty years, according to rumors. Apparently, the rumors were true. Recently, the society came out of hiding and opened an office in Anaheim. Based on information that I overheard, they plan to set up offices in several other cities soon."

"What does the Dar Lumbre Society advocate?"

"Changing the world through medical science."

An edge touched Crane's voice. "Change is a word that NatGov doesn't like. With the help of the news media, they'll brand the society as a bunch of fanatics, and the IRS will be auditing their books for years to come."

"Elmore Larson doesn't sound like a fanatic to me," Larry retorted. "I didn't hear much, but what I heard makes sense."

"What else did he say?"

Larry's eyes sparkled with fervor. "When Dar Lumbre returns, he'll resume his research. That kind of work is legal now, and it can be used to help people in many ways. The society has political ambitions as well. Right now, they're encouraging Outsiders to register so they can vote in the upcoming presidential election."

"A noble cause," Crane said, "but one which has already been attempted without much success."

Andrew joined the discussion. "Previous attempts failed because both political parties opposed any change in the status quo. They paid lip service to the registration of Outsiders, but instead of helping, they threw up obstacles."

Crane nodded. "Probably so." The point was hard to refute. Fifty years after the massive data loss, millions of people still hadn't registered. He looked back toward Larry and asked, "What other claims did this guy make?"

"I heard something about a Methuselah gene," Larry said, "but that part was garbled."

Crane's chin dropped in astonishment. "Ever since Gregor Mendel's day, geneticists have toyed with the idea of finding a Methuselah gene."

Larry went on forcefully. "Word in the street is that Dar Lumbre will introduce a gene that will lengthen the life of everyone who receives it. It's similar to the religious doctrine of eternal life. In fact, waiting for Dar Lumbre's return seems to be evolving into a new religion."

Crane scoffed. "New religions are against the law. No more messiah-prophets allowed. You know that."

"Most people think that law will be overturned. It'll probably go to the Supreme Court next year."

"What makes you think they'll hear it?"

"Congress overstepped their authority when they attached a rider to the First Amendment making it illegal to add another messiah-prophet to the approved list consisting of Jesus, Mohammed, Buddha, the Dali Lama, and L. Ron Hubbard."

"What are you getting at?"

"The list is short," Larry said. "Maybe Dar Lumbre will be added some day."

## Chapter 5

Crane and Annie entered CellTech's observation gallery a half-floor above Operating Room Number 12. A dozen fellow geneticists had already claimed the best seats in the house along the front window, and others were pouring into the room. The air rippled with excited chatter.

"Those seats down there are fine," Crane said, with a wave of his hand. "Let's grab them before somebody else does."

"This is a big crowd for Monday," Annie said, as they made their way down the steps.

Crane knew why the audience was larger than usual. Word of the problem with DL-666 had spread throughout the Mediplex, and leaked out into the street as well. Rumors abounded, one of them claiming that today would be the last transplant using the famous tissue. Crane hoped the rumor was wrong, but after a short and intense investigation, he had no basis to refute it.

A group of newly-minted MD's sat on the opposite side of the operating room in a second observation gallery facing CellTech's suite. The surgeons-in-training whispered among themselves and glanced around in anticipation of the drama about to unfold. Nearly all of them keyboarded iTabs while they waited for the show to start. Crane studied their faces across the room. Most of them were a couple of years younger than him, and looked more like online gamers than doctors.

Show time arrived.

Hallway doors swung open with a pneumatic hiss, and a bustle of activity hit the operating room. Lights brightened, buzzers sounded, and Dr. Sean Tanner marched in. A cadre of green-clad personnel flanked him with military precision that rivaled a well-trained color guard. Even the most casual observer could tell that the team was ready.

Dr. Tanner was the best-known transplant surgeon in the United States, and had dramatic flair to match his surgical credentials. Paparazzi and gossip columnists often waited near the exits of the Houston Mediplex, hoping to get a photo or an interview with the charismatic surgeon.

His high visibility was a boon to CellTech. For years, he had maintained close ties with the company's top management, particularly Dr. Rosenfield, the Technical Director and CEO.

"He's the best in his field, isn't he?" Annie said.

Crane shrugged. "Yeah, I guess."

"You don't like him. Why?"

"You saw the way he walked in--like a peacock."

"He has credentials."

"Credentials?" Crane scoffed. "Wasn't that what the Scarecrow wanted in *The Wizard of Oz?*"

Annie shook her head. "Not so--he wanted a brain. Instead, the Wizard gave him an *Honorary Doctorate of Thinkology.*"

"A paper document," Crane said with a smirk. "Like a Mensa card."

"Give it a rest."

Without further conversation, they directed their attention to the brightly lit operating room where Dr. Tanner's assistants stood at attention. The wax-like patient was wheeled into the room in a Cryo-Unit, a device resembling an open sarcophagus fused with an old-fashioned pinball machine. Crisp blue LEDs blinked along each side of the unit, creating a halo. The C-Unit was a magic box, and Dr. Tanner was the top-ranked magician ready to display his legerdemain to an appreciative audience.

Surgery had made a dramatic change more than seventy-five years ago when C-Units became as much a part of the operating team as surgeons and robotic assistants. Prompt use of the device kept trauma victims alive until the medical community could decide on a proper course of action. The complex machines saved thousands of lives every year, and were common equipment in all major hospitals. No competent surgeon would think of operating without one.

Dr. Tanner began, "The patient is Richard Hunter, a male Caucasian. He has suffered from coronary disease for several years, and has anticipated this surgery for six months. NatGov approval for this transplant was granted late last week, and preparations were begun immediately. Yesterday, he was placed in a C-Unit in preparation for today's surgery." He paused to look at the ring of hypnotized faces above him. No one moved a muscle as the renowned surgeon spoke.

"My office obtained a synthetic heart from CellTech," Dr. Tanner resumed his lecture. "We'll remove the patient's defective heart and replace it with one fabricated from the tissue we know as DL-666. When we complete the procedure, this subject should fully recover and be able to resume his normal life after a short rehab. If he maintains a heart-healthy lifestyle after this surgery, there is no reason he can't live to be well over a hundred years old…"

As Dr. Tanner lectured, Crane wondered what Dar Lumbre would have done in the face of uncertainty such as this. He was fairly certain the legendary doctor would have pressed on in spite of the recently-discovered anomaly. DL-666 was proof that Dr. Lumbre was not afraid to take chances. Besides, what other choice was available? Doing nothing was hardly acceptable.

"While my team is making the final preparations," Dr. Tanner continued, "I'll make a few comments on the use of Cryo-Units during surgery. As you know, in the past, this type of surgical procedure required considerable effort to control blood loss. This is no longer a major concern today. The C-Unit reduces vascular and pulmonary complications, thus providing surgeons with additional time. As a result, complex thoracic surgery has become routine in major medical facilities throughout the country."

Dr. Tanner cleared his throat and invited questions.

A young doctor in the observation booth stood. "Yes, Sir. I have a couple of questions about C-Units, and cryonics in general."

Dr. Tanner nodded. "Go ahead."

"How long can a person survive in a C-Unit?"

"A good question," Dr. Tanner said, "but one that has no exact answer. Survival time depends primarily on the condition of that individual's health upon entering the unit. A healthy person could survive for several months, perhaps even a year or more, with little or no damage. An elderly subject, or one in poor health, would experience rapid tissue degeneration. Does that answer your question?"

"Not completely, Sir," the young man said. "I have another question on the same subject. What about those people stored in cryonic suspension in Scottsdale, Arizona? That famous baseball player's head is stored there--Ted Williams. Whole bodies are frozen there as well. I've even heard that Walt Disney is in cryonic suspension. Can any of these people ever be revived?"

Tanner shook his head. "Not likely, although several companies in the United States have cryogenic storage facilities open to the public, and claim to use procedures which can preserve human bodies for decades. Their claims can't be verified, and the procedure is expensive. Basically, the subjects are stored in giant flasks filled with liquid nitrogen. In some cases, an antifreeze solution is used to prevent ice crystals from rupturing the cells, but long-term exposure to the antifreeze solution would likely be toxic.

"By contrast, the C-Unit we are using produces a state of suspended animation, rather than a deep-freeze condition. Our process bears very little resemblance to commercial cryogenic storage offered to the public for a fee. We use an antifreeze solution, too, but not one expected to keep the subject in a viable condition indefinitely. We consider it temporary--a year or two at most, even in exceptional situations."

Another young doctor raised his hand and Dr. Tanner acknowledged him.

The man stood. "Doctor, do you think Dar Lumbre is stored in a C-Unit at a secret location, and about to make some sort of messianic second coming?"

Dr. Tanner glared at the questioner. "Young man, you're wasting my time, and your own as well. I'm trying to teach you to become a surgeon, not a theologian or philosopher."

"Sorry," the young man said. He slumped in his seat amid derisive stares from his fellow student doctors. Everyone fell silent at that point, waiting for the surgeon to take his station.

Signaling that the Q & A session was over, Dr. Tanner sat down at the surgical console and grasped the master controls with both hands. He flexed his fingers, and the operating pod hovering above Richard Hunter bent all four arms slightly, indicating the system was functioning properly.

"The first robotic system approved by the FDA was the da Vinci Surgical System in 2000," Dr. Tanner said. "That system was used laparoscopically. Today, robotic surgery has advanced so much that it can be used for highly invasive surgery, such as the one you are about to witness today. Remember, during this process, the surgeon is in control at all times. Surgery cannot be done by AI."

At Dr. Tanner's command, the robotic surgical system sprang into action. One robotic arm flourished a laser scalpel and cut open the patient's chest in one deft move. A second arm inserted an endoscopic camera into the pericardial cavity and began transmitting images to strategic locations in the Mediplex, and into university classrooms throughout the country. A third arm attached a hemostat to the external mammary artery to control the slight flow of blood. As the procedure continued, Dr. Tanner and the surgical system morphed into a symbiotic organism so perfectly synchronized that the robot appeared to be acting of its own accord.

Crane studied the faces of the young doctors in the gallery. They had fallen under Dr. Tanner's magic spell. In the coming months and years, they would try to emulate the master surgeon's skill and coolness in the operating room. Most would succeed to some degree, but only a scant few, maybe one or two, would reach Tanner's status. Crane tried to pick out the future super-docs, but couldn't. They all looked alike.

With Dr. Tanner at the controls, the robot finished opening the patient's pericardial cavity to expose the swollen heart surrounded by yellowish fatty tissue. Working in unison, three flexible arms began the process of removing the damaged heart. They clamped off the anterior and posterior vena cava, pulmonary trunk, and aorta. Finally, they severed vessels and supporting ligaments to free the heart from its moorings. When all connections between the heart and the rest of the body were eliminated, one arm lifted out the heart and placed it in a container of saline solution.

Another robotic arm picked up the new heart fabricated from DL-666. At first glance, the heart appeared to be a plastic model from medical school, but it was considerably more complicated, having been produced by a 3D printer from living heart tissue. A series of thin platinum wires dangled from the dorsal portion of the organ. When the new heart was securely in place, surgeons would connect an electromagnetic pacemaker to the severed nerve endings. The resulting product was so precise that the subject's brain would never realize it was sending messages to a lab-produced organ.

The robotic surgeon placed the synthetic heart inside the subject's open chest and began to reestablish connections. The process was tedious, but finally the operation ended, and Dr. Tanner got up from the surgeon's console and turned to face the audience. A murmur of approval, accompanied by light applause, buzzed through the gallery. Dr. Tanner bowed slightly and continued, "This patient will be transferred to CCU where the C-Unit will gradually raise his temperature back to normal. The process will take four hours, or longer. It must be done slowly in order to avoid unnecessary strain on the new organ."

After another brief round of questions and answers, Dr. Tanner excused himself and retreated from the room, leaving the rest of his team to finish post-operative procedures.

The big show was over. Everyone in the observation gallery got up simultaneously and pushed toward the exits.

Annie returned to the lab, and Crane went to the cardiac surgery waiting room to join Kim and Larry.

He sat down beside Kim and the interminable waiting started.

One hour…no word from Dr. Tanner's team.

Two hours…still no word.

Three hours…nothing yet.

At the fourth hour, a buzzer shrieked, and a mechanical voice blared over the PA system. "Code Blue…Code Blue…Code Blue Emergency Team to CCU immediately!"

As the Code Blue sounded again and again, the waiting room occupants snapped to attention, all fearing the worst. Conversation ended abruptly, and everyone looked around in frightened expectancy. Faces were taut and drawn. All eyes fixed on the door leading to the operating rooms, and everyone knew a bearer of bad news would burst in at any moment.

The big question—whose name would he call?

Kim sat between Crane and Larry. She put her head against Larry's shoulder and closed her eyes. Tears trickled down her pale cheeks. Larry placed his arm around her. No one spoke. There was little to say, and nothing to do but wait.

Finally, the door opened. A green-clad doctor from Sean Tanner's team stepped into the room and said, "Hunter family?"

Kim, Larry, and Crane jumped up and approached the doctor.

"We have a problem," the doctor said. "The artificial heart is not performing properly. It exhibited arrhythmia when the C-Unit reached ambient temperature. We have lowered the temperature of the C-Unit again, and it must remain low until the problem is solved."

Kim began to sob fitfully and tried to speak, but couldn't control her voice. Both Larry and Crane put their arms around her as her body wrenched with each sob.

Crane turned toward the doctor and asked, "How long can he survive in the C-Unit in his current condition?"

"Everything rests on the performance of the new heart," the doctor said. "If it does not respond properly, we will have to repeat the procedure with another heart, either a new artificial heart, or one from a human donor, if one can be found."

"Is he in immediate danger?" Larry asked.

"He's stable."

Kim regained her composure sufficiently to ask, "When can I see him?"

"Not before tomorrow," the doctor said. "I suggest you go home and get some rest."

"Let me know if anything changes," Kim said in a trembling voice.

The doctor assured Kim that he would keep her informed, then turned briskly and left the waiting room. Kim turned toward Crane, despair showing in her eyes as she said, "Please help my father."

"I promise I will," Crane said. He hoped his words sounded reassuring, but feared they didn't, particularly since he was experiencing a growing uncertainty about DL-666. And, even though the doctor mentioned the option of obtaining a heart from a human donor, Crane knew such a possibility was remote. DL-666 had been so successful over the years that organ banks no longer sought heart donors. A mechanical heart might offer a temporary fix, but rejuvenated DL-666 was the only permanent solution.

Stark reality struck Crane--*Richard Hunter's life was in his hands.*

## Chapter 6

Sunday afternoon was crisp and clear as John Stone drove northwest along Highway 36 in his ancient Ford Expedition. John was fifty years old with short-cropped salt and pepper hair covered by a baseball cap matching his camouflage fatigues. He was lean and tan from working outside.

Both sides of the highway displayed a checkerboard of small fields in a range of colors, an indication that fall crops were doing well. Toward the end of the week, local farmers would turn out in force to harvest beans, onions, tomatoes, and anything else that was ready. Most of the produce would be sold on Saturday at the Farmers' Market, with the remainder available Sunday afternoon for sale to the locals. This cycle repeated itself until the last harvest of the year, which was just around the corner. Winter was on its way.

John considered the people living in this area to be modern-day pioneers, although they lived less than twenty miles from one of the largest cities in the United States. Most homes in the area utilized stand-alone septic systems and water wells, and some stored rainwater in cisterns. A few generated their own power with windmills. Farm machinery dotted the landscape, and a barn stood a short distance from nearly every house. The residents of this area survived by hard work. Most of them gave little thought to which party occupied the White House. Neither party had treated them very well.

Just outside the city limits of Richmond-Rosenberg, John passed a faded sign announcing that he was entering the small town of Orchard. He turned onto Simonton Road, which like many other rural roads in the area, was not magnetized to accommodate vehicles on autopilot. John grasped the steering wheel firmly and resumed control of his vehicle. The red F150 currently displayed 525,196 miles on its odometer, which was on its second time around. John loved his old Ford. Externally, it was in show-room condition, but had begun to sputter at every stop sign and red light, a situation he hoped to correct soon.

The dilapidated buildings on each side of the road

---

were reminders of days gone by. Most had flaking paint and cracked windows. The residents of this area were Outsiders, and HUD money was not available to refurbish buildings where the populace had not joined either approved political party.

The usual Sunday afternoon crowd was forming with people whose attire parodied the buildings. Men in khaki pants and denim jackets mingled with amorphous women in faded print dresses and sweaters. Teenage boys, many with hands in their pockets, lounged in doorways and ogled the pubescent girls passing by. Young children ran amok, shrieking as they darted from one hiding place to another, happily playing peekaboo. Women pushed creaky grocery carts from one small shop to another to pick over the wilted produce still available after the Farmers' Market sale on Saturday.

John understood the system that kept these people poor. It had been in place since the early 2000's, maybe longer, depending on whether you believed the Republicans or Democrats. Under current law, two options existed—either sell your vote to NatGov for chump change, or exist as *little people* forever. The perpetual scheme had been worked out to perfection in a joint agreement between the power brokers in both political parties. NatGov claimed the system was working well, and for them, it was.

Against prevailing logic, John believed the system was about to change. It would change because a lot of Outsiders expected Dar Lumbre to return someday and take up their cause. John hoped to convince them that *someday* referred to the near future.

He pulled into a gravel parking lot surrounding a row of tan buildings joined at the front by a vinyl façade. Separated by a gravel driveway, a lone warehouse stood at the left end of the strip center. The building stood out from its tan-colored counterparts. It sported a fresh coat of paint in red, white, and blue depicting the American flag. The corrugated plastic siding of the building distorted the image somewhat, but all fifteen stripes and fifty-two stars on the flag were clearly visible. A large sign with foot-high black letters hung just below the roofline of the building. The sign read:

## THE DAR LUMBRE SOCIETY
### Register To Vote

John parked beside a small green pickup in front of the building. He knew the pickup would be there. It belonged to Emilo Lopez, his mechanic friend who constantly hunted parts for old cars, many of which still operated in the truck farming region northwest of Richmond-Rosenberg. As usual, Emilio was early.

Each man got out of his vehicle and moved to the graveled area between them. Emilio stuck out his hand and said, "Hey, Juan. How's it going?"

"It's going well," John said, grasping Emilio's outstretched hand. "Did you find the parts for my SUV?"

"I've got them," Emilio said." Take a look." He pointed toward a plastic box in the back of the pickup.

John went to the pickup and looked in the box. The fuel injectors were laid out neatly on red shop rags. John took one of the injectors out of the box and examined it carefully. It was in mint condition, as were the remaining five.

"They look great," John said. "Thanks for tracking them down."

While John and Emilio were talking, two men separated from the crowd next door and joined them. They were members of the Cizek family, Bob and his son, Robbie, both local truck farmers whom John had known for years. The Cizeks were the salt of the earth, poor but proud, like so many others in the Richmond-Rosenberg area. They shared many of John's beliefs, and both had joined the Dar Lumbre Society recently.

Bob said, "Hi, Rocky," and Robbie said, "Hello, Mr. Stone."

They shook hands and chatted for a few minutes. John liked the names the local residents affixed to him. Emilio, like many Hispanics in the area, called him *Juan Piedra*, while Bob and other Czech, German, and Polish friends often morphed his surname into *Rocky*. Some polite teenagers, of which there seemed to be fewer each generation, still called him *Mr. Stone*. He believed that the variety of names certified him as a prototypical *every man*,

49

a concept that should be helpful during the sociopolitical revolution, which—hopefully--was just around the corner.

John turned toward Emilio and asked, "When can you fix my truck?"

Emilio thought a few seconds and answered, "I can do it tomorrow, but you'll have to miss a day's work."

John shrugged. "That's okay. I don't think there'll be much produce to haul early in the week. Do you need a down payment?"

Emilio shook his head. "Your word is good with me."

"Okay, I'll bring it to your shop in the morning."

Before he turned to leave, John pointed to the Dar Lumbre sign on the building and said, "Don't forget the rallies."

The three men gave affirmative nods, and Bob said, "We'll be here."

Thirty minutes after leaving the Dar Lumbre Society office, John parked in front of his tiny garage apartment on Second Street, which ran along the Brazos River in the Richmond community. Although the small town was primarily Outsider territory, NatGov controlled several historical locations in the area, including picturesque Morton Cemetery across the street from John's apartment. The ashes of John's father rested there in a vault beneath a spreading live-oak tree, and several Texas pioneers were interred nearby. It was a quiet and peaceful place.

Lugging a basket of wilted produce, John went up an outside staircase leading to a small landing at his front door. He hesitated and glanced across the river to the east. The gleaming high-rise condos stood in bold contrast to the modest buildings on his side of the river. John Stone, an eternal optimist with a strong conscience, was dismayed that a small river could be the boundary of a caste system created and perpetuated by the government. He entered his austere one-room apartment. On a white plastic dining table serving as his desk, a lamp glowed dimly. The lamp was powered by a solar panel on the roof, one of the few luxuries that John afforded himself.

As John sat his shopping basket on the floor, his archaic cellphone played its California ringtone. He flipped open the cover with his thumb and saw that the caller was Elmore Larson. John was expecting the call.

"Hello, Mr. Larson," he said.

"Hi, John. Can you talk a few minutes?"

"Sure. Go ahead."

"How's the membership drive going?"

"Couldn't be better. A lot of people are joining the society, and next week we'll have our first rally. I'm expecting a good crowd."

"We're getting that same response all over the country," Larson said, "so, it's time to print and distribute the flyers. Do you have everything you need to begin that project?"

"I've rented office space and set up the printer that you sent," John said. "All I need to do is get some more paper. We're ready to go into action on a moment's notice, but some trained workers would be a big help."

"That's the main reason I called," Larson said. "I'm going to send two of the people you met when you came out here last spring, Julie Gilchrist and Jerry Legrand. They'll be arriving in Houston in a few days, so I called to give you a little information on each of them before they get there."

"I remember them. Nice young people."

"They're some of the top operatives in the society," Larson said. "Still, there are a couple of things you should know about them before you start working together. I've found full disclosure is the best way to operate."

"That makes sense to me," John said.

Larson continued, "I'll start with Jerry. He was born into the society, so it's ingrained into his psyche. He's always tightly wound and ready to go, but he engages people very well and works hard. When out in the community, he'll remind you of a street corner preacher from last century. He has a lot of zeal--evangelical zeal, I would call it."

"I'm okay with that. We'll need plenty of zeal to pull this off. I'm looking forward to working with Jerry...and with Julie, too."

"Now, let's discuss Julie a bit," Larson said. "She's

one of my most trusted assistants. She works harder than anybody else in the office…gets in early…works late…totally dedicated. She can do anything, and do it well. Her only possible downside—she was divorced recently."

"That shouldn't cause a problem."

"I don't expect it to," Larson said. "It hasn't affected her performance at all, but since her divorce was finalized only two weeks ago, I thought you should know about it."

"I'm sure they'll both work out fine," John said, "but, I appreciate the heads up. It'll keep me from getting caught off-guard."

After a brief exchange of small talk, Larson said, "Okay, John, that's all I had. Nice talking to you. If there's anything I can help you with, let me know."

"Okay, Mr. Larson."

When they ended the conversation, John began to ponder the situation. He had spent a large part of his life developing rapport with the Outsiders around the Richmond-Rosenberg area. Being *every man* was his strong suit, and he believed that he had played it well. Consequently, he couldn't help but wonder how the operatives from California would interact with the locals.

Still, it was Mr. Larson's call. He had successfully managed the organization for a long time while it was underground. In John's ex-military eyes, Elmore Larson was a four-star general commanding the entire theater of operations. Basic training was over, and General Larson had given orders to begin the campaign. Captain John Stone was ready to deploy and lead the troops into battle.

John lay his iTab on the table next to a well-worn copy of Dar Lumbre's only published work, *The Double Helix Odyssey*, a publication banned by NatGov fifty years ago. He picked up the dog-eared booklet and thumbed through it.

As he often did, he stopped on Page 10 and read it again.

Chapter 7

Kim leaned against the wall of her checkout station and looked down the aisles of Party Town Novelty Shop while thinking about her father. Over a week had passed since his surgery, and Kim's life had defaulted to a structured daily routine. Every day before work, she went by the hospital to check on his condition. Lying comatose in the C-Unit, his appearance never changed. Likewise, the doctor's report never changed. It was always the same short sentence, *Mr. Hunter's condition is stable.* She didn't see *stable* as a very descriptive word, but the doctors recited it like parrots. Hopefully, Crane would be able to tell her something more definitive in the near future.

From her vantage point, Kim could see only two customers, a skinny young woman browsing in the party balloons section, and a man wearing camouflage fatigues looking at paper and printing supplies. With Thanksgiving just around the corner, she'd been expecting a surge of customers, but it hadn't happened yet. If more people didn't start trickling in, the day would drag by at a terribly slow pace.

She wondered if the constant talk about recession was scaring customers away. Something had. For some reason, people didn't seem to be giving many parties these days. And when they did, they bought only a few party favors and other small trinkets, not a shopping basket full of fancy decorations like Betty Hopkins bought for Andrew's birthday party.

In spite of what she saw and heard about the economy, Kim seldom gave much thought to financial matters, even though she and Larry lived from paycheck to paycheck. Who didn't do it these days, especially people their age?

Larry didn't earn a regular salary like she did. A few years ago, he won several internet gaming tournaments, after which he began to develop programs on his own. To date, all of his sales had been desktop applications sold through the Apple-Disney's App Store. Not a lot of money to be made that way, unless he hit one out of the park, maybe something like the recent mega hit, *Angry Pterodactyls.* She knew that was a one-in-a-million shot, not something they could hang their financial future on.

Her husband kept telling her that he was about to hit pay dirt with the program he was working on currently, a multi-player game called *Global Cooling on Mercury*. She hoped he could sell it to Apple-Disney. That would bring a nice payday, and might land Larry a job with Apple's Houston Software Group. She might quit work and go back to college. On the other hand, maybe she would just stay home and play with Mickey, the Jack Russell terrier that Larry bought yesterday. The thought made her smile.

"Hey, Kim, are you okay?" Sandy asked from the next checkout station.

Kim stood up straight. "I feel fine. Why?"

"You were leaning against the wall. I thought maybe you weren't feeling well."

"Oh, that was nothing," Kim said. "I was just looking to see how many people are in the store. When we're busy, the day goes faster."

Concern showed in Sandy's face. "Remember how busy we used to be on Saturday afternoon? It's not that way anymore. Even with the holidays approaching, we haven't had a big crowd in weeks. That's scary."

"Everybody says we're in a recession," Kim said. "Maybe we are."

"If business doesn't improve, Party Town might replace us with robo-checkers."

Kim shook her head. "Machines can't replace us."

"Why not?" Sandy asked. "They can do anything we can do."

"Not so. They can't smile at customers."

*"Touché!"*

"I asked Larry about robo-checkers," Kim said. "He said it would be illegal to replace us with them."

"Why? Amazon-Walmart uses them right down the street."

"Larry looked up Party Town's corporate documents and found something interesting," Kim said. "The building we're in is over a hundred and fifty years old. The Historical Society protects it, just like they protect the old River Oaks

Theater up the block. When they leased the building, Party Town agreed to use real people at all checkout counters. They can use robots everywhere else in the store, but not as checkers—not now or ever."

"They could still go bankrupt."

"They won't," Kim said. "Party Town is one of the few retailers that hasn't been bought by Amazon, and they're doing okay."

Kim didn't worry much about losing her job. She had always been able to find employment with some small independent company or one of the fast food establishments. Still, maybe Larry was right about the importance of the E-Points she would receive for registering. Soon, she would be a fully registered Republican, and could apply for a job with one of the huge conglomerates affiliated with NatGov if she wanted to. It would be legal for them to hire her now.

The man in fatigues approached the checkout stations pushing a shopping cart loaded with printer paper and toner cartridges. He hesitated, as if unable to decide between Kim and Sandy.

Kim motioned for the man to enter her station. "I'll help you, Sir."

"Thank you, Miss."

He lay his purchases on the countertop. "Will you be getting any more of this paper soon?" he asked. "I need some more, and it's hard to find. Most stores don't carry it any longer."

"We'll have more in a couple of days," Kim said. "Would you like for us to notify you when it comes in?"

"No, thanks, Miss. I'll check back."

"You bought more paper than we normally sell in a month," Kim said. "What kind of printing project are you working on?"

"Uh…it's a promotional campaign."

"Do you have enough toner cartridges?"

"I think so."

Kim picked up one of the cartridges and read the label before scanning the price. "Wow!" she said. "The label claims one of these cartridges will print 10,000 pages, and you have a basket full. You'll need a lot more paper."

"I'll be back in a couple of days."

"When you took the last package off the shelf, the inventory robot noted it and automatically placed an order with Amazon," Kim said. "We might possibly get it tomorrow."

"Thanks, Miss."

"Thank you for shopping at Party Town."

The man paid for his purchases and left the store. Kim's eyes followed him as he walked along the glass storefront. He got into a red SUV, and pulled out of the parking lot. She wondered what kind of printing project required so much paper. Virtually nobody printed anything on real paper anymore. The Tree Destruction Tax had made it prohibitive.

Kim would be glad when the work day ended. She was looking forward to studying her Texas Driver Education Course when she got home. Several weeks ago, Larry purchased a car, even though they barely could afford one. He bought it from a starving artist--oddly enough, named Rembrandt. Far less talented than the original, this Rembrandt's specialty was pencil drawings of pets, mostly dogs. He'd painted his car to match one of his beloved subjects shortly before Larry bought it. Kim enjoyed the car, and was determined to get a license. The four lessons remaining dealt with driving on non-magnetized roads. They would be difficult, but she planned to finish one of them tonight, and then play with Mickey until Larry got home.

The prospect brought comfort to her after a long day of little to do except worry about her father.

## Chapter 8

The Starbucks adjoining CellTech's main lobby was crowded when Annie entered. Like nearly everyone else in the coffee shop, she wore white scrubs. She had accessorized the generic company-issued clothing with a lime green headband to keep her short Manga hairstyle from falling across her forehead. The iTab bag slung over her shoulder matched her headband. She wouldn't have felt fully dressed without a splash of color.

The coffee shop was the pre-work gathering place for employees of the Mediplex, especially for those thirty-something and under. Most of the early arrivals were already linked to their offices via iTabs and were multitasking while sipping various caffeinated drinks. The caffeine intake of Mediplex personnel was so far above the national average that they joked about adding it to Aristotle's list of four essential elements, thereby creating a five-component list consisting of earth, wind, fire, water, and caffeine.

As she approached the counter, Annie greeted someone at nearly every table she passed. She ordered green tea and a blueberry scone, and stepped to the serving area to wait. She looked around and spotted Crane seated alone at a table in the corner. He was squinting at the screen of his iTab, and a coffee cup sat in front of him. Annie could see that he was totally absorbed in his own thoughts, and hadn't noticed her enter the shop. When her order arrived, she picked it up and headed toward Crane's table.

After working with him for a year, Annie believed that she understood how Crane thought. He was inexorably linked to DL-666. It occupied his every waking moment, and many of his sleeping moments as well. She'd begun to do the same thing herself. She believed everyone who had worked with the tissue in the past felt the same attachment to it. It was an all-encompassing assignment.

The enigmatic tissue exhibited the most irritating eccentricity Annie had ever seen—it couldn't be stock cultured by ordinary cold storage techniques. Instead, the culture existed as living, growing tissue in an incubator maintained at 37 degrees Centigrade. Faced with such difficulties, every researcher with curatorial responsibility for it, including Crane, had tried to develop a technique for maintaining stock cultures in some more conventional manner. No one had succeeded, although Annie believed she and Crane would do so eventually.

DL-666, then, was old. It had aged in real time. It never rested. No wonder it was having problems. Senility had crept up on it. It was the senior citizen of all known synthetic tissue. Still, in spite of the problematic issues with DL-666, it was the only tissue culture in the world that could grow a living heart.

Annie reached Crane's table. "Greetings, Protein Man."

He looked up and motioned to the chair next to him. "Morning."

Annie placed her tea and scone on the table and sat next to Crane. "What are you dissecting?"

"Dar Lumbre's reading list."

"His archived medical journals again?"

"Uh-huh."

"We've looked at them a dozen times," Annie said. "Thousands of other scientists have done so as well, and no one has found anything worthwhile."

Crane nodded. "I know it's probably a waste of time, but I keep pouring over them. It's strange that no records of his research ever surfaced. These old journals were the only thing in his archives when NatGov seized his digital records."

"Did you see anything different this time?"

"Possibly."

"Talk to me."

"His library covers a time frame of nearly a hundred and fifty years," Crane said. "From 1950 to the late 2000's. When I looked at the titles again, I noticed a large number of publications from 1986 and 1987. Just those two years. Does that seem odd to you?"

Annie processed the timeline of scientific history etched in her mind as a teenager. "1986 and 1987...that's when the scientific community was working on the genetics of muscular dystrophy."

"Big years for genetic researchers."

"So, what's the connection?" Annie asked, her dark eyes showing puzzlement. "Do you think DL-666 has the symptoms of muscular dystrophy?"

Crane shook his head. "I doubt it's going to be that simple, but I suspect that Dr. Lumbre knew the tissue would fail at some point, and the problem would be related to the X chromosome. What other reason would he have for archiving so many publications from those two years?"

Annie leaned toward Crane and put a hand on his arm. "If this leads to the solution to the problem, you win the blue ribbon for serendipity."

"I'm just looking for a place to start. The repair of DL-666 has the potential of turning into another Human Genome Project."

Annie shook her head. "We don't have time for that. We're in a crisis and need to find a short cut. The clock is ticking on Richard Hunter, and before long, a lot of other people will be in the same situation."

Crane nodded, but didn't reply.

"Dar Lumbre had a good reason for archiving those old journals," Annie said. "Maybe you've tapped into his thinking."

"This is somewhat of a back-door approach, but it's better than nothing," Crane said. "We need to tie the man to his invention in some way."

Annie took a bite of scone and a swallow of tea. She placed her iTab on the table and her nimble fingers danced on the screen for a moment. "You know," she said, looking up at Crane, "a lot of people believe NatGov erased all vital information about Dar Lumbre. They think the government has some kind of eradication council like the old movie, *Counterclock World*. Maybe that's why nobody found lab notes on DL-666."

"I don't know whether NatGov erased anything or not, but they turned against Dar Lumbre and others like him."

"They shot the messenger."

Crane nodded agreement. "A government fiasco-- one of the biggest."

Annie scrolled through her mental list of malefactors who blocked the use of data from the Genome Project. It consisted primarily of presidents, senators, representatives, and other government officials. She dubbed these people the *catalog of weasels*; history had not been kind to them.

Annie considered the Human Genome Project, completed in the early 2000's, to be one of the greatest accomplishments in the field of science. The international effort produced a map of all human genes—together known as the genome. For the first time in history, scientists were able to read a complete genetic blueprint of the species *Homo sapiens.*

The project, albeit a scientific success, caused a social upheaval when industry and government began to misapply the information. Insurance companies demanded genetic proof of insurability, employers required DNA testing, the FBI profiled ordinary citizens, and the CIA drew up lists of good genes and bad genes. On and on. The list of genetic atrocities seemed endless. When genetic discrimination led to demonstrations and riots, NatGov tried to reverse the damage by passing legislation making it a felony to use Genome Project data without a court order—a solution that caused more problems than it cured.

"It's still hard to believe," Crane said, "that NatGov would ban the use of such useful data for twenty-five years and make further genetic research on humans illegal during that period of time."

"The government caused a genetic dark age."

"Dark and light," Crane said. "Maybe that's a clue."

Annie looked puzzled. "What are you talking about?"

"How's your Spanish?"

Annie shrugged. *"Muy bien*, I guess. I had a couple of Puerto Rican friends in middle school, and we spoke Spanglish all the time, just for fun."

"Then you know the name, Dar Lumbre, means *to give light* in Spanish."

"Affirmative."

"It sounds like a fictional name."

Annie shrugged. "Why would he make up a name?"

"Maybe he was taunting his critics. Lumbre and 666—light and dark."

"I've always wondered why he didn't just skip that

number," Annie said. "He could have used DL-667 instead. Number 666 raises eyebrows."

"Did you know one of Apple's first computers was priced at $666.66?"

Annie's arched her eyebrows. "Did anybody give Apple a hard time?"

"Not that I know of."

"I think DL-666 was just the next number in a series," Annie said. "But if anyone wants to, he can read a theological concept into the number. Many people are doing it, right or wrong."

"It seems pretty far-fetched to me."

"It's similar to the doctrine that led to controversies in early church history," Annie said. "Some theologians did not accept the teaching that Jesus has two natures, one divine and the other human. Maybe Dr. Lumbre utilized the same concept."

They dropped the discussion about theological concepts and continued their iTab search, but found little of interest. Over the years, Annie had spent a lot of time pouring over the scant medical history related to Dar Lumbre. One thing was clear--Dr. Lumbre's star, though it burned brightly, burned briefly. His early work enjoyed strong support from President Charles Garwood. But Garwood was a one-term president, rejected by his own party, and not allowed to serve the normally-allotted second term. Under the next president, NatGov turned against Dar Lumbre and others like him. Many of his supporters believed the government action was altogether political, and had nothing to do with scientific experiments, legal or illegal. During the widespread chaos following the solar flare, Dr. Lumbre vanished. Yet, from the time he vanished until the present day, millions of people awaited his second coming, a messianic concept, to be sure.

"Dar Lumbre's story is weird, even to scientists," Annie said. "In spite of NatGov opposition during his day, the American people loved him, and he's considered to be the founder of CellTech. The board of Directors mentions him in every Annual Report, and his pic is displayed in the lobby along with other company memorabilia."

"What a paradox."

---

"Only in America."

"I've always wondered why Dr. Lumbre abruptly left the University of Nevada, Las Vegas, after his freshman year and finished his education at the University of Mexico," Crane said.

Annie took another bite of scone before answering, "I'm sure he had relatives living in Mexico."

"It's too bad no one ever found any records of his time in Mexico, especially at the university."

"Their records were destroyed, too," Annie said. "Probably a lot worse than ours. They'll never be able to reconstruct them,"

"His UNLV transcript turned up," Crane said, "and it shows a perfect grade point average, *four point zero*. Nothing but A's in every subject."

"All of his biographers claim he had a photographic memory," Annie said. "Total recall. Still, I don't see how he could do scientific research—especially genetics--without keeping detailed lab notes."

Crane rubbed his chin thoughtfully, but said nothing.

Suddenly, Annie's eyes lit up. "Have you heard about those studies at UNLV where human genes were spliced into sheep ova before fertilization?"

"Uh-huh. I've heard rumors, but never found a valid report."

"Those studies remind me of that old movie, *The Fly.*"

"Now, that's one old movie I know," Crane said. "My favorite scene is when the fly with a human face gets caught in the spider web and yells, *Help me, help me.*"

"There's a similar story about sheep with human DNA," Annie said. "According to the story, some pre-med students at UNLV were walking beside a pasture where genetically modified sheep grazed next to the fence. A young ram peeked through the fence and said, *Please, help me*. It was just like the movie."

Crane chuckled. "Do you really believe that story?"

"Of course. I read it on the internet."

"Maybe it's true," Crane said. "Something like that might be why Dar Lumbre left UNLV and went to Mexico to continue research that NatGov had banned."

"Something related to splicing human and animal chromosomes?"

"Exactly--and we both know that DL-666 is not entirely human."

## Chapter 9

Kim sat before the iTab docking station on her student desk with Mickey asleep on her feet. The condo was small--only 500 square feet--but comfortable. Unlike most units of its size, it had a separate bedroom which doubled as an office. She and Larry had moved into the efficiency unit after getting married a year ago. If Larry sold his computer program to Apple-Disney, he could request a housing upgrade from HUD. They should be able to afford it then.

At long last, Kim was about to start the final lesson of the Texas Driver Education Course. It had taken longer than she anticipated. The last four lessons involved driving on non-magnetized roads where the driver was in complete control of the car. Studying the lessons had given her greater appreciation for autopilot functions. She couldn't imagine what driving was like before smart cars. She wanted to finish the lesson tonight, and thought she could do it if Mickey didn't wake up and start nipping at her toes.

The iTab was linked to a thirty-inch monitor showing every detail in crystal clear resolution. Kim could have used virtual reality goggles for a simulated hands-on driving experience, but she preferred the flat screen projection. It was less intimidating. The clock in the upper menu bar showed seven o'clock. Larry would be home in about an hour, and she wanted to finish the driver education video before he returned. If she pressed on, she could do it.

She gazed at the monitor. The picture showed a two-lane road with orange construction cones positioned at periodic intervals along the right lane. She recognized the narrow highway as one which intersected Highway 36 out in the country. It was one of the busiest non-magnetized roads in the Houston area, and had been under repair for several years. She assumed the video was shot in a construction zone to test students over a wide range of traffic conditions.

The monitor flickered and the scene switched to a panoramic view. Several vehicles appeared in the wide-angle shot, then the camera zoomed in to focus on a small black and white car.

Kim was taken aback.

The car looked exactly like the one that Larry bought a couple of months ago. She stared at the image. The paint job was unmistakable—white with black spots, like a Dalmatian. Kim wondered if Larry's car was featured in the training video before he bought it, or after. She leaned closer to the screen, but couldn't read the number on the license plate. The plates of all cars in the video had been blurred digitally, along with the faces of everyone on camera.

Onscreen, the spotted car overtook a small blue pickup carrying a rusty clothes dryer. The car swung to the left, slipped past the pickup, and cut in front. Instantly, the pickup's collision avoidance system reacted and steered the vehicle onto the shoulder of the highway. It hit one of the plastic cones and sent it flying into the ditch. At that point, the road scene disappeared, and a digitized police officer appeared on the monitor.

"What violation did the driver of the mini-car commit?" the simulated officer asked.

Kim responded immediately. "He didn't give a signal."

"That is correct. What else?"

Kim hesitated. She wanted to get it right. "He was speeding in a construction zone."

"That is correct," the digital man intoned.

After affirming her answer, the officer faded like the Cheshire cat, and the road scene reappeared. A State Trooper riding a Hover-Harley appeared behind the spotted car. He turned on a siren and flashing red light. Obediently, the driver eased the small car onto the shoulder and stopped. The motorcycle floated to a stop behind the car. The uniformed officer dismounted and approached the driver's side of the vehicle.

"License and insurance, please," the officer said.

The driver picked up an iTab from the seat beside him, touched the screen briefly, and held it out of the window. The officer glanced at the screen and asked, "Do you know how fast you were going, Sir?"

The driver answered, but his voice was electronically distorted.

Kim replayed the first five minutes of the video, and

saw the same thing again--blurred license plates, pixelated faces, and distorted voices. The Texas Highway Department had done a good job of editing, except for one thing—the paint job was a dead giveaway.

The man getting the ticket was Larry. There was no doubt about it.

Kim glanced at the clock in the menu bar. It was nearing eight o'clock. Her husband should be home in a couple of minutes. She stared idly at the monitor until she heard the ringtone announcing Larry's entrance into the apartment. A moment later, he came into the bedroom.

He looked toward her. "Hi, what's up?"

"I want to show you something. Come over here."

"Just tell me," Larry said, as he tossed his jacket onto the bed.

Kim shook her head. "No, I want to show you."

Although Larry hesitated for only a split second before walking toward her, Kim thought she saw some reluctance in his demeanor.

She pointed to the monitor. "Is this you in the video?"

Larry stared at the picture on the monitor. "Where did you get that?"

"It's the Driver Ed program I'm studying, but you didn't answer my question—is that you?" Kim gazed at Larry, waiting.

He remained mute.

"Is it?" Kim asked again, her voice rising.

He breathed a long sigh. "Yes, I got a ticket."

Kim was piqued. "Why didn't you tell me?"

"I didn't want you to worry."

"Well, I worry more when you hide things from me," Kim said. "Besides, what were you doing running around late in the evening when I thought you were at Starbucks?"

Larry's tone was defensive. "Don't make such a big issue out of it," he said. "I didn't do anything wrong. All I did was drive out past Rosenberg to an old strip center where the Dar Lumbre Society was holding a rally."

"Did you go to the rally?"

"No. It was ending when I got there," Larry said. "I turned around in the parking lot, and got into a traffic jam.

The State Troopers stopped nearly everybody leaving the strip center and gave us tickets, whether we were speeding or not."

"Why would they do that?"

"They're harassing the society."

"Well, you shouldn't have been out there in the first place."

Larry gave a dismissive shrug. "What harm was there in driving by the society's office?"

"Well, for one thing, you got a ticket that will cost money we don't have," Kim snapped.

"A ticket is not a capital offense," Larry shot back, "so, stop treating me like a criminal."

"Where will we get the money to pay it? That's what I'd like to know."

"I'll sell my new program soon, and we'll have plenty of money."

"That's what you always say," Kim said, "but it never happens."

"Stop nagging me."

"I've got a right to nag. We're living from one paycheck to the next—my paycheck, I might add."

Larry glared at Kim a few seconds and stormed out of the room muttering under his breath.

## Chapter 10

Annie entered the T-shaped laboratory and strode toward Crane's office cubicle near the intersection of the two wings. She passed between parallel lab benches containing racks of sparkling glassware in a myriad of shapes and sizes. Beyond the glassware storage, she walked by incubators, centrifuges, autoclaves, DNA sequencing equipment, and other sophisticated equipment that was beeping, humming, and clicking. A constant rhythmic blinking of multicolored LEDs accompanied the polyphony.

This was Annie's world.

She went to Crane's cubicle where he sat hunched over his desk, staring intently at an image on his desktop monitor. She sat down on a lab stool beside his desk and said, "Any progress?"

"Maybe."

"Talk to me."

"Let's put this on the big screen," Crane said, getting up from his desk.

She bobbed up and followed him back into the main lab. They took their seats in the viewing area with Annie at Crane's right. She had occupied the spot since day one, subconsciously claiming it as the traditional spot for a trusted assistant.

Annie pointed toward the monitor. "I installed a new screensaver yesterday afternoon."

Crane looked at the screen. It displayed an African veldt complete to the last blade of grass and grain of sand. The waving grass surrounded a turquoise water hole. A lion approached, vultures circled, and the sun shined brightly.

"Even though the scene is different, this reminds me of that Disney ride, *Soaring Over California*," Annie said. "Do you like it?"

"Yeah, I guess."

"So…why don't you like it?"

"That kind of shifting scene makes me seasick."

"The pharmacy next to Starbucks sells Dramamine."

Crane ignored Annie's friendly jibe and motioned toward the monitor. A hidden sensor read his palm. The veldt dissolved into colorless fog for a brief moment before metamorphosing into an image of a winged staff with two strands of DNA coiled around it, CellTech's familiar logo. He gave another hand signal and the logo faded away, to be replaced by the pink image of a striated muscle fiber, the building block of DL-666. The slowly revolving image expanded until it was as tall as Crane.

"This first image is from Dar Lumbre's early work," Crane said. "We looked at it numerous times before the problem occurred. Our perspective might be different now that we're concentrating on the X chromosome. I think it's worth another shot."

Annie got up from her stool and stood beside Crane. She studied the image intently. It was in perfect focus. The mysterious Dr. Lumbre's slides were impressive. It would be impossible to make better ones today.

Crane signaled, and the magnification increased in stepwise fashion until it focused on a single elongated cell that was turgid and ready to divide. He motioned toward the cell. Obediently, it moved toward him, stopping in the 3D field where it appeared close enough to touch.

"Getting these cells to morph into usable heart muscle was a miraculous feat," Annie said. "No one else has ever come close to duplicating it."

"It's still mind-boggling."

"We'll figure out how he did it," Annie said, gazing at the gigantic image before them. She was convinced that Dr. Lumbre had used a virus for the final transformation, after a lot of gene splicing in the early stages. In effect, he tore the X chromosome apart piece by piece and reassembled it like a jigsaw puzzle. But now, a piece was missing, and they had to find it.

"Ready to tackle the X chromosome?" Crane asked.

"X's are my specialty. I've got two in every cell."

He signaled again, and the magnification increased, showing individual chromosomes. Slowly, the computer sifted through the maze of chromosomes until the X came into view. The X chromosome was paired with its Y counterpart, indicating that DL-666 was derived from male tissue, Dar Lumbre's own heart, by all indications.

---

Annie studied the pink chromosome standing out in bold relief against the black background. It floated in 3D space, the same height as Crane and only slightly thinner. She loved to work with chromosomes, and had mapped and manipulated them since middle school when she developed her first chromosome model of the American bullfrog. Her exhibit, *Genome of Bufo Americanus*, won first place in regional and second place in the State Science Fair of California. First place went to some tall guy with a project based on butterfly DNA. By some quirk of fate, the winner was a Crane Hopkins doppelganger. She was still peeved at the judges.

Annie had never thought of working in a field other than genetics. As far as she was concerned, there was no other field worth pursuing. She liked Crane's game plan for moving forward on the DL-666 project by focusing on the X chromosome. Hopefully, that shortcut was the right way to proceed. When they pinpointed a defective DNA base--assuming that was the problem--the next step would require a blending of science and art beyond anything she ever imagined in college. What Dar Lumbre did was more than genetic engineering; it was genetic artistry, and the artist had painted the Mona Lisa on a strand of DNA.

Crane adjusted the controls. "Do you see anything unusual? Anything at all?"

Annie's voice was barely a whisper. "Maybe...I'm not sure. This is an excellent angle on the X chromosome. That uncoiled element looks a little unusual, even for heavily spliced DNA. Don't you think so?"

Crane nodded. "I agree. It's totally atypical, which is probably the cause of the problem."

"Let's see what we can do with this," Annie said. "Why don't you split the screen into quadrants, and put the old specimen in the upper left quadrant with its DNA fingerprint in the upper right quadrant. That'll leave room to display the new specimen in the same manner below it."

Crane completed the maneuver.

"It's a shame the BLAST App wasn't more useful," Annie said, as she studied the chromosome and its accompanying fingerprint. The idiosyncratic nature of the tissue hindered the usefulness of the *Basic Local Alignment Search Tools* App, forcing them to rely more on old-school techniques to search for anomalies on the DNA strand.

"The DNA in this tissue shows little similarity to Human Genome maps," Crane said. "Dar Lumbre tweaked it so much it's barely human."

He signaled again, and the image of another X chromosome appeared at the lower left of the screen, directly below the first X chromosome. Another signal, and a second chromosome map appeared at the lower right.

"Okay, let's see how they compare," Annie said.

Crane advanced the video at high speed until the new image began to resemble the initial one directly above it. He instructed the computer to search for an exact match. With a series of whirring noises, the computer synchronized the images. A beep announced that the electronic detective had completed its search. The match was good. The images on the left of the screen seemed identical, but they were separated by a time span of fifty years.

"Superimpose the images," Annie said.

Crane signaled and the images overlapped. "Are they identical?"

"It's hard to tell for sure," Annie said, as she stared at the images. "Rotate the most recent image clockwise a little." She thought she saw something out of place, perhaps a bit of missing DNA on the short arm of the chromosome. If so, the fingerprints should pinpoint the differences in the two samples.

Crane adjusted the controls. "What do you see?"

Annie pursed her lips thoughtfully. "The fingerprints look exactly alike, and if that's the case, the malfunction can hardly be chemical in nature."

"It could be a mechanical problem brought on by the configuration of the molecule."

"Hindrance caused by the lengthy uncoiled section?" Annie said.

"Maybe."

After staring at the same area of the molecule for several minutes, Annie breathed a long sigh. "This molecule is tangled up. It's getting in its own way."

"Look at Band 21," Crane said. "There appears to be a breakpoint on the short arm adjacent to it, regardless of what the fingerprint says."

"The famous Xp21 location," Annie said. "You may be right about the muscular dystrophy connection. So…does DL-666 have MD? Or something similar?"

"Possibly," Crane said. "But, I don't understand why the problem is just now beginning to show up if the defect has been there for a long time."

"Let's channel the first MD researchers," Annie said. "What would they do?"

"We have a tougher job than they did," Crane said. "They had plenty of MD cases to study—case histories from large populations. DL-666 is one of a kind."

Annie grimaced. "No mother, no father, no sisters, no brothers, no aunts, uncles, or cousins. This freaky tissue is an orphan."

Crane joined the negative diatribe. "No lab notes, no DNA libraries, no markers, no probes."

Annie stared at the image frozen on the monitor. DL-666 was the biggest enigma she'd ever seen. The culture was known by name in the streets, yet little else was known about it, other than the fact that Dar Lumbre developed it during a time when such research was illegal. She wondered if some aspects of its use would become illegal again when President Keynes' latest Supreme Court nominee was confirmed? Who could tell? Nobody knew what NatGov would do next in the health care field. They had bungled it for more than a century.

"Okay," she said, "we've vented our frustrations. What next?"

"I think we should continue to focus on the Xp21 location," Crane said, as he gazed at the image. "If it's not the source of the problem, we'll have to start over."

"That would take a lot of time."

"I know," Crane said, fearing it would take more time than Richard Hunter had left.

## Chapter 11

The autopilot guided Larry's car across the Brazos River Bridge into Richmond-Rosenberg, a transit which made him feel like he was travelling in a time machine to the previous century.

Along both sides of the uneven street, historic downtown Richmond displayed holiday splendor. Every surface boasted a fresh coat of paint in a primary color, and twinkling lights beckoned sightseers and shoppers alike. The old buildings housed an eclectic mix of vendors--arts and crafts, antiques, gifts, and food. Houstonians and others came here to buy time-tested holiday favorites, or simply enjoy the sights and sounds of the season.

The residents of this area lived a rather drab existence for nearly eleven months of the year, but starting in November, most of them pitched in on a community rejuvenation project to make the historic area sparkle. While growing up, Larry and Crane often came to this area with their parents around Thanksgiving and Christmas, holidays which NatGov called Harvest Festival and Winter Solstice Celebration. He remembered how special these outings were when he was a child.

To his left, the old Richmond courthouse came into view. The building was protected by the Historical Society, and as an annex of Houston, it was maintained by NatGov funds. Three small museums occupied the first floor of the courthouse, the Museum of Tex-Mex History, the Museum of African-American History, and the Museum of Asian-American History. The remainder was divided into a beehive of small offices and apartments available for lease under GSA and HUD supervision. Most of the units were leased, and the area was turning into a pocket universe.

Behind a wrought iron fence covered with ivy, a bronze statue of Sam Houston on a horse watched over the grounds. The statue originally faced east toward the San Jacinto Battleground where General Houston defeated the Mexican army under Santa Anna. Ten years ago, the Racial Equality Bureau ordered the statue to be rotated to the north so it wouldn't denigrate Mexican-Americans any longer.

---

73

Five minutes past the courthouse, Larry approached a group of corrugated steel buildings which had housed a cottonseed processing plant during the 1900's. He'd passed this complex dozens of times, never giving it more than a precursory glance. Today, it was his destination, and he took a close look at the cluster of sturdy buildings which made up the complex. They resembled Aztec pyramids covered in rusty sheet metal. Breezeways made from the same material linked the pyramidal structures together, and a steady flow of foot traffic on the paths between the buildings gave an air of purpose to the dull-looking location.

He touched the screen of the autopilot and resumed control of his vehicle. Dodging a pothole, he squeezed his car into a space near the largest building and got out. Most of the people on the paths were wearing sturdy khaki and denim, clothing characteristic of manual laborers--farmers, plumbers, carpenters, cooks, maids, mechanics, and others who worked with their hands. Their abilities had been acquired through years of hard work, yet according to NatGov they were failures—Outsiders, because they had not registered to vote.

Larry went into the building, and walked down the linoleum-lined corridor leading through the ground floor. After passing by Muy Pronto Bail Bonds, Cookie's Dulces, and Kolache Heaven, he entered Jose's Hamburgers and looked around.

John Stone sat alone at a corner table. He stood and extended his hand as Larry approached. After exchanging greetings, the two men sat down facing each other, and John signaled the waiter.

The waiter approached John's side of the table and asked, "The usual, Mr. Stone?"

John said, "Yes," and turned toward Larry. "What would you like?"

"Coffee...black."

The waiter withdrew, and John said, "Thank you for meeting me."

Larry felt cold sweat on his palms. "I have a lot of questions."

"Could I ask you a couple of questions first?"

Larry nodded. "Go ahead."

"When did you begin to believe that Dar Lumbre will return soon?"

"I've always been inclined to believe it," Larry said, "and something happened recently that totally convinced me."

"What happened?"

Larry told John about picking up Elmore Larson's voice transmission from Anaheim via the hot mike incident. As he finished the story, the waiter appeared carrying two coffees on a tray. He set the cups on the table along with a bowl of Mexican sugar and a pitcher of non-dairy creamer.

John added two heaping teaspoons of beige colored sugar to his coffee and pushed the bowl toward Larry.

"No, thanks."

"Do you have family living in this area?" John asked, as he stirred his coffee.

"My wife, my parents, and my brother."

"What do they think about your interest in the Dar Lumbre Society?"

"Kim--my wife--is worried about it."

John made a dismissive hand gesture. "Why would she be worried?"

"Her father is in a C-Unit awaiting a second heart surgery," Larry said. "Needless to say, she doesn't want me to get mixed up in anything illegal."

"At the moment, all we're trying to do is get Outsiders registered to vote," John said. "That's not illegal. NatGov claims they're doing the same thing. They're suspicious of us, though, because we're not affiliated with either of the approved political parties."

"Why the secrecy?" Larry asked. "I mean...why didn't we meet at the society building out on Highway 36?"

"We're meeting in Jose's Hamburgers," John said. "A public place. No secrecy in that."

John paused, and a moment of silence passed as Larry waited for him to continue.

"The fact is," John went on, "NatGov would try to block our efforts, if they understood the full extent of our plans."

Larry leaned forward. "Will Dr. Lumbre really bring an M-gene when he returns, or is that a red herring tossed out to distract NatGov's attention away from what the society really intends to do?"

John smiled faintly. "We expect Dr. Lumbre's genetic discoveries to lengthen the life-span of many people, but not necessarily through the use of a Methuselah gene."

"Then, why's there so much Outsider buzz about it?"

"Outsiders aren't stupid," John said. "They know NatGov will take control of any medical innovation that Dar Lumbre brings with him, or any he develops after his return. If Outsiders want access to these new developments, they'll have to register. We're making that clear to them, and they're responding to our message."

"Universal health care is a political football, and always has been," Larry said.

John looked around furtively and pulled an ancient cellphone from the pocket of his camouflage jacket. It was a flip top with a short antenna, the kind seen only in museums. He opened the phone with his thumb, and punched in a number into the keypad. It buzzed, and someone answered in a garbled voice.

"Are you ready for us to come?" John asked.

When John paused, Larry could hear a muffled answer.

"Okay," John said. "I'm bringing the guy I told you about."

Larry heard the unintelligible voice again.

"Of course, I'm sure he's okay, "John said. "He and I have talked a lot about the society and its goals. He's a high-tech guy, the kind we need to enlist. We'll see you in a few minutes." He closed the phone and slipped it back into his pocket.

"What kind of phone is that?" Larry asked.

"Analog. A very old model."

"The National Security Agency can monitor analog."

"I know they can," John said, "but they don't. The agency's monitoring system is so overloaded with digital transmissions that they can't process the data they have in storage now, but they keep on collecting more. They don't bother with analog anymore."

Larry's concern was not assuaged. "They might start monitoring it again if they get suspicious."

"We have operatives in the NSA," John said. "*Moles*, some people would call them. They're secret members of the Dar Lumbre Society, and will warn us if the policy changes."

Larry was impressed.

"We're hiding in plain sight," John said, "and will continue to do so until the movement is too big to stop,"

"How long will that be?"

"Very soon," John said. "We're about to launch a sociopolitical tsunami. In the next couple of weeks, millions of Outsiders will register to vote, largely because of the society's efforts. That will change the way things run in Washington. NatGov won't be able to check our momentum then, no matter how hard they try."

Larry took a deep breath. "I'm almost convinced."

"Okay, let's go," John said. "I'll show you what we're doing right now. Then, we'll talk about our future plans and how you could fit into them."

Larry waited as John swung by the counter to pay for the coffee, and they headed toward the elevator. He admired the clever way the Dar Lumbre Society was playing cat and mouse with NatGov. He understood the society's desire to help those neglected by the government for so long. Still, he didn't understand many ramifications of the new movement that was drawing him into its vortex.

They took the elevator to the fifth floor. Larry followed John down the dimly lit hallway, and they stopped before an unmarked door. John glanced around and knocked.

The door opened. A young man with long red hair stood facing them. "Hello, John. Come in."

Larry and John stepped inside.

John made the introductions. "Larry Hopkins, meet Jerry Legrand from our Anaheim office."

The two men shook hands.

"Where's Julie?" John asked.

"She's in the printing room," Jerry said. "She'll be out in a minute."

They stepped into the living area of the apartment.

As they entered, a scraping sound occurred from the rear wall, and a panel slid away to reveal a spacious room. Clicking and whirring noises emitted from the room.

A young woman came out of the room and entered the living area. Looking directly at Larry, she approached the three men. He returned her gaze. She was a bold-looking woman about his age, with thick dark hair and barely-visible freckles. She was wearing black jeans and a blue denim work shirt. Tan and fit looking, she exuded competence and authority. Larry could tell immediately that she was not an Outsider from the Richmond-Rosenberg area.

"Hello," she said, extending her hand. "I'm Julie--like the Julie in *1984*. I don't suppose you're Winston Smith?"

Larry was surprised by the woman introducing herself in terms of the George Orwell classic. He'd used the *big brother* analogy frequently himself, but only in the presence of his immediate family. He wondered how the woman had managed to get such a quick read on his political psyche? It was unnerving.

He recovered his composure and grasped her outstretched hand. "Hi. I'm Larry Hopkins."

"John says you'll help us distribute these tracts," Julie said. "We're printing them by the thousands, and need a lot of help handing them out."

She handed one of the booklets to Larry. It was one of the *Register To Vote* tracts he had seen at the society office, a leaflet so innocuous in appearance that he couldn't understand why secrecy was necessary.

Larry frowned. "Do you think NatGov will ban...*this?*"

Julie's eyes sparkled. "If they planned to, they've missed their chance."

"Why do you need my help? Anybody can hand out tracts."

"This is just the beginning of our campaign, and as you said, anybody could do it," Julie said. "But, soon, we'll begin working on projects which require a high level of technical expertise. John told me you're a computer expert with a desire to help Outsiders. Is that right?"

"I guess that's how I'd describe myself."

"The *Dar Lumbre Society Wants You*—have you

seen the poster?"

"Yeah...I like it."

"Do you think it's effective?"

"It must be. A lot of people are joining."

Inexplicably, Larry felt a strong connection to Julie, even though he knew nothing about her beyond his first impression. The only thing they had in common was the Dar Lumbre Society, where he was a total novice and Julie a pro. Yet, something had clicked between them instantly. He didn't understand it.

Julie opened a metal cabinet to reveal dozens of plastic boxes with snap-on lids. "These are ready, John."

"We'll load them in my Expedition," John said, "and start handing them out the first thing in the morning. Other volunteers with pickups and SUV's will meet us at the office to help blanket the Richmond-Rosenberg area."

Larry was puzzled at the timing. "Is Saturday the best day to do this?"

John nodded. "For Outsiders, it's a good day. Surveys show more of them will be home early Saturday morning than any other time. If they're not at home, they'll be taking produce to the Farmers' Market. If not there, we'll look in the fields. We'll find them tomorrow or another day soon."

John took a grocery cart from the printer room, and for the next thirty minutes, the three men hauled the contents of the cabinet to John's SUV, one cartload at a time. When they finished, Larry went back into the printer room where Julie was working on the next batch of tracts.

He watched as Julie loaded another ream of paper into the old printer. It clicked again and again. At each click, a sheet of paper popped out of a slot and dropped into the document tray. The setup was primitive, but effective.

Julie turned toward Larry. "See what we're doing here?" she said, motioning with her hand. "There are hundreds of other locations throughout the U.S. doing the same thing right now."

Larry was astounded. "Hundreds? Wouldn't it be simpler to put commercials on TV?"

Julie shook her head. "A lot of Outsiders don't have TV, so this is still the best way to get information to them en masse, maybe the only way. We're going to spend a week handing them out. It's old fashioned, but it works because NatGov isn't paying attention to our stone-age methods."

"What will you do next?"

Julie looked directly at Larry. "Do you mean me, or the society?"

"Uh...both."

"I won't be passing out any more of these flyers. From now on, I'll be working to arrange interviews and speaking engagements for Mr. Larson when he arrives in Houston. I just landed a plum. Monday morning, he'll appear on the Carolina Herrera Show."

"That's a big one," Larry said. "In Houston, Carolina is the queen of daytime TV, and stations all across the country pick up her show as well."

"In addition to TV, we intend to start utilizing every kind of social media available," Julie said. "We'll tag, poke, invite, request, text, phish, Instagram, and tweet everybody we can find."

"How many people work for the society?" Larry asked. He was amazed at Julie's grasp of the sociopolitical aspects of the project.

"Thousands," Julie said. "And we have hundreds of operatives like John Stone working in Outsider communities where they've lived for a long time. We've worked on this plan for years."

"How can that be?" Larry asked. "I've never heard of this movement until recently, except for a few rumors which seemed unbelievable."

"You can believe the rumors now," Julie said. "Right after the solar flare, the society formed and helped Dr. Lumbre disappear. Today, there are many second and third generation members in the society."

A dozen or so questions popped into Larry's head simultaneously, but before he could voice a single one, John said, "We're going to get something to eat--maybe some Texas barbeque. Would you like to come with us?"

Larry hesitated briefly before answering, "I can't. I have to get home."

"That's too bad," Julie said. She did an about face

and marched toward the rear of the printer room.

Larry watched the intriguing woman recede into the shadows. He'd never met anyone like her. She was bold and brassy--possibly dangerous, as well.

He looked forward to seeing her again.

## Chapter 12

Larry stopped the car in front of Party Town. Before Kim could unbuckle her seat belt, a car backed out of a parking slot directly in front of them. "Wait," he said. "I'll get that place."

"Just let me out here," Kim said, "unless you want to come into the store."

"I want to show you something."

"I need to scan in before noon."

Larry was insistent. "We have plenty of time. He pulled into the parking space, and they got out. "Come with me over to the poster wall."

Officially, poster walls were known as *Public Graffiti and Poster Walls*. Numerous such sites were constructed thirty years ago by the PubWorks Administration following a Supreme Court ruling that many citizens had no way to exercise their constitutional right to freedom of speech without help from NatGov. The walls were part of the court's answer to this inequity.

Kim was reluctant. "What do you want to show me?"

Larry caught Kim's hand and led her to the huge electronic screen shimmering with hundreds of holograms ranging in size from a sticky note to a TV monitor. The images on the wall waxed and waned in screen-saver fashion, displaying moving pics surrounded by every color of the rainbow. At one end of the wall, two young graffiti artists worked on iTabs linked into the wall via Wi-Fi. They spoke softly in Spanish as they drew a portion of their dream world on the wall.

Larry pointed to a large hologram. "Look at that."

The screen showed a man, apparently late middle aged, but handsome and charismatic. He was pointing a finger in the pose reminiscent of Uncle Sam's *I Want You* poster displayed in armed forces museums throughout the country. A caption blinked beneath the photograph:

THE DAR LUMBRE SOCIETY RALLY

"Who is the guy in the picture?" Kim asked.

"That's Elmore Larson, the leader of the society."

"Really?"

Larry nodded. "Yes, and he's in Houston right now."

Kim winced. Larry's infatuation with the Dar Lumbre Society was beginning to grate on her nerves. "What are you suggesting?" she asked.

"We should go to one of the rallies."

"I wouldn't walk across the street to see one. I've told you that before."

"Think about it."

"I already have."

"They're registering a lot of Outsiders," Larry said passionately. "That's a good cause."

Kim glanced at the caption beneath the picture. "This outfit sounds like a cross between a new political party and a new religion. Aren't both illegal?"

Larry shrugged. "Sometimes it's difficult to determine what's legal and what's not."

"I have to get to work," Kim said. "One of us has to earn a paycheck." She turned away and started along the sidewalk toward the entrance of Party Town.

Larry watched as Kim disappeared into the store without glancing back.

Once inside, Kim went to the time clock near the manager's office and thumbprinted in as the clock struck noon. Directly in front of her, Sandy touched her thumb to the sensor plate a microsecond before noon, and they walked away together.

"Hey, Kim," Sandy said. "I didn't think you were here."

Kim sighed. "I'm here, but just barely."

They retrieved freshly laundered red smocks from the supply locker near the clock and started toward their respective checkout stations. After tying on her smock, Sandy looked at Kim for several seconds, and asked, "What's wrong?"

"I'm worried about Dad," Kim said, as she clipped on her nametag.

"How's he doing?"

"He's stable--that's all the doctors ever tell me when I ask."

---

"What about Larry?" Sandy asked. "I saw you guys at the poster wall. You were having a lively discussion. Is something wrong?"

Kim shook her head. "Everything's okay."

They reached their stations and began to prepare for the day's work, another slow one according to early indications. The store was practically deserted except for workers, a situation that resurrected the discussion about the economy and jobs. Finally, a few people drifted in to break the monotony.

Sandy checked out a customer and looked across the aisle toward Kim as the customer left the store. "We've worked together too long to keep secrets," she said. "I know something else is wrong. Tell me what's bothering you."

Kim was not surprised at Sandy's insistence. They'd worked together for nearly two years and had shared many secrets. Moreover, Sandy wasn't above prying from time to time, albeit in a friendly way. After hesitating briefly, Kim decided to accept the invitation to talk. In one sentence, she blurted out the story about Larry getting a ticket and not telling her until she saw his car on the Driver Ed video.

"I would have thrown a major hissy fit," Sandy said. "Maybe that's why I'm twice married and twice divorced."

"We had a minor argument, that's all," Kim said. "We're okay now. He wasn't doing anything really bad when he got the ticket--maybe speeding a little. It could have happened to anybody, but I wish he'd told me about it, instead of letting me find out on my own."

"Anything else?"

"Recently, Larry got interested in the Dar Lumbre Society. I'm sure you've heard of it."

"Who hasn't?" Sandy said. "Their commercials are on every news screen I pass. That organization is growing like wildfire, particularly among Outsiders. It's probably just a fad that will pass quickly."

"Larry is committed to the Outsider's cause, too," Kim said. "For that reason, and maybe others, he doesn't think the movement is going away anytime soon."

"Maybe not," Sandy said. "But whatever they do, it won't affect us. We're doomed to be low-paid cashiers at

Party Town until we start collecting social security."

"Well, at least we have jobs."

An elderly woman carrying a shopping basket approached and placed a few small items on Kim's counter.

Kim put on her *happy-cashier* face and said, "Good afternoon. Thank you for shopping at Party Town." She was glad to see a customer in the store.

The day crept along at a snail's pace. In the middle of the afternoon, Kim's iTab played the first line of *Beautiful Dreamer*, her favorite ringtone at the moment. She retrieved it from beneath the counter. The screen showed Larry's avatar.

"Larry? What is it?"

"Hey, Kim. What's up?"

By his tone, Kim knew Larry wanted to tell her something important. "Why are you calling me at work?"

"I'm thinking about attending the meeting of the Dar Lumbre Society tonight."

"Will that guy be there?"

"What guy?"

"The old dude on the poster wall."

"Oh…you mean Elmore Larson," Larry said. "I'm not sure whether he'll be there, or not. Still, I'd like to go."

"That area is run down. Do you think it's safe out there after dark?"

"Most of the people are farmers. How dangerous could they be?"

"What time will the rally be over?"

"I don't know for sure. A little after eight, I think."

"Are you going by yourself?"

"Of course," Larry said in a defensive tone. "Who would be going with me?"

Kim shrugged. "I don't know, but you're getting obsessed with that stupid society."

"They're trying to help Outsiders. I think that's a good cause."

"Since when did you become a crusader?"

"I've always supported the underdog."

"Well…if you go, don't come dragging in late. I don't like that after I've worked all day."

---

85

"I won't."

"I have to go. A customer is coming," Kim said, logging off.

The afternoon dragged by incessantly. The lack of customers at Party Town was getting to be an everyday occurrence, and had become Sandy's main topic of discussion. A few weeks ago, when Sandy first mentioned a recession, Kim didn't give it a second thought. But now, Party Town traffic seemed to indicate that something was wrong with the economy.

The idle time gave Kim the opportunity to rethink the events of the last few days. Although she'd told Sandy otherwise, she feared her relationship with Larry may have developed a few hairline fractures, even though they'd stopped arguing about the speeding ticket. Telling her coworker part of the story made her feel better momentarily, but the feeling was wearing off, and she wondered what to do next.

The work day dragged to a close, and Kim took the Metro back to the West Gray Condos. It was ten o'clock when she opened the front door of the unit. She stood at the entrance for a moment to allow her eyes to adjust. Something was wrong. The living/dining area was dark. From where she stood, Kim could see into the bedroom. Larry's workstation was dark, as was her iTab docking station. A tiny LED glowed on the smoke detector above the bedroom door, the only source of light in the entire condo.

Larry was not home.

## Chapter 13

Crane dawdled along the aisles of the Village Antique Bookstore, one of his favorite Saturday morning hangouts. The tiny shop specialized in novels and short stories from the era when publishing houses printed on real paper. He'd spent countless hours in the shop searching for classic science fiction, and was constantly on the lookout for works by Philip K. Dick, Kurt Vonnegut, and Ray Bradbury— the top three SF writers of all times in his opinion. In addition to the three old masters, he liked Don Johnston a lot. Johnston wrote in the early years of twenty-first century. Unfortunately, he didn't start writing until he was eighty, so his entire body of work consisted of two novels and seven short stories. Crane sensed that he would find something special today, perhaps a novel by one of his favorites.

Out of the corner of his eye, Crane detected movement. He turned and saw Lily Long, the owner of the shop, approaching. Lily was a good friend, even though she was about the same age as his parents. A bibliophilic connection between Crane and Lily negated the age difference.

"Hi, L.L.," Crane said. "What's up?"

Lily's eyes twinkled. "Good morning, Crane. I've got something special for you."

"Something about to be banned?"

Lily beckoned and smiled slyly. "Come."

Crane followed Lily down the aisle to the rear of the store, and they stopped before a door covered with musty-smelling orange drapes. Lily pulled the drapes aside and motioned for Crane to enter the short hallway beyond the door. Once inside, they went to a floor length mirror at the end of the hall. Lily touched the screen of her iTab, and the mirror slid aside to reveal a small bookshelf hidden behind it. The shelf held fewer than a dozen books, Lily's private stock, each wrapped in clear plastic.

At the bookcase, Lily knelt and removed one of the books from the bottom shelf. "I thought of you when I acquired this one."

She stood and handed her selection to Crane.

---

"*Ubik*, by Philip K. Dick…incredible," he said, rubbing a finger across the title. He examined the book carefully. The cover was faded, but the caption, *One of Time's 100 best English-language novels*, was still clearly visible. The binding was intact and felt sturdy. A real find, he thought. A bona fide collectible by any standard. He wanted the book if he could afford Lily's price, which wouldn't be cheap.

"NatGov will ban the sale of this book in the near future," Lily said. "They're considering it now."

"Why? *Ubik* is not anti-government."

"They're linking it to *The Zap Gun* by the same author. Both are about to be banned."

"*Zap Gun* is political satire," Crane said, "but not *Ubik*. I don't understand why NatGov would ban it."

"My ears in Washington tell me *The Zap Gun* ban is based on the use of two words, *pursaps* for regular citizens, and *cogs* for government officials," Lily said. "These words don't pass the politically correct smell test. NatGov sees these words as derogatory, rather than empowering."

Crane shook his head in disbelief.

Before he could broach the subject of Lily's asking price for *Ubik*, his iTab buzzed.

A glance at the screen revealed that the caller was Kim. Crane was surprised. She hadn't contacted him directly since she and Larry started dating nearly two years ago. Something was wrong, or she wouldn't be calling now.

"Excuse me, L.L. I need to take this call."

"Sure, go ahead. I'll wait here."

Crane stepped through the curtained doorway into the main store, and touched the screen of his iTab. "Hi, Kim. What's up?"

"I need to talk to you."

"Is your dad okay?" Crane asked, fearing the worst.

"As the doctor tells me every day, he's stable. But, that's not why I'm calling--I need to talk to you about something else."

"Go ahead. I'm listening."

"I'd really like to talk to you in person."

Crane was puzzled. "Can't you tell me what's wrong over the phone?"

Kim hesitated before answering. "It would be much easier face to face."

"Are you at work?"

"Yes," Kim said. "I'll get a break in twenty minutes. Could you come to the store?"

Crane knew he was hearing a plea that required his immediate attention. "I'll grab the Metro," he said. "Where will you be when I get there?"

"I'll wait in the employee's break room," Kim said. "If we can't find a quiet corner there, we'll go back to one of the stockrooms."

"I'll be there in a few minutes."

"Thanks, Crane. I really appreciate it."

Crane stuck his head back through the curtains. "I've got to leave. My sister-in-law needs me to meet her at work. Don't sell *Ubik* out from under me."

"Okay, I'll hold it until I see you again," Lily said. After a pause, she added, "Unless I get an offer I can't refuse."

"If that happens, text me."

Lily nodded. "I will."

Crane left the bookstore and hurried to the Metro stop at the end of the block.

Fifteen minutes later, he entered Party Town and located the employee break room. The odor of stale French fries overlaid with air freshener greeted him as he walked in. Near the back of the room, Kim sat at one end of a rectangular table surrounded by folding chairs. The only other occupant of the room was a young man about twenty. He was seated at a table near the entrance, playing *Angry Pterodactyls* on an iTab.

When Crane approached, Kim stood and they hugged.

Kim smiled faintly. "Thanks for coming."

"Glad to do it."

The iTab gamer got up to leave. He nodded at Kim as he walked out.

"He works in the stock room," Kim said. "A nice kid...very reliable...never misses a day."

"Can we talk here?" Crane asked. "Or do we need to find some place more private?"

---

89

Kim glanced around the room. "This will be okay. Everybody has gone back to work."

"What happens if you return late?"

"Sandy is covering for me. Anyway, the store is nearly empty. I won't be missed."

Crane motioned toward the chairs. "Let's sit down." He was anxious to hear why Kim called, but didn't want to rush her.

Kim leaned toward him. "I hated to call you."

Crane turned his chair sideways to face Kim directly. "We've been friends a long time. You can tell me anything."

Kim nodded. "I know--and I appreciate it."

After a brief silence, Crane said, "Take your time." Being reticent about personal matters himself, he understood Kim's reluctance.

Kim regained her composure and continued, "Larry has been acting strange lately."

"How so?"

Kim told Crane about seeing Larry get a ticket in the Driver Ed video, and added, "We argued about it. Finally, he convinced me that everything was okay. I was willing to let it go until he came home late a couple of nights ago."

"How late?"

"About ten o'clock," Kim said. "That might not sound late to most people, but he's usually home much earlier. On days when I have the afternoon shift, he works on his program at Starbucks until around eight o'clock, but never much later."

"Did he call or text?"

"No," Kim said, shaking her head. "I tried to call him, but his iTab was on mute--accidentally, he said."

"Did he tell you where he'd been?"

Kim pulled a wrinkled booklet out of her iTab bag and lay it on the table in front of Crane. "Larry was helping print these *Register To Vote* flyers. I hope it wasn't illegal."

Crane picked up the booklet and flipped through it. "NatGov is having a conniption about this," he said, "but there's not much they can do about it now."

"Is it illegal?"

"No, but NatGov opposes any political literature not

sanctioned by one of the approved parties. You probably shouldn't have it here at work--I'd better take it with me." Crane folded the leaflet in half and stuck it in the hip pocket of his jeans.

After a moment, Kim continued, "Larry brought the flyer home to show me, and it looks completely harmless. He claims the society isn't doing anything illegal, but the whole concept seems radical to me. I wonder what he's gotten himself into."

"The Dar Lumbre Society is spreading rapidly all over the country," Crane said. "I don't have any problem with what they're doing. To the contrary, I think registering Outsiders is a worthy cause. NatGov never put much of an effort into it, although they claimed to."

Kim's expression was glum. "It's more than that, Crane."

"What are you trying to say?" Crane asked, realizing that Kim hadn't yet told him why she'd called.

"I'm afraid Larry might be seeing another woman— maybe one in this organization," Kim blurted out.

"What makes you think so?"

"Just the things I've told you about…the speeding ticket…coming in late."

"Anything else?" Crane was out of his comfort zone.

"That's all--except my woman's intuition."

"Do you trust your intuition in matters this serious?"

"It's usually right."

"Have you confronted Larry about this?"

"Not really," Kim said, "and it's not my nature to accuse him unless I have evidence—which I don't. We've been arguing a lot lately, and I'm suspicious, but that's all."

"How long have you been suspicious?"

"A couple of weeks."

"What do you want me to do?" Crane asked. Even before he finished speaking, he wondered how to proceed. Larry wasn't going to play twenty questions, or sit still for a Roman Inquisition. Crane knew this kind of investigation was not his forte. He was a DNA detective, not a gumshoe. Still, he had to do something to help Kim. Her problem had defaulted to him.

—

"Keep your eyes and ears open when you're around Larry," Kim said. "Maybe you can find a tactful way to bring up this subject."

"I'll try to find out what's going on," Crane said, "but I'll have to wait for the right opportunity. This is a serious accusation."

"Thanks, Crane. I knew I could count on you."

## Chapter 14

Dr. Helena Cartwright stepped out of a robo-cab onto the sidewalk in front of the Sausalito Bay Condos. She was wearing a sky-blue pantsuit made from ersatz silk, the de facto uniform of the day for modern women in positions of authority. Her short jacket was expertly tailored to conceal the fact that she was fifteen pounds overweight, and her dishwater blonde hair was cut in the latest unisex style. Her manner was brisk, confident, and businesslike.

For fifteen years, Dr. Cartwright had hoped to become director of the Office of Financial Stability by the time she was fifty years old, but that career milestone passed her by a month ago when she turned fifty. She still aspired to the position, but had the feeling her career had reached the do-or-die point. The current OFS Director planned to retire after next year's presidential election, a time-frame which seemed advantageous to her since a new assignment was coming her way. That would give her about a year to outshine her counterparts, several of whom were also vying for the directorship. As far as she was concerned, the current director had climbed the ladder of success while others held the ladder. She didn't want the same thing to happen again, and vowed to do whatever it took to stand out from the crowd.

Dr. Cartwright entered the lobby of the condos adjacent to the Casa Madrona Historical Museum. She crossed the smoky marble floor to the glass elevator and glanced at the retina scanner beside the door. The scanner recognized her, began to play *I Am Woman*, and the door slid open. She stepped inside and, as the capsule rose, looked out across San Francisco Bay toward Tiberon Island. The view was spectacular, the proper ending to another successful week.

Two years ago, Dr. Cartwright had purchased the condo in anticipation of several consecutive assignments in the Bay Area, but such wasn't the case. She would be moving soon. Due to her status with NatGov, selling the unit wasn't a concern, even in an economic downturn. If she needed to, she could use her accumulated perks. NatGov owed her.

---

Her specialty was restructuring companies in the medical field under the auspices of the OFS. The authority of the office was vested in her when she took on a project, and with the office's backing, she had resurrected five companies in fifteen years. As she saw it, one rescue every three years should be deemed outstanding by anybody's measuring stick. She knew some people called her ruthless, but that was of little concern to her. Instead of worrying about what others thought, she stayed focused on her job and career.

Dr. Cartwright left the elevator on the sixth floor and went down the hallway to her luxury condo. She thumbed the sensor plate on her door, and it glided open with a whisper. Upon entering the condo, she walked through the living room to her secluded study, a cozy and functional niche designed by a talented architect who knew how to utilize angles and glass. On clear days, she could the Oakland Bay Bridge and the Golden Gate Bridge at the same time. Sometimes, haze prevented her from seeing past Tiburon Island, but even reduced visibility could not hide the charm of San Francisco Bay. She felt a little sad to be leaving the bay area, but her work in California was finished. It was time to move on to the next project.

In all likelihood, her next assignment would be Houston, a city that she knew well. Nearly ten years earlier, she had worked on an OFS project in the Bayou City. Upon completing that assignment, she remained in Houston on a short sabbatical to lead a fruit fly study in affiliation with Rice University. The two back to back projects produced mixed results—total success on the OFS venture, but a subpar outcome on the fruit fly research due to problems with a student assistant.

Still, she would welcome a Houston redux. If things went well, she could relocate and settle in before the Winter Solstice Celebration.

Dr. Cartwright looked at the incoming posts on her iMessenger linked to a NatGov secured server. As always, some junk popped up that the security system was unable to filter—text blasts from politicians, pleas from charities, and other assorted spam and phishing. Even a text from the Dar Lumbre Society urging her to register to vote. Nothing from Washington yet. NatGov was getting bigger and bigger, and slower and slower. The layers of red tape had multiplied over the last few years, and the government functionaries couldn't keep up. Although she worked for NatGov, Dr. Cartwright considered herself to be an outside-the-beltway operative. She hadn't spent much time in Washington, and didn't expect to move there ever, unless she became the next OFS Director.

She picked up a pair of binoculars and zoomed in on a clump of sailboats anchored in the marina. The scene below her was a microcosm of Marin County, a classroom to study local culture. Observations made here helped her understand sociological changes before they went viral nationwide. She enjoyed being ahead of the curve, and would strive to do the same thing in Houston, if the OFS relocated her there.

The iMessenger on her desk sounded a ringtone, the first eight notes of *"Mona Lisa."*

She turned toward it. "Dr. Cartwright speaking."

Activated by her voice, the monitor coalesced into a picture of a blue-suited man in his mid-fifties. "Hello, Dr. Cartwright," the man said. "Howard Jefferson here. How are you this evening?"

Something about Jefferson annoyed her. He had low-level clerk written all over him, but NatGov had promoted him to an important job. Probably as payment for being a devoted serf, she surmised. Dr. Cartwright had to work through functionaries like Jefferson every time she relocated. He handled loose ends for turnaround specialists who were changing locations; hopefully, he was about finished with the details concerning her move. She was ready to get started on the next project as soon as possible, and was seeing San Francisco Bay in her rearview mirror already.

Dr. Cartwright eschewed all small talk. "Hello, Mr. Jefferson. Do you have the information on my next assignment?"

"Yes, and the Director is sure you'll like it," Jefferson said. "It's CellTech in Houston, as you suspected it might be. They manufacture artificial hearts and other...."

"I know what they do. You don't have to tell me."

---

95

"Sorry. What information do you need?"

"When do I start?"

"In two weeks, if that's satisfactory with you."

"That will be fine, Mr. Jefferson. And you'll take care of the details with HUD regarding this condo?"

"Of course," Jefferson said, "and I'll send you all of the background information about CellTech--organizational charts, financials, products, and so forth. Everything you'll need to get started."

"I'd like the info by Monday."

Jefferson cleared his throat. "I'll try."

"Do it," Dr. Cartwright said, touching the screen to break the connection.

She opened a cabinet beside her desk to reveal a wet bar stocked with mineral water and ice. After pouring a glass of Evian, she swiveled her chair around to examine a trophy case on the wall behind her. The case contained her MVP awards. Rather than glittery hardware like that collected by athletes, the case held a display of logos from the companies she had managed to a successful turnaround. She loved the trophies and expected to add another at the end of her Houston assignment. Failure never crossed her mind.

She was struck by an urge to take a closer look at CellTech's logo. She turned back to the iMessenger, touched the screen, and stared at the image that materialized. At first glance, the logo appeared to be an ordinary caduceus common in the medical field, but closer examination revealed chains of DNA, rather than snakes, coiled around a winged staff.

Original, interesting, and informative, she thought. Duly impressive.

She leaned back in the chair and took a sip of Evian, her mind making the transition to Houston.

Chapter 15

Disappointed that Crane was too busy to join her, Annie left the CellTech complex on Friday evening and headed toward her favorite restaurant, the Palace of Oriental Delights. She despised eating alone because she enjoyed conversation along with her food, although eating with Crane could be a one-way conversation at times. Even at that, she enjoyed his company and thought she understood him well, even though she'd overheard others say that he was too idiosyncratic to figure out.

The Palace boasted the most eclectic mixture of customers she'd seen anywhere, including Marin County. That was part of its appeal. The way Annie opined, if she couldn't have conversation, she might as well have a show, and a show was always in progress at the Palace--not a floorshow, but a sideshow put on by bizarre clientele who often utilized the sushi bar to showcase their exhibitionist tendencies. To Annie, it was nearly equal to the cantina scene in *Star Wars,* the third best movie of all times, according to her *Top 100 List*.

Unless the weather prevented it, Annie always walked to the Palace. CityGov was studying the possibility of installing a PedMover along this stretch of Main Street. She didn't like the idea, and hoped the Historical Society could prevent it. The short walk was invigorating. She and Crane took this route frequently on days they worked late, which recently, was nearly every day. They'd seen some strange sights in the Palace and had eaten a lot of tasty food. The crab sushi with avocado and mango was out-of-this-world delicious, and she hadn't eaten any in a couple of weeks. She needed a sushi fix. The thought of it fired up her salivary reflexes like Pavlov's dog, and she quickened her pace.

To her left, the wooded property of Crane's alma mater, Rice University, ran along South Main Street. She knew that both Cal Tech and MIT had offered Crane full scholarships, but he wouldn't leave Houston. He was a home-town boy who thought he could learn all he needed to know at Rice. Apparently, he was right. Four years ago, CellTech promoted him to curator of DL-666 over a number of geneticists who had PhD's. Obviously, the company knew he was an exceptional geneticist.

Moments later, Annie entered the Palace of Oriental Delights. The aroma of fried calamari enticed her as she picked her way through the clump of patrons loitering near the entrance. The Palace was always crowded for dinner, and she believed it would continue to do well, even in the economic downturn. She passed through the front dining room to a glassed-in patio where serious sushi-eaters convened every night. A kaleidoscope of colors greeted her. Waitresses with hibiscus in their hair glided to and fro in color-changing geisha costumes. The head bartender, who was also the bouncer, was a gigantic sumo wrestler dressed in a green loincloth.

The big man bowed. "Good evening, Miss Lee. Welcome."

"Hello, Tokyo. How's it going?"

Several customers spoke to Annie as she picked her way to the sushi bar. The Palace boasted an extraordinary collection of movie-cult patrons. Lauren Bacall was sipping a martini with Humphrey Bogart at a corner table covered with a red-checkered tablecloth, and nearby, Clint Eastwood accompanied Elizabeth Taylor. At the bar, Peter Sellers was picking at a bowl of fried rice. Several Marilyn Monroes smiled blankly at no one in particularly. The wannabes are out in force tonight, Annie thought. She loved old movies and enjoyed identifying stars from the twentieth century, but it was impossible for her to understand the current fascination with cosmetic alteration. It used to be face-lifts, now it was new faces altogether, with many of the new-face recipients going Hollywood retro. The fad had swept the nation, and the Cosmetic Surgery Association was lobbying NatGov to add cosmetic alteration to Universal Health Care. Congress was considering it on the grounds that a person has the right to look like whomever he or she pleases. Many claimed it provided a form of empowerment that was a constitutional right. Several suits had been filed already, and attorneys seemed to think it might be the next *bird's nest on the ground*.

Annie sat down at the end of the bar next to a ficus tree which had dropped a couple of brown leaves on the countertop. A geisha placed a cup of green tea and a menu in front of her. She flicked away the dry leaves and took a sip of the tea, but before she could open the menu, a figure appeared from the shadows and stood like a specter at her elbow.

She looked toward the man, expecting to see one of the cosmetically altered patrons. Instead, the interloper was Jerry Legrand, an old classmate from Berkeley. Annie recognized him instantly, even though she hadn't seen him since their university days. He had barely changed. His red hair, well below his shoulders, was neatly trimmed, as was his beard. He wore faded jeans, T-shirt, and sandals. A tiny gold caduceus dangled from his left ear. Annie surmised that he was representing himself to be a modern-day John the Baptist, and had dressed in a style consistent with street-corner preaching in the twenty-second century. Annie always thought he was rather odd, but they'd been semi-friends in college.

"Jerry Legrand! What are you doing here?"

"I was looking for you."

Tokyo was standing six feet away with an inquisitive look in his eyes. Annie motioned him back. "It's okay, Tokyo. This guy is a friend of mine…sort of, anyway."

"Thanks, Annie," Jerry said. His voice was polite and well-modulated--a speaker's voice.

Annie took a sip of tea. "So…why are you looking for me?"

Jerry moved out of the shadow of the ficus tree, and for the first time, Annie saw the lettering on his T-shirt: THE DAR LUMBRE SOCIETY.

Jerry touched the imprint on his chest. "I'm spreading the good news—Dar Lumbre will return in the near future."

Annie scoffed. "That story pops up every few years, but it hasn't happened yet."

"It will be different this time," Jerry declared.

"Why so?"

"Because the Dar Lumbre Society is involved this time, and they hold the key to his return."

Annie mulled over Jerry's statement. "Are you telling me that the society can bring Dr. Lumbre back any time they want to?"

"That's correct, and they'll do so at the appointed time."

Annie shook her head in disbelief. "Why don't they bring him back now so he can correct the DL-666 problem?"

"The age of DL-666 has passed. There is a new and better way," Jerry said.

"Are you proclaiming a new religion?"

"The movement is spreading like a religion. Could I tell you about it?"

"I know about it," Annie said. "But, new religions are against the law, and it's illegal to proselytize in a public place. Besides, I'm Roman Catholic--moderately devout--as you might remember from our days at Berkeley."

"Then you know how rapidly religion is changing," Jerry said, seemingly oblivious to the fact that he was getting the brush-off.

"What changes are you talking about?"

"Lots of them. For example, your church just named a new Pope. What do you think about their choice?"

Annie shrugged. "I thought Mother Mary Magdalene was a good choice."

"However, electing the first woman Pope does prove that religion is changing."

"It's 2135 AD," Annie said. "Time for some changes, perhaps." She took another sip of tea and pursed her lips thoughtfully. "Now, get to the point. I'm going to order dinner, and I'd like to eat it without distractions."

Jerry continued in a calm voice. "I'm not trying to get you to change your religion, but I need your help."

"I'm not making a donation, either."

Jerry leaned closer. "Annie, in the near future, Dar Lumbre will return. In the meantime, DL-666 should not be used for transplants because it's deteriorating rapidly. In fact, it should be destroyed immediately."

"Why are you telling me this?"

"Because you work at CellTech," Jerry whispered. "You could destroy the culture."

"You must be bonkers," Annie said sharply. "I'm dedicated to the preservation of that tissue. It has saved thousands of lives. There's no way I'd destroy it. In fact, I'd do my best to stop anyone else from doing so."

Jerry's façade cracked microscopically, and he became more animated. "DL-666 shouldn't be used," he insisted. "It's extremely dangerous. Dar Lumbre will return soon and bring its replacement."

"Surely, Dr. Lumbre is dead," Annie said, although she would have liked to believe otherwise.

Jerry shook his head vigorously. "Not so. He'll return soon. Many people believe that, upon his return, he will develop a Methuselah gene as the next step in human progress. We are striving for constitutional equality through medical science, and I'm asking for your help. Will you destroy DL-666?"

"Absolutely not," Annie snapped.

Jerry fixed Annie in his gaze, as if repeating his request without using words.

Annie returned the stare. "You'd better leave."

"I'll find another way," Jerry said, his voice resolute.

Annie stood and faced Jerry. "Beat it pronto, or I'll get Tokyo to toss you out."

Jerry cast a quick glance in Tokyo's direction, then did an about face and walked out.

Annie watched him leave, wondering if he would try to find some other way to destroy DL-666, as he had threatened to do. She realized that her old classmate had changed considerably. He was always eccentric, but his eccentricities had turned into fanaticism. His approach didn't seem consistent with the Dar Lumbre Society's stated purpose of helping Outsiders. Was he the average society member? she wondered. Or an outlier?

## Chapter 16

Annie stood before a fume hood plastered with yellow and purple radioactive signs. Behind the clear shield, a half-dozen trays of miniature test tubes sat on the lab bench. She placed one of the trays on a conveyer belt linked to an automatic pipetting machine. When the tray emerged from the apparatus, each tube held one milliliter of precisely measured liquid containing radioactive DNA fragments. Annie was preparing DNA probes to utilize in searching for anomalies along the X chromosome.

She planned to incorporate the probes into rings of bacterial DNA known as plasmids. Geneticists had used this technique for more than a century and a half, practically since the discovery of the DNA structure. Unlike Annie, early researchers had little access to automated equipment, and the testing of a single probe could take as long as a month. With today's technology, she could grow probes in twenty-four hours and prepare them for use in an additional thirty minutes. Still, in spite of available cutting-edge technology, DL-666 was so unique that many of the modern procedures were of limited value. Dar Lumbre had given the tissue a facelift, and with something other than Botox.

The geneticists still believed the problem was on the X chromosome near the Xp21 location where the two strands of DNA joined. The strands appeared to be unraveling like a frayed rope, a situation which created sites where problems could occur during cell division. As Annie had said weeks ago, the molecule was getting in its own way.

Annie stared at the miniature tubes, mentally visualizing what was happening at the molecular level. Adenine was joining thymine, cytosine was joining guanine, and so on along the multitude of bases making up the DNA chain. When the reaction was complete, she would have a supply of mirror images of the DNA from DL-666's X chromosome. According to the laws of genetics, each of the new fragments would bind to any complementary segment of DNA from the original culture. Radioactive probes would flag the sequence she sought, allowing her to examine it with an electron microscope linked to a 3D monitor.

Annie stepped away from the lab bench, stripped off her surgical gloves, and placed them in the biohazard receptacle. With the stages of the experiment set up as they were, the rest of this study would be performed at a computer terminal. She set her iTab alarm for thirty minutes and went to Crane's cubicle at the rear of the lab.

Crane sat at his desk with his attention fixed on a desktop monitor. He glanced toward Annie and grunted a greeting as she entered.

"Okay, Protein Man, talk to me."

They discussed their findings and exchanged ideas until Annie's alarm chimed, informing her that her probes were ready to view. Together they went back into the main lab and sat on their adjoining stools in front of the wall monitor.

"My turn to drive," Annie said, raising her right palm toward the screen. The computer acknowledged her with a beep, and a double helix of DNA formed on the 3D screen. The molecule turned slightly each time Annie gave a signal.

Crane and Annie felt sure that the short arm of the chromosome, known as the *p arm*, was from Dar Lumbre himself. All data indicated as much, and nothing else made sense. The long arm of the chromosome, the *q arm*, was another matter. It wasn't from the same source, nor was it human. All data tagged a reptile, probably a snake, as its origin. But, what species? The sequencers were set up to address this question.

"DL-666 has turned into a house of cards," Crane said. "The first card fell when the growth rate slowed, and the whole house came tumbling down right after Mr. Hunter's surgery."

"This is not the typical DNA you would have expected Dr. Lumbre to combine with his own chromosomes," Annie said. "He produced DL-666 when he was less than fifty years old, but it has aged in real time since then. It's amazing that it has functioned for so many years."

"He chose it for one reason," Crane said. "It produced functioning cardiac muscle under lab conditions. No other tissue has ever duplicated that feat, so he was stuck with it in spite of its eccentricities."

Annie nodded. "He had to live with it, and so do we."

She gave a signal, and the image on the screen changed. "I'll tell you one thing," she said, "CellTech's original management team, and ours as well, has to take a *mea culpa* for what happened. Over the years, all they did was take a caretaker approach with DL-666. As profitable as it is, you'd think they would have unraveled all of its secrets in order to be ready for problems like the one we're having now. Surely, they knew problems would pop up at some point."

"They knew it from the beginning," Crane said. "When Dr. Lumbre donated DL-666 to CellTech at startup, both NatGov and CellTech knew the tissue was produced by illegal techniques. But, it was such a miraculous product they decided the best course of action was to covertly ignore the law."

"Don't ask--don't tell," Annie said, as she leaned forward and stretched her back. "That was the agreement."

Crane nodded. "A tacit agreement. One that left the company reluctant to address the exact composition of the product for fear of having incriminating data on hand if NatGov changed their minds."

"So, all they did was kick the can down the road fifty years," Annie said. "But when the road dead-ended, the can bounced back and landed in their laps."

"Our laps," Crane said solemnly.

He stood and pointed toward the non-human arm of the chromosome. "Let's see if there's a reptile fingerprint in the data bank that matches this portion."

Annie motioned toward the upper menu bar. A submenu dropped down to reveal a list of DNA fingerprints. She selected a folder titled SERPENTES and it appeared in the center of the screen. She circled the long arm from DL-666 and dropped it on the reptile database folder. Instantly, a spinning beach ball appeared, indicating a search was in progress. Two seconds later, the ball stopped spinning and the words NO MATCH FOUND appeared.

Annie gazed fixedly at the images on the screen. "What do we do now?"

"We have to find the source of this reptile DNA."

Annie started to speak, but the central PA system interrupted her. The geneticists looked at each other, both knowing that an important announcement was in the offing.

"Attention, please," a mechanical voice intoned. "All personnel are requested to turn to CellTech Channel 321 for important breaking news. Attention, please..."

Annie signaled and the news article exploded into view, filling the entire screen:

### DR. TANNER--CELLTECH SPLIT

*Houston--Renowned organ transplant surgeon, Dr. Sean Tanner, withdrew his endorsement of CellTech's tissue culture products thereby ending a twenty-five-year relationship with the company and dealing a blow to CellTech's stock on the New York Stock Exchange. Dr. Tanner's surprise announcement came amid rumors of problems with CellTech's flagship product, DL-666, but he would neither deny nor confirm the rumor. CellTech officials would not comment on the dissolution of the long-standing arrangement with Houston's best-known surgeon. Details to follow when available.*

Annie shook her head in dismay. "How could he withdraw his support? Didn't he have a contract?"

"It must have been only a verbal agreement," Crane said. "I'll bet he endorses a competitive product."

"Genomes Incorporated--that's who he'll endorse," Annie said. "Their stock went up five points yesterday. CellTech's stock fell five."

"They must have offered him the moon."

"I never liked that Genomes outfit, anyway," Annie said. "They're newcomers in the biotech industry, and their artificial heart is more mechanical than biological. I don't see how they ever competed with CellTech."

"They'll likely be more competitive now that DL-666 has fallen from grace," Crane said.

He pondered the gravity of the situation. The implications were clear. If Sean Tanner had lost faith in DL-666 after the recent failure, no other surgeon would use it either. It made little difference whether the beneficiary of CellTech's problem was Genomes Incorporated, or some other biotech company. The financial blow to CellTech would be huge. A storm of trouble was roiling on the horizon.

"A NatGov shakeup is in the making," Annie said. "It's inevitable."

"The only question is when?"

"I'm sure Washington has been working on this for a while," Annie said, "and have their ducks lined up for the next step. We won't have to wait long for them to post the rest of the bad news."

Crane started to speak, but stopped abruptly when another news banner scrolled across the screen. Again and again, it repeated the words:

OFFICE OF FINANCIAL STABILITY TO
ASSUME CONTROL OF CELLTECH...

"Just like we thought," Crane said.

Annie's voice was urgent. "Keep reading. The article says that OFS is sending someone here named Dr. Helena Cartwright to manage the company. I know that name. You've mentioned her."

Crane said nothing.

"Tell me who is she?" Annie demanded.

"I worked for her just before I started grad school."

Annie rolled her eyes. "You told me that before, but when I started asking questions, you got evasive."

"What else do you want to know?"

"I want to know the truth, the whole truth, and nothing but the truth, so help you God."

"Sounds like you're swearing in a witness."

"I am. Talk to me."

Crane shook his head. "She won't be easy to get along with."

"Tell me everything about the time you worked for her," Annie said. "And don't give me a text message version. I want to know the whole story."

Crane knew it was time to tell Annie everything. "I worked for her right after I got my bachelor's degree."

Annie leaned toward Crane, her eyes wide. "Keep going."

"I was taking it easy before starting grad school," Crane said. "Just bumming around and biohacking butterfly DNA for fun. Dr. Cartwright showed up at Rice University. She was with the OFS at the time, but was waiting for her next assignment. Somehow, she got a NatGov grant to work on a study with one of my professors, and they needed a gopher. The professor recommended me because I did well in a couple of his classes. I needed money, so I took the job."

"What was she working on?"

"A fruit fly experiment."

"I thought they'd been studied to death."

"I thought so, too," Crane said, "but she managed to get a grant for another study, and asked me to work for her. I agreed, but after I signed on, she expanded the project considerably. It changed to *The Effects of Zero Gravity on The Reproductive Organs of Drosophila melanogaster.* How's that for a project funded by NatGov?"

"Better than some I've heard about. What happened next?"

Crane shook his head. "This is so bizarre you're not going to believe it. She obtained permission to conduct a portion of the study on the International Space Station. Before I knew what Dr. Cartwright had in mind, she obtained approval for both of us to go to the station, but I didn't want to go."

"Why not? It was the opportunity of a lifetime."

"Not for me. I get motion sickness--you know that."

Annie stared at Crane in disbelief. "You let that stop you?"

"I have to face forward on the Metro bus to avoid getting sick," Crane said. "I'd never survive in space."

"I would have worn a barf bag all the way there and back, if need be," Annie said. "You let a fantastic adventure slip through your fingers."

"It didn't seem that way to me."

"So, you quit?"

"No, she fired me."

"Uh-oh."

Chapter 17

Kim was peering into the refrigerator when Larry dragged into the dining area wearing rumpled pajamas. His hair was disheveled, and he sported a three-day growth of beard. For the last couple of weeks, he'd stayed up late every night trying to finish his new game, *Global Cooling on Mercury*. Kim was glad that he was working more at home, instead of spending so much time at Starbucks. Lately, her fear that he was seeing another woman had diminished, and she regretted mentioning it to Crane. One thing still bothered her, though--Larry mentioned Apple-Disney and California every day.

"I tried to be quiet when I got up," Kim said. "I don't go to work until noon today. You could have slept late, if you wanted to."

Larry rubbed his eyes. "I couldn't. Too much on my mind." He sat down at the tiny breakfast table in the corner of the living/dining area.

"I'll make coffee," Kim said, still holding the refrigerator door open.

"I thought we ran out."

"I thought so, too," Kim said, taking a small bag out of the refrigerator, "but I found some behind a mayonnaise jar. It's a generic brand--pretty bitter, as I recall, but better than nothing." She removed two coffee cartridges from the bag, dropped them in the coffee maker, and pushed the start button. The machine gurgled briefly and produced two cups of dark hot liquid. Kim sat one in front of Larry.

"What do we have for breakfast?" Larry asked.

"Toast and plum jelly," Kim said. "The jelly is delicious. Your mom bought it in Richmond when we went down there to do some Christmas shopping."

"Sounds good to me."

Kim took out the last four slices of San Francisco sourdough bread, scraped a small patch of mold off the corner of one piece, and popped them into the toaster. "It's a good thing today is payday," she said. "We're out of everything, but we can restock the cupboard tonight."

A noticeable silence passed, and Kim looked at

Larry to see what he was doing. He returned her gaze, and she could see a question mark on his face.

"Kim?"

"What is it?"

"I heard from Apple-Disney last night. They offered me a job."

Kim's heart skipped a beat, and she almost dropped the margarine dish. She had anticipated this dilemma for a long time. She wanted to be happy for Larry, but was apprehensive about where his job prospect was leading.

"Does Apple expect us to move to California?" she asked.

"We'd have to move if I went to work full time for them in Cupertino," Larry said. "The other option is to continue working freelance from here and sell them the first rights to anything I develop, but that wouldn't pay as much."

Kim's face was long. "I can't move now because of Dad's heart problem. I have to stay here."

"Honey, this is a great opportunity, particularly in these tough economic times," Larry said. "The salary in California would be far more than I earn working from home."

"The cost of living is high out there," Kim said in a gloomy voice. "I've heard that a tiny efficiency condo in Silicon Valley rents for five or six thousand dollars a month. I don't see how we could afford to live there, even with you working full time."

"I'd like to talk to them, anyway. It's a once in a lifetime opportunity."

"What do they want you to do?"

"Software development."

Doubt showed in Kim's voice. "You'd have to work a regular eight-hour day."

"Don't be so pessimistic," Larry said. "I worked hard on my new game. This offer didn't just fall into my lap. I earned it. Apple really liked my assassin droid program. They said it was one of the best they've ever seen."

Kim was determined to have her say. "We've just barely settled into this condo."

Larry's voice rose. "Are you afraid I couldn't handle the job with Apple?"

In spite of Larry's assurances, Kim was having difficulty with the idea of him working a full-time job. He'd never done it before. "Maybe they offered you a job to get your new game at a lower price," she said.

"That's ridiculous," Larry snapped. "Apple is not trying to save a few dollars by low-balling an independent programmer. They do very well, even in a stock market slump. They have trillions of dollars in the bank. This is a good job opportunity--the pay would be great. You've said that you wished I had a regular job, rather than freelancing. They wouldn't have offered me this job if they didn't think I could do it."

In Kim's mind, moving to California was the equivalent to moving to Mars. "Doesn't Apple have a software development group here in Houston?" she asked.

"They do a little work here," Larry said, "but the job they offered me is in Cupertino--their main office. They won't hire you to work there unless you're really good."

"Couldn't you at least talk to them about a full-time job here?"

"The Houston group works on desktop applications," Larry said. "That's boring. The one in Cupertino designs software for multiplayer games and other complex systems. That's what I like to do."

After a long pause, Kim asked, "What did you tell Apple?"

"I told them I'd come for an interview," Larry said. "They'll pay my way, so I don't see how it could hurt to go talk to them. And I think we should consider moving out there if my interview with them works out."

"I can't move, Larry," Kim said. "Not now. I have to stay until Dad's out of danger, no matter how long that is."

"This is the best job opportunity I've ever had. If I give Apple the brush-off this time, they won't give me another chance. I'll be a freelance programmer the rest of my life."

"The timing couldn't be worse for me."

"What about me? I can't put my career on hold indefinitely."

Kim felt her world crumbling. "Go for your interview whenever you want to," she said glumly. "But don't plan on me moving out there any time soon. If you move to California now, it'll be without me."

## Chapter 18

Crane sat at his desk, re-checking data from the previous week. As he saw it, no matter what the data indicated, the status of the DL-666 project was in limbo. Dr. Helena Cartwright had arrived. She would impose her input upon all aspects of the work; such was her modus operandi. He didn't look forward to seeing her again, but the waiting was sheer agony. He was ready to get it over with.

At eight-thirty, a ringtone sounded simultaneously on the central PA system and on Crane's iTab. The tone was CellTech's *all-hands-on-deck* signal, indicating that a general meeting was being called.

"May I have your attention please," a computerized female voice chimed. "Dr. Rosenfield requests all personnel to report to the Technical Director's conference room immediately. Attention, please. This is not a drill. All personnel report…"

This is it, Crane thought. The NatGov takeover and inevitable face-off with Helena Cartwright. What a way to start the week. He looked up, and Annie was approaching, her eyes wide.

"A summons to the TD's conference room the first thing Monday morning," she said. "We don't get many of those."

"Thank goodness."

Together they walked into the hallway and joined a group of their white-clad colleagues trudging toward the elevator. The mood in the hall was somber with the normally-chatty scientists having little to say to each other.

"This looks like a zombie movie scene," Annie said.

Crane didn't respond. His mind was in a spin. He hoped his second genetic venture with Helena Cartwright went better than the first one. Much more was riding on the line this time. Eight years ago, fruit flies' lives were at stake. Today, it was human lives.

At the end of the hall, they took one of the elevators to the twelfth floor and entered the conference room, which was filling with anxious-looking scientists.

Crane looked around. The room hadn't changed

since his first visit with the company. The centerpiece was a long oval table constructed of imitation mahogany. Straight-backed chairs with padded burgundy seats surrounded the table, and several rows of matching theater-style seats occupied the rear of the room. The incoming arrivals jockeyed for position in the theater section. Not a single one chose a chair around the table.

Looking rather grim, Dr. Sam Rosenfield stood at one end of the conference table. Two people flanked him. One of them, as Crane expected, was Dr. Helena Cartwright, his nemesis on the *Drosophila* project. The other was a tall middle-aged man emitting a bureaucratic aura--the typical NatGov functionary-for-life, Crane surmised.

Dr. Rosenfield beckoned to Crane and Annie as they entered the room. They approached the trio standing at the head of the table, and the Technical Director made the introductions. "Crane Hopkins and Annie Lee, meet Dr. Helena Cartwright and Howard Jefferson."

Dr. Cartwright nodded toward Annie and looked directly at Crane. "Nice to see you again, Mr. Hopkins. Please sit down." She motioned toward the chairs near her, which put them directly in her line of sight.

Mutely, they took the chairs indicated. As discretely as possible, Crane sized up Dr. Cartwright. Except for a few gray hairs, she hadn't changed much. The jaw line was the same, set so hard that she appeared to be gritting her teeth. Steely blue eyes which never seemed to blink. Unsmiling lips that were a little thinner. Not a single feature had softened since the fruit fly project. Overall, she looked like the same over-achiever who could fire a student assistant without a second thought. He hoped his five-second evaluation of her was wrong, but doubted that it was.

Tension permeated the air, and all eyes were fixed on Dr. Cartwright. Crane glanced sideways at Annie. She raised her eyebrows slightly.

Dr. Rosenfield began, "I'm sure you're aware that the Office of Financial Stability has declared CellTech to be an essential business which cannot be allowed to fail. NatGov fears we are on the verge of bankruptcy, so we have been brought under the oversight of OFS. Later today, each of you will receive a brief report explaining this office's oversight policies and procedures. Documents have been executed by NatGov to transfer operating authority to Dr. Helena Cartwright, who will act as CEO and Technical Director. At this time, she would like to give you some information. Please give her your undivided attention."

Dr. Helena Cartwright replaced Dr. Rosenfield at the head of the table, a move that, to Crane, signaled both a symbolic and literal change of power.

"Thank you, Doctor," Helena Cartwright said in a slow and deliberate pace. She glanced briefly at Crane before continuing, "Many factors contributed to CellTech's problems. One factor was the sudden decline in financial indicators, a situation that caused economists to believe a recession is imminent. Still, the main problem at CellTech was brought on by the failure of DL-666, the artificial heart fabricated from Dr. Lumbre's discovery fifty years ago. We must solve the problem, and we must solve it quickly."

She paused, as if allowing time for her words to sink in thoroughly.

"I know this situation is difficult for some of you," she continued. "But let me assure you, we all have the same goal--the survival of CellTech. We must work together to achieve that goal. For the time being, I want each of you to continue with his or her current assignment. I will review all projects in progress, as well as those in the planning stages, and determine what changes need to be made in projects and personnel. Are there any questions?"

One of the newly-hired cytologists from MIT raised his hand. "Can you give us any information regarding job security?"

"I haven't had time to evaluate CellTech's personnel requirements," Dr. Cartwright said, "but I have asked the HR Department for a report on current staffing. When I receive that information, I'll determine if a reduction in force is necessary. Hopefully, this will not be the case. Are there any other questions at this time?"

No one spoke, and Dr. Cartwright said, "This meeting is adjourned." She looked at Crane and Annie. "Please wait. I'd like a word with you in private."

The two geneticists kept their seats while other CellTech lab personnel jumped up and vacated the room in record time. Dr. Rosenfield and Howard Jefferson both hesitated until Dr. Cartwright cast a dismissive nod in their direction. They walked out immediately.

Dr. Cartwright sat down across the table from Crane and Annie. Again, she looked directly at Crane and said, "Mr. Hopkins, I won't allow past differences to prevent us from solving this problem."

"My only concern is DL-666," Crane said, wondering if Dr. Cartwright's words were a threat, or a promise to cooperate. More likely the former, he feared.

"Obviously, restoring the functionality of DL-666 is our primary goal," Dr. Cartwright said, "but, as a secondary goal, we need to determine how Dr. Lumbre produced the tissue originally. Do you think that is possible, Mr. Hopkins?"

"Yes, I do," Crane said, "but, I believe the two goals are inseparable. I doubt there's a way solve the current problem without determining how DL-666 was produced originally."

"You don't think that some stop-gap measure is feasible?"

Crane shook his head. "We tried a couple, but they didn't work. So, we plan to concentrate on discovering Dr. Lumbre's original methodology, rather than trying to patch up the failing tissue."

Dr. Cartwright looked toward Annie. "Are you comfortable with this approach, Miss Lee?"

"Affirmative. I don't think there's a quick fix."

After a noticeable pause, Helena Cartwright said, "That's all I have for now. Do either of you have any questions?"

Crane shook his head, and Annie said, "No, not at the moment."

"Good. Let's get to work," Dr. Cartwright said. "I'll visit you in the laboratory after I look over your reports."

Crane and Annie returned to the lab and went to their adjoining stools in front of the big screen monitor. After staring at the blank screen for a moment, Annie swiveled to face Crane and said, "We can solve this mystery, and I'm confident we will."

"We will if Dr. Cartwright gives us enough time and elbow room," Crane said, struggling to push aside the foreboding feeling hanging over him like a black shroud.

Annie raised her eyebrows. "What else can she do? You've had more experience with DL-666 than anybody else at CellTech."

"I'm not sure that counts much with her."

Crane gave a signal to the monitor, and it glowed to life. Annie went to the fume hood at the opposite end of the lab. In two minutes, each of them was lost in the world of protein molecules.

Early that afternoon, after an abbreviated lunch break, Crane was back at the lab bench when he sensed movement out of the corner of his eye. He looked toward the entrance of the lab. Dr. Cartwright was entering. She carried an iTab and wore a white lab coat complete with a nametag reading H. CARTWRIGHT, PhD.

Crane was dumbfounded at the lab coat. What was Dr. Cartwright up to? Surely, she didn't intend to belly up to the lab bench between him and Annie and do some hands-on cytology work. Did she really think she could become one of them by donning a white lab coat? The thought was disconcerting.

"Good afternoon, Mr. Hopkins," Dr. Cartwright said.

Crane nodded a mute greeting.

"This situation may be awkward for both of us," Dr. Cartwright continued, "but we have to work through it."

"That's what I intend to do," Crane said. "I've already indicated as much." He resolved to keep his mind focused on lab work and leave company politics to others. Many lives depended on CellTech's geneticists. He had to get along with Dr. Cartwright, no matter what. Even so, it was hard for him not to consider his old nemesis to be his new enemy.

Annie approached and stopped beside Crane.

Dr. Cartwright touched the screen on her iTab. A page of data appeared. "I'm reviewing your recent reports on the DL-666 problem, and I have a question."

Crane shifted uneasily. "What is it?"

"Have you reviewed the Duffy-a and Duffy-b blood

groups related to uncoiled elements in chromosomes?"

"We've looked at it briefly."

"I didn't see anything in your report."

"There was nothing new to report," Crane said defensively. "We reviewed studies on various kinds of tissue. No known data connects Duffy genes to heart disease, so we didn't go any further. With the new data available from the Updated Genome Project, the Duffy approach doesn't offer anything significant." He wondered if his new boss was nitpicking, or just wanted to show she could speak the lingo. He didn't like either scenario.

"You don't think it's worth looking into?" Dr. Cartwright asked.

Crane shook his head. "There's no possibility of the problem being related to a Duffy antigen."

Dr. Cartwright bristled slightly. "Merely a suggestion, Mr. Hopkins."

Crane bit his tongue, but didn't express a rejoinder.

Annie edged closer. "We both think that continuing our pursuit of the Xp21 anomaly and the genes adjacent to it is the most logical approach."

Dr. Cartwright looked at Annie and nodded. "You're probably right, Miss Lee, but don't rule out anything completely." She turned abruptly and strode out of the lab.

When their new boss was out of sight, Annie turned to Crane. "So...is the Hopkins diplomatic approach going to get us canned?"

Crane smiled faintly. "Not yet. Who could replace us?"

"How about those two new guys from MIT--Sanders and Thomas?"

Crane shook his head. "Not them. They're newbies."

"I've talked with both of them several times. They're plenty smart."

"All book learning," Crane said. "They haven't been tested by fire. Dr. Cartwright would incinerate them in a nanosecond."

Annie nodded. "She's a major force. I can see that."

"We can't allow ourselves to be lured off track," Crane said. "No matter what Dr. Cartwright suggests, we have to stay focused and keep pressing ahead."

"I'd like some more information on Dr. Cartwright. You still haven't told me very much."

"What kind of information?" Crane asked tentatively.

"Everything you know about her. Is she married? Does she have children? That kind of stuff."

"She's married and has a daughter," Crane said. "At least, she was married when I first met her, but wasn't living with her husband. He's a big-time political operative."

"A political operative?"

"Yes."

Annie's eyes widened. "Is her husband Ahab Cartwright?"

Crane nodded.

"*The* Ahab Cartwright?"

"Yes—that one."

## Chapter 19

Helena Cartwright sat in her office, eyes fixed on a desktop monitor. She touched the screen, and the image of coiled DNA strands rolled across the monitor like tumbleweeds in a New Mexico desert. At midday, she was still unable to see anything beyond the features discussed yesterday during her lab visit. Her scientific skills had waned somewhat during her years of working as a turnaround specialist, and she knew it. She wanted to regain those skills as quickly as possible. Contributing to the cytology of DL-666, while serving as CEO, should carry considerable weight when the next Director of the OFS was selected.

For the time being, she had to concede that the fate of DL-666, the fate of CellTech, and her own fate as well, were in the hands of the taciturn Mr. Hopkins and his ebullient cohort, Miss Lee. Not exactly a good thing, even though the Hopkins-Lee team thought they were the best geneticists at CellTech. Maybe they were, and until she got her scientific feet back on the ground, she hoped they were right. Time was of the essence. If they didn't produce results quickly, she would have to make changes in work assignments. That would ruffle feathers, but she would do whatever she had to.

Dr. Cartwright got up from her desk and looked at the street below. The intersection was buzzing with activity. People milled about on the sidewalks and along the edges of the street. Some sat on the curb. A few robo-cabs eased through the gathering throng of people, and police officers posted at strategic intervals kept a watchful eye on the proceedings.

Today was *Peaceful Protest Day*, a day of historical significance in the struggle for freedom of speech. Over a hundred years ago, in an effort to empower those whose voices were seldom heard, NatGov authorized Peaceful Protest Day. The language of the bill was based on Article 19 of the Universal Declaration of Human Rights passed in 1948 by the United Nations. In the United States, any organization wanting to be heard could get a permit to march along a  designated  route on Peaceful Protest Day.

In this part of Houston, the protest route was South Main Street. With the passing of so many years, the event had become more of a parade than a protest, but many felt it still had political validity. Organizations could promote their cause, state their case, or object to laws they thought were unfair. Unless it rained, Peaceful Protest Day always drew a crowd.

Dr. Cartwright had watched a few protests in San Francisco, but this would be her first time to see one in Houston. She expected social causes in Houston to differ considerably from those in Marin County. Normally, she paid little attention to such events, believing they were a waste of time. But, today was different. She was a newly-minted Houstonian, whether she liked it or not, and had a vague feeling something unusual was about to happen. She decided to watch for a few minutes, in spite of the workload facing her.

From her vantage point high above the intersection, she studied the crowd of observers lined up along Main Street. Nearly all of them were looking north, an indication that marchers would approach from that direction. A trio of Houston Police officers astride black Hover-Harleys appeared from a side street and herded the scattered pedestrians to the curb. The scene was set for a group of protesters to appear at any moment.

Returning to her desk, she touched the screen of the desktop monitor, and the DNA image was replaced by that of a tall African-American woman. Dr. Cartwright recognized the reporter as Carolina Herrera, Houston's favorite talk-show host.

The Star-Spangled Banner was playing in the background, and a U.S. flag waved in the upper left quadrant of the screen. Carolina stood on the sidewalk at the intersection of Main and Dryden, the identical scene Dr. Cartwright saw through her window. The peaceful protesters were about to hold a rally in CellTech's front yard.

The camera zoomed in on Carolina, who was leaning into a stiff December breeze. "Today we have six organizations participating in the parade," she said. "That's two more than last time. Here comes the first group now, the Asian Language Society. They are marching to bring awareness to the language needs of Asian-Americans. A spokesman for the group reported they're working with two members of congress, one a Democrat and the other a Republican, who are both willing to co-sponsor a bipartisan bill to add Mandarin Chinese as the third official language of the United States."

The camera pulled back to show a panoramic view behind the reporter. The Asian group, a hundred strong, marched briskly to recorded music from an unseen source. At intervals, the music was drowned out by the synthesized sound of ladyfinger firecrackers exploding. The marchers took the intersection with theatrical flair. Women wearing red body-hugging Mandarin gowns led the way, followed by men wearing white Karate uniforms with red sashes. A short dragon, made up of six people under a tubiform costume, brought up the rear. The dragon was blue.

"Red…white…blue," the group shouted in unison. "U.S.A. U.S.A."

They repeated the slogan in Spanish and Mandarin Chinese and continued their march along South Main Street until they passed out of camera range. The appreciative crowd applauded

Another group moved into view.

"Next, we have the Sharia Law Coalition," Carolina said, "a group of Muslims petitioning congress to allow the application of Sharia law in communities with a population consisting of fifty-one percent Muslims. This proposed law has been presented to congress more than a dozen times, but has yet to gain traction. Expecting to pick up more congressional seats in the upcoming election, Muslims plan to continue pushing for passage of this law. President Keynes also supports this cause. The Sharia Law Coalition marchers outnumber the Asian Language Society marchers"

The camera made a broad sweep of the Muslim marchers. They were dark and somber in their mid-eastern clothing complete with the traditional headdress, and several of them carried signs written in Arabic. All of the marchers were men, but from the curb, a group of women wearing burkas cheered them on.

*"Allahu Akbar, Allahu Akbar,"* they chanted in rhythm with their marching cadence. Moments later, the Muslim activists moved out of camera range, and a few onlookers clapped lightly.

The next band of marchers was several hundred strong, a high count for any Peaceful Protest Day demonstration. Many of them shouted and waved their hands. Some carried signs and placards scrawled with messages indicating a renewed interest in Dar Lumbre and the legends surrounding his life and work. TV cameras zoomed in on the signs:

DAR LUMBRE WILL RETURN SOON
GENETIC EQUALITY FOR ALL
REGISTER TO VOTE

Carolina continued her play-by-play description of the street scene. "A group of social activists known as the Dar Lumbre Society is the largest group marching today. They burst on the scene a few weeks ago and immediately generated considerable interest among Outsiders. Recently, the movement has begun to gain large numbers of supporters within the city, as well. This group is attempting to prepare the world for the return of Dar Lumbre. A spokesman for the movement said the failure of the well-known cardiac tissue, DL-666, is the signal that Dr. Lumbre will return soon, bringing a gene with him to increase life expectancy by a quantum leap. Some followers also claim he will bring a revised edition of his book *The Double Helix Odyssey*, which is currently banned by NatGov. This book is said to promote religious aspects of a Methuselah gene, but the society's spokesman would not confirm that such a publication exists. Some detractors claim…"

Carolina spoke faster and faster as she described the scene in the street.

Dr. Cartwright was fascinated. She kept her eyes glued to the monitor until the parade ended and the crowd began to disperse. When the show was over, she put on her white lab coat and headed toward the lab. She wondered what the Hopkins-Lee team thought about the cult springing up around Dar Lumbre. Clearly, word about the DL-666 problem had spread into the street and was growing exponentially with all kinds of bizarre ramifications.

A quick resolution was needed, and she was determined to make it happen.

## Chapter 20

The first Monday of the New Year, Crane sat at his favorite table in the Starbucks adjoining CellTech. Thanksgiving and Christmas had passed in a blur, and were not the festive occasions he remembered from holidays past. He was glad to ring out the old and ring in the new. Hopefully, 2136 would be a better year.

With his parents on vacation, and the rest of his family and friends going their separate ways, Crane had Thanksgiving dinner delivered by an Amazon drone. The food wasn't bad, but dining in Lone Ranger mode left a lot to be desired, and he vowed he would never eat a holiday meal alone again.

Christmas was not much better. The family had dinner together, as planned. In spite the fancy French cuisine, with stuffed lamb chops as the main course, Crane felt like he was going through the motions by force of habit. He sensed that every family member felt the same way. Too many personal concerns had put a damper on the holiday spirit.

A movement beside him interrupted his mental replay of the holidays, and he looked up to see Annie approaching.

"Happy New Year," she said, as she reached the table.

"And to you. How was California?"

Annie placed her roll and latte on the table and sat down in the chair opposite Crane. "It was okay."

Crane sensed something amiss. "Just okay?"

Annie hesitated before answering, "It was nice to see my mother again, but I think we've drifted apart."

"Really? What happened?"

"I didn't stay in contact with her very well last year," Annie said, "and she surprised me with news that she's planning to remarry this June."

"Why would you object?"

"It was a major shock."

"Obviously, she doesn't want to be a widow the rest of her life," Crane said.

Annie's eyes glistened. "I miss my father so much. I

was closer to him than to my mother."

Crane put his hand on Annie's arm. "You're her only child. It's up to you to give moral support when she needs it." He was stunned at his own words; it wasn't his nature to mime an advice columnist.

After a pause, Annie said, "Thanks, *Dear Abby*. You're probably right."

*"Probably?"*

"I'll text her later today and congratulate her."

"Good. It'll make you feel better."

Annie smiled faintly. "Now that you've granted me absolution, let's get to work."

"I want to show you something," Crane said. He picked up his iTab and turned the screen toward Annie. "Does this guy look familiar?"

Annie peered at the pic. "That's Elmore Larson. Of course he looks familiar. His face is on every news screen 24/7."

"Let me rephrase that question. I was asking if he reminds you of anybody else."

Annie glanced at the pic again. "Well…he looks a lot like Dar Lumbre."

Crane nodded. "That's what I thought, too. If they're related, we might learn something from Larson's DNA."

"Before we start trying to get a sample of Elmore Larson's DNA, let's get some pics of Dar Lumbre and make a detailed comparison between the two men," Annie said.

"There's a good pic of Dr. Lumbre in the lobby display case," Crane said.

"Probably Photoshopped. We'd better look online."

They finished their breakfast snacks in record time, and five minutes later, they were seated in front of the wall monitor. Annie, who by tacit agreement assumed operation of the computer, gave a hand signal and a half-dozen pictures of Dar Lumbre appeared on the screen in a millisecond. They all showed the mysterious Dr. Lumbre in the company of Hollywood starlets at charity fund-raisers shortly before he fell from grace and disappeared. Crane touched his iTab screen and exported the recent pic of Elmore Larson onto the big screen amid the old pics of Dr.

Lumbre. Annie signaled and the flat photographs morphed into 3D images.

Crane pointed at one of the images. "That's a good picture of Dr. Lumbre. Keep it and move the rest of them out of the way."

Annie selected the pic indicated by Crane and moved it into position beside the recent pic of Elmore Larson. "They're posed in exactly the same manner," she said, "and are about the same age in the pics."

Crane studied the screen intently. "These look like pics of the same person."

"Let's run the Facial Recognition App," Annie said, as she selected the program from a drop-down menu. She pointed an index finger toward Elmore Larson's pic, highlighted his face with a circular motion, and repeated the procedure with Dar Lumbre's pic. Images of the two men blinked, signaling that the app was on standby.

Crane gestured toward the screen. "Have you used this program before?"

"A couple of times," Annie said. "Nothing to it." She opened the preferences menu and read the principal component list aloud. "Eyes, nose, forehead, cheekbone, jaw, chin and ears. Pretty complete. I'll select them all."

At her command, the computer whirred briefly and posted its findings for each of the components selected. The matches ranged from fifty to ninety percent.

A caption blinked at the bottom of the screen:

MATCHING COMPONENT AVERAGE: 73 %

A chill went down Crane's spine. "Larry and I wouldn't match that closely. These two guys look like twins."

"Well, no matter how much these pics match, Elmore Larson can't be Dar Lumbre," Annie said. "The results are close, but not one hundred percent."

Crane looked back at the monitor. "This gets weirder all the time."

"We've got to find out how they're related," Annie said. "We need a sample of Elmore Larson's DNA to compare to DL-666."

"We missed the boat. Larson was in the Houston area for several days, holding rallies everywhere. He returned to Anaheim recently."

"Then, we need to go to Anaheim," Annie said, "or contact him and ask for a sample."

Crane thought for a moment. "We'd better take this up with Dr. Cartwright."

Annie raised her eyebrows. "Above our pay grade?"

"I think so.

## Chapter 21

As Larry's flight approached John Wayne Airport, he picked up his iTab and placed a long-anticipated call. The moment was bizarre. Mentally he was standing at the nexus between his old world and a new world represented by the Dar Lumbre Society. The new world was pulling at him with the gravity of a black hole, and he wondered if he'd already passed the event horizon.

"Dar Lumbre Society," a female voice answered on the first ring. "How may I direct your call?"

"Julie Gilchrist, please."

"Whom shall I say is calling?"

"Larry Hopkins."

"Is she expecting you?"

"I believe so."

"Okay, I'll connect you."

The circuit hummed, and Julie said, "Hi, Larry. You did come."

"I told you I would. Is Mr. Larson going to be in the office today?"

"That's his plan, and he can see you late this evening."

"Great," Larry said. "We'll be on the ground in fifteen minutes. I'll grab a cab and be there in less than an hour."

"Forget the cab," Julie said, her voice firm. "I'll pick you up in thirty minutes."

"That's too much trouble," Larry protested, although he knew his objection was not likely to deter Julie.

"No, it's not," she said with an air of finality. "I'm going to pick you up."

Larry, feeling reluctant, gave in. He didn't want to hurt his chance to meet Elmore Larson, and it seemed that Julie was Larson's doorkeeper. She was a forceful woman. What else could he do?

"What kind of car do you drive?" he asked.

"A green Eco-Micro, Asian Auto's smallest car."

"Isn't that what everybody out here drives?"

"Pretty much," Julie said. "I'll come to the ground transportation area. See you in a bit."

128

Larry's plane landed on schedule, touching down with barely a bump. He reviewed his plans. The rest of the day in Anaheim was open for his visit to the Dar Lumbre headquarters and his appointment with Elmore Larson. He was apprehensive, but knew he'd never be satisfied if he backed out now. The society was helping Outsiders, a cause he believed in. After the meeting with Elmore Larson, barring some unforeseen event, he would take a commuter shuttle to San Francisco and keep his appointment with Apple. If the Silicon Valley interview went as scheduled, he could catch the red-eye out of San Francisco and return to Houston tomorrow night. A tight schedule, but he thought he could keep it.

He couldn't decide which aspect of his California visit meant the most to him, the Dar Lumbre ramifications, or the employment possibilities. Either one could be a life-changing event. California was beckoning him, but with Kim stuck in Houston mindset, he wondered if he'd be able to answer the call.

When the seat belt sign blinked off, Larry retrieved his carry-on luggage and checked around his seat to see if he had all of his belongings. Moments later, he exited the plane and walked up the concourse leading through the main terminal to the ground transportation area. He zipped up his windbreaker and stepped out onto the sidewalk.

Shuttle buses, robo-cabs, and tiny smart cars inched along the passenger pickup area. The collective humming of the electric vehicles sounded like a swarm of bees and created static electricity in Larry's polyester jacket, making it cling to his arms like a one-size-fits-all garment. Several green Eco-Micros edged along the curb, but Julie's car was not among them. He moved back against the building to wait.

The air was cool and fresh. Typical California weather, Larry thought, beautiful nearly all the time. Who wouldn't want to live here? Well…Kim, for one.

Sunlight reflected off the windows and warmed the area next to the wall where Larry stood. After a few minutes, he began to feel conspicuous. Every pedestrian that passed by seemed to be staring at him, as if knowing he was supposed to be in San Francisco, rather than Santa

Ana. He was a stranger in a strange land. He hoped Julie would show up soon.

Another green Eco-Micro approached. This time, Julie was at the controls. The small car eased to the curb, and the passenger door slid open. "Sorry I'm late," Julie said. "I got caught in traffic."

"No problem," Larry said, as he squeezed into the small car. "Thanks for picking me up."

"Glad to do it. It gives us a chance to talk before we get back to the office."

She touched a button to return the car to autopilot. It pulled away from the curb and eased into the line of vehicles leaving the airport. Moments later, they were on the Santa Ana Freeway headed toward Anaheim. Traffic was light and moving at a fast pace. The Micro moved to the inside lane and increased its speed to sixty miles per hour. When the vehicle reached cruising speed, the AutoPilot icon on the control screen glowed bright green. The car hummed along, giving off a high-pitched whine like a toy racecar.

Julie turned toward Larry. "I drove on a couple of non-magnetized roads in Houston. It was the first time I'd done so in a long time. It was a little scary."

"We have a several of them west of Houston. I drive on them all the time, and enjoy it."

A serious look crept into Julie's eyes. "You know I didn't pick you up just to discuss roads in California and Texas."

Larry nodded. "I know. You're going to give me a sales pitch."

Julie flashed a winsome smile. "Something like that. Are you game?"

"Sure...go ahead."

"I'll get straight to the point. I want to convince you to get more involved in the society."

"I'm involved," Larry said, "I handed out thousands of Register to vote  tracts, even though I thought it might be illegal at the time."

"We're past that stage," Julie said, "and it went exactly as we hoped. We're out in the open now, and have registered millions of new voters.  The movement is too big for NatGov to squelch, even if they try. Washington thinks we're harmless kooks because we're not an approved political party, but they're in for a big surprise. We got off to a good start, but to keep moving forward, we need to enlist people like you."

"What are you suggesting I do?"

"You should move to Anaheim and work full time for the Dar Lumbre Society."

He pondered the proposition. "That could cost me a lot, and maybe cause family problems. What would I get out of it?"

"You'd get the satisfaction of knowing you're working for a good cause," Julie said. "I can see your concern for Outsiders. You should join us."

"Do you speak for Elmore Larson?"

"He authorized me to speak to you."

"He doesn't even know me."

"He knows about you," Julie said. "Another part of my job is to scout for talented people, especially those in the high-tech fields. I told him you're a computer genius."

"I'm a free-lance computer programmer. Mostly in the area of gaming--that's all."

"Don't sell yourself short," Julie said. "The society can use your computer skills for something better than developing internet games for pimply-faced teenage boys. We've completed the first phase. Our next move will be high-tech, and we'll be concentrating on big cities this time. You can help."

"But you don't really know what I can do," Larry protested. "You've never seen my work." He was still doubtful that Julie was able to accurately judge his creative talent based on the few times they had talked. She seemed to think she could, and more importantly, she claimed Elmore Larson trusted her. Larry was not sure about her full intentions. She was smart and attractive, but pushy. He had to be careful.

"I know you better than you think," Julie said. "I have a sixth sense about people. That's one of the main reasons Mr. Larson sends me out into the field on a regular basis. I'm like the Marines, looking for a few good men. You might be one of them. Let's face it--you're not what most people think you are, some happy-go-lucky computer gamer. That's a disguise, and I can see right through it."

His curiosity was triggered. "What do you think I am?"

"You're a secret activist, and a closet intellectual as well," Julie said. "Those two qualities are needed in the Dar Lumbre Society. You have the insight to recognize injustice, and the intellectual capacity to do something about it."

The talk sounded somewhat high-minded to Larry. "This is new to me," he said. "I've never thought of myself as a politician. This movement is political, and always has been. As for me, I vote regularly as a Republican, but that's all. I've never been involved in the party in any other way."

Julie answered with passion, "You can be a lot more than a computer programmer. You've never been challenged to rise to the occasion."

"And you're challenging me?"

Julie nodded emphatically. "Yes, I am. The whole Dar Lumbre approach is based on getting people to work together to claim what is rightfully theirs. That's a big undertaking, and it will take all kinds of people, including educated professionals, as well as Outsiders. We're signing up Outsiders by the droves. You know that—you helped do it. But they're like sheep without a shepherd. We need to find people to lead them."

Larry mulled the idea over in his mind as they passed mile after mile of faux-stucco houses. The houses were the same size, the same style, and the same color—all clones from one original pattern. He wondered if the inhabitants were clones, too. He conjured up an image of cookie-cutter citizenry steadfastly hanging on to their Democratic and Republican registration cards in order to build up E-Points for their own benefit, without a thought about those outside the system. Could large numbers of them be persuaded to join the Dar Lumbre Society as they were doing in the Houston area? It seemed possible, even probable.

After a brief silence, Julie said, "You look pensive. What are you thinking about?"

"I'm thinking this is a dream. That it's not really happening to me."

Julie's eyes sparkled with conviction. "Believe me, this is real. It's happening right now at this intersection of time and space. It's not a metaphysical experience in some alternate universe. The Dar Lumbre Society will change the world."

"What's your story?" Larry asked. "How'd you get involved in the society?"

Julie answered glibly, as if expecting the question. "I was born into it, but didn't find my niche for a while. I went to UCLA for two years, then dropped out and went to the Anaheim Police Academy."

Larry was taken aback. "I can't see you as a police officer."

Julie laughed. "That's what everybody says when I tell them my story. But, as strange as it seems, I was with the Police Department for two years. All I ever did was sit behind a desk and process data. It was a boring, dead end job."

"So, you quit?"

Julie nodded. "I went back to UCLA and graduated. A short time later, Mr. Larson decided it was time to bring the Dar Lumbre Society out of hiding. I went to work full time for the society. Thousands of other underground members did the same thing."

Larry stared at Julie as he pondered the situation. She shot a quick glance his way, then returned her gaze to the road ahead where a knot of traffic appeared, triggering the autopilot to apply the brakes.

"Tell me the truth," Larry said, as the Micro slowed and switched lanes. "Is Dar Lumbre still alive?"

"Absolutely."

"Where is he now?"

"In a secure location."

Larry grimaced. "That's a non-answer. Surely you can tell me more than that."

Julie shook her head. "I can't tell you where he is, because I don't know."

"Who knows?"

"Only Elmore Larson and his top lieutenants—three or four people, at the most."

Larry was exasperated. The more he learned about

the society, the more mysterious it sounded. He believed Julie had told him all she was authorized to tell, probably all she knew, as well. If he learned more, it would have to come from Elmore Larson himself, and that opportunity seemed to be approaching rapidly.

The Micro eased into the right lane as Disneyland loomed ahead. Larry gazed at Cinderella's Castle and recalled visiting the amusement park when he and Crane were in their teens. The memory was vivid in his mind...the sounds of happy people...the metallic clank of magical machinery...calliope music...the smell of hot dogs and cotton candy. Sometimes he wished he could go back to that time. Life was much simpler then--no big decisions to make.

They turned off Interstate 5 onto Anaheim Boulevard and went left on West Ball Road. A moment later, an old-fashioned strip center appeared on the left.

Julie motioned toward the building. "This is it. We're here." The Micro pulled into the nearly-empty garage, and chose a parking space on the ground level.

"We can go into the side entrance," Julie said.

Larry felt a knot in the pit of his stomach as they approached the building, but was anticipating meeting the man who had inspired a nationwide sociopolitical awakening just by talking about a famous doctor who disappeared fifty years ago.

Julie touched her right thumb to the sensor plate, and the heavy plate-glass door slid aside. They went inside and Julie led him to a waiting area.

The room was sparsely appointed with sturdy furniture in earth-tone colors--utilitarian, functional, business like. In spite of the simple furnishings, Larry was impressed. A few weeks earlier, Dar Lumbre's followers were printing leaflets in secret locations on obsolete equipment. Now they occupied office space near Disneyland, an impressive move up the ladder in a short time span. He wondered what the next move would be, and if he would be a part of it. A few people were preparing to leave for the day. Julie made introductions and chatted briefly with some of them. Everyone seemed to be the same age, about thirty. They all seemed pumped up about the progress the society was making. Zealots, all. Larry could see it in their eyes. Their detailed knowledge of political machinations made him realize he was a babe in the woods, yet he was intrigued by what he saw and heard.

Julie motioned to a small table surrounded by four wooden chairs. "Let's wait here. Mr. Larson will be out shortly."

Obediently, Larry sat down.

Julie went to a refrigerator in the corner, opened the door and peered inside. She looked back at Larry. "Would you like something to drink? Maybe a Coke, or water?"

Larry's realized his mouth was dry. "Just water-- thanks"

Julie took two bottles of water out of the refrigerator and went back to the table. She handed one to Larry and sat down across from him.

Larry twisted in his chair. The wait was an ordeal. He felt as if some cosmic revelation was unfolding at a snail's pace, and being merely an observer, he couldn't do anything to speed up the process.

Presently, a man stepped into the waiting area.

The man, tall and white-haired, was wearing olive drab pants and a matching short jacket in the oft-revived WWII style. He strode into the room with a lively step, and a magnetic aura about him announced *Commanding Officer* when he entered the room.

It was Elmore Larson.

Larry jumped to his feet, and the two men met in the center of the room.

Julie moved to Larry's side. "This is Larry Hopkins, the computer guru I told you about."

The men shook hands.

"Pleased to meet you, Mr. Hopkins," Larson said. "Thank you for your help in the Houston area. I'm sure Julie has told you a lot about the society."

Larry was made a conscious effort to relax. "Yes, and the story is inspiring." It was difficult to deal with the pace of the events unfolding in his life. He could scarcely believe he was face to face with Elmore Larson, the charismatic man whose picture he had seen for the first time only months ago.

135

"Julie is one of my confidential assistants," Larson said. "I trust her explicitly. She knows everything about the society except the details of Dar Lumbre's location and the date for his resuscitation. From the beginning, the society has kept that kind of information on a *need-to-know* basis."

"Let's sit," Julie said. She motioned, and they moved back to the table and sat down.

Elmore Larson gazed at Larry. "Tell me, what attracted you to the society?"

Larry thought a moment before answering. "I think it was the way your speeches made the opening words of the Declaration of Independence come alive."

Larson smiled faintly. "You mean the Jeffersonian statement that all men are created equal?"

Larry nodded. "Yes—self-evident truth, according to Thomas Jefferson. Until recently, they were just words on an old document archived in some museum. Today, they're associated with voter registration among Outsiders."

"The fate of this movement rests with Outsiders," Larson said.

"They're hanging on to every word you say."

Larson spoke with religious fervor. "My job is to set the stage for Dar Lumbre. He will become the true leader when he returns. I'm just paving the way."

"A comparison to John the Baptist and Jesus is inescapable," Larry said. "Was that intentional?"

Larson shook his head. "Not really, but we didn't discourage those who embraced the concept. It helped us spread the word."

Larry was beginning to feel more relaxed. The man across the table from him was easier to talk with than he'd expected. Even so, he was biding his time, waiting for the opportune moment to ask more specific questions about Dar Lumbre's return. Larry hoped Elmore Larson would bring up the topic, but if not, he planned to do so himself.

"We're disappointed by the lack of response from the medical community," Larson continued. "Dar Lumbre was a legendary doctor. We expected support from doctors and other medical professionals when we announced his return, but it didn't happen."

"I know. My brother is a doctoral candidate in genetics, but he doesn't believe Dr. Lumbre will return."

"Your brother, and others like him, are in for a big surprise."

Larry felt that the opportunity to press the issue had arrived. "When will Dr. Lumbre return?"

Larson's expression was unreadable. "Soon."

"Is that all you can tell me?"

"Unfortunately, yes."

Larry motioned toward the offices surrounding them. "Do these people know?"

Larson shook his head. "No, they don't, but they're convinced that it will be soon. I assure you, they won't be disappointed. He will return, indeed. So, why don't you move to Anaheim and work full time with us?"

"What kind of work? I'm not really political by nature."

"We're going to expand our high-tech capabilities rapidly in the near future," Larson said. "We plan to build our own social network to take us far beyond anything available now. We need computer experts like you."

A sense of belonging began to come over Larry. These people held many of the same beliefs he held, and they were doing something about it. He wondered if he had the temerity to do likewise.

Larry wanted the movement's policies and politics to have meaning, and he fully accepted them with a portion of his brain. Still, in another part of his brain, the thought persisted that he was nothing but a small-time computer programmer who had fallen down the rabbit hole into Wonderland. Only time would tell which part of his brain was in contact with reality.

Abruptly, Elmore Larson stood, ending the magic moment. "I have to go now," he said. "Please give careful consideration to the things we've discussed. If our brief conversation has convinced you to work with us here at the national headquarters, let me know after your trip to Silicon Valley. You'd fit right into this organization."

Larson extended his hand. Larry jumped up and grasped it. "I'll give it some serious thought, Mr. Larson."

Larson left the room, and Larry sat down again.

Julie stared at him. "Well…?"

Before he could respond, a young brunette burst into the room. "Julie, could I borrow your car to run a quick errand?" she asked. "It would save me a taxi fare, and I'll have it back in less than fifteen minutes."

"Sure, Angie. No problem." Julie held her iTab toward Angie, who touched the screen to log in as a guest operator of Julie's Micro. "It's parked near the end of the walkway--space three."

"Thanks," Angie said, as she walked away.

Julie turned back toward Larry. "Let's go for a walk."

"Where to?"

"Just down around Disneyland for a few minutes while Angie is using my car."

"The entrance is at least a mile away. I don't have enough time. I need to catch a flight to San Francisco.

Julie flashed an amused smile. "No problem. The city installed a PedMover along Disneyland Drive a couple of years ago. We can say hello to Mickey Mouse, and I can still get you to the airport quicker than the shuttle."

Larry gave in. "Okay, lead the way."

Julie and Larry left the office building via the front entrance and walked east on West Ball Road to the PedMover station. They stepped onto the moving belt, and moments later, arrived at the entrance gate of the Magic Kingdom. A few people loitered near the entrance, but to Larry's surprise, the front gates were locked.

"What's going on?" he asked. "I didn't know Disneyland ever closed." At that moment, he saw a sign on the front gate:

CLOSED TODAY FOR CITYGOV INSPECTION

"CityGov inspection?" Larry said. "What's that?"

"A new law just went into effect in California," Julie said. "All amusement parks have to shut down one day every quarter for an inspection by various labor unions working for CityGov. The city is tight with the unions. Even Mickey Mouse carries a union card."

"We didn't have time to go inside, anyway," Larry

said, "but, I liked the PedMover ride."

"Let's get some coffee and sit on one of the benches over there for a few minutes," Julie said, motioning as she spoke. She started toward a street vendor's colorful cart. "The day is too nice to get in a hurry."

"Just a few minutes. Then, I have to go."

They approached a red cart decorated with lemon-yellow smiley faces. The young woman behind the counter wore a smock duplicating the colors of the cart. Dispensers for lemonade and tropical punch were standing upside down on the counter near the cash register. Napkins, sweetener packets, and stirring sticks had been collected and placed in a rectangular box next to the drink dispensers. The refreshment stand was in closing-time mode, and the attendant didn't seem pleased to see customers approaching as she was shutting down.

Larry cast a quizzical look toward Julie. "Why are these street vendors closing so early?"

"They do it every CityGov inspection day. Without Disneyland traffic, they don't have enough customers to justify staying open later."

They had to settle for regular coffee, the only drink still available at the stand. After being served, they moved to the bench that Julie pointed out earlier. By the time they sat down, all of the nearby refreshment stands had closed their windows, and the area around the entrance of the Magic Kingdom was turning into a ghost town.

They sipped their coffee and watched as several street vendors hurried out with garbage bags and deposited them in trash cans near the entrance of Disneyland. Two minutes later, robotic garbage trucks appeared and emptied the cans.

"Disney has everything synchronized like a dance troop," Larry said. "Even garbage pickup. I've never seen anything like it."

Twenty minutes later, after finishing their coffee, they tossed the empty cups into one of the recently-emptied trash cans and zipped back to the office on the PedMover.

"I'll drop you off at the airport," Julie said

"That's too much trouble."

"It's right on the way," Julie insisted. "No use wasting money on cab fare, if you don't have to. Out here, we share everything to save money."

Larry gave up. "Okay."

He tried to replay the last thirty minutes in his mind, but his mental video was blurred and out of focus. He didn't understand what was happening to him. Seemingly, he was in the cross hairs between a determined woman and a charismatic politician bent on changing the world, and they both wanted to bring him to Anaheim. The ramifications boggled his mind.

Angie emerged from a small room adjacent to the waiting area and looked toward Larry and Julie. "Your car is parked in the same spot," she said. "Thanks a bunch."

"No problem," Julie said.

They retrieved the Micro from the garage and headed north along Euclid Street. In less than a half hour, they were approaching John Wayne Airport.

"My condo is right over there," Julie said, motioning toward a stucco building to her left. "Let's run by it and I'll give you a copy of the new TV commercial that'll hit the airways soon. You might find it interesting. It's the type of thing that you could help us with."

"Just email or text it to me."

"Mr. Larson won't let me."

"Why not?"

"He doesn't want it to fall into the wrong hands."

"Who would that be?

"The National Security Agency monitors all digital transmissions," Julie said. "The Department of Justice and IRS are probably doing it, too. There are plenty of wrong hands out there."

"I'm in a hurry," Larry said, but was beginning to wonder if he really was.

Julie ignored Larry's objection and swung the Micro into a narrow alley leading to the rear of the building.

"We'll go in the back way. I live on the second floor about half way down."

The old two-story stucco building had an early California look, and was attached by a breezeway to a modern condo facing the interstate. The grounds around both buildings were landscaped with sedum, lavender, juniper, and other plants requiring little or no water, as required by California law.

"This is it," Julie said. "I moved into this place a few months ago."

"It's nice," Larry said, immediately realizing how lame his comment must have sounded.

Julie led Larry up a flight of stairs. She thumbed the screen of her iTab, the door opened, and she motioned him to follow her inside.

A light came on as they entered, illuminating the typical HUD refurbished studio apartment with a living/sleeping/kitchen area and a bathroom. Julie's furniture was utilitarian, with a green sofa bed and student desk in the living area, and a tiny dinette suite near the kitchen. The overall effect was austere, but comfortable looking.

Julie went to the desk and opened a small drawer. A moment later, she produced a thumb drive and handed it to Larry.

"This is the opening salvo of a new publicity campaign," she said. "We're out in the open now—well past the door-to-door salesman approach. This new video is the next step. Let me know if you think it makes a strong appeal to tekkies. They're one of the groups we're not reaching, and Mr. Larson intends to change that by recruiting people like you."

"I'll let you know what I think," Larry said. He was flattered, but uncertain about the value of his input. As Julie had correctly surmised, most of his contacts were internet gamers. Maybe he could devise a way to help draw them in. He was about ready to give it a try, even though it would be a giant step outside of his comfort zone.

"You'd be great at this," Julie insisted.

"I'll let you know what I decide."

Julie motioned toward the kitchen. "Would you like something to drink? I make a mean margarita--blue agave tequila straight from Jalisco."

Larry shook his head. "I really need to go. I've got to catch a plane."

Julie gazed incredulously at Larry. "Are you afraid of me?"

"No, of course not."

Julie feigned a pout. "You don't like me?"

"I like you fine."

"You're married, aren't you?"

"Yes."

"You're not wearing a wedding ring."

Larry shrugged helplessly.

Julie crossed the room to the sofa bed and sat down, leaning her back against a stack of lemon yellow pillows. She pulled her feet up and tucked them underneath her legs.

"Why don't you sit down?" she said. "You look ridiculous standing there."

Julie's persona was hypnotic, but Larry remained standing.

"You'll have to decide for yourself," she said. "No one else can do it for you."

They stared at each other until Larry flinched. "I have to go," he said solemnly. "I'll call a cab."

## Chapter 22

The high-pitched whine decreased a few decibels, and the airplane shuddered slightly as the captain resumed control. Crane repositioned his lanky frame, leaned across Annie, and looked out of the window to his left. The ground below was a brown and green checkerboard, and beyond the land, the blue Pacific Ocean accentuated the earth's curvature along the hazy horizon. The plane began its descent.

"You're quieter than usual," Annie said, "and that's pretty quiet. What's on your mind?"

Crane managed a weak smile. "I was thinking about how the Dar Lumbre Society caused a rift between Larry and me. We haven't talked to each other in a couple of weeks."

"Maybe this California adventure will give you something to talk about. Wasn't Larry coming out here to talk to Apple-Disney?"

"The last I heard, that was his plan," Crane said. "He could be in California right now, and I wouldn't know it. We've been out of touch lately."

"Remember the advice you gave me concerning my mother?" Annie said. "It would work for you, too."

Crane changed the subject. "There's John Wayne Airport. Time to track down Elmore Larson's DNA."

He was dismayed at the paltry data available on the leader of the Dar Lumbre Society. According to census bureau information, Elmore Larson was born and raised in the farming area of Salinas Valley and lived as an Outsider until five years ago, at which time he came into the system with minimal background information. He was registered as a Republican, but had always marked his ballot *present, not voting,* a situation which led Crane to suspect the society had political aspirations they were keeping under wraps to minimize problems with NatGov.

"Fasten your seatbelt," the intercom blared. *"Abroche su cinturon."* After the seatbelt warning, a message in English followed by Spanish stated the aircraft would arrive at the terminal shortly.

Fifteen minutes later, the plane docked. Crane and

Annie took a robo-shuttle to the Amazon-Holiday Inn on Walnut Street near Disneyland. The location was perfect for their purpose. The Dar Lumbre Society's office was less than a mile away. Crane felt confident they could obtain a sample of Elmore Larson's DNA within a day or two. Larson was appearing at public forums on a regular basis, and had no reason to suspect that anyone was after his DNA. Surely a couple of experienced geneticists could pull off the caper. Reflexively, Crane touched the DNA kit in the pocket of his windbreaker, hoping that he would get the chance to use it soon.

They arrived at the Holiday Inn at 8:30 a.m., too early to check in. After depositing their bags with the bell captain, they left the lobby via the Walnut Street exit.

"I'm hungry," Annie said, as they stepped out into the morning chill, "and I could use a big cup of strong coffee. Southwest must be serving decaf."

"I saw a McDonald's just before we turned into the hotel driveway," Crane said. "Let's grab something there and move on. When we get a sample of Elmore Larson's DNA, we'll reward ourselves with a meal at a nice restaurant—some place where movie stars and other celebrities go. Real stars, not the wannabes manufactured by plastic surgeons."

"Sounds good to me," Annie said, as they walked away from the Holiday Inn. "Now it's BOLO time--*be on the lookout* for Elmore Larson."

The morning haze was dissipating rapidly, and sunlight bathed the buildings around them. Cars were filling the streets. Pedestrians appeared. The major flow of traffic in the street, as well as on the sidewalk, moved toward Disneyland. The PedMover along Disneyland Drive was near capacity. Crane was surprised at the size of the crowd. Apparently, theme parks weren't affected by recessions.

They walked north on South Walnut Street, stopping at McDonald's for one of their time-tested favorites, Egg McMuffins and coffee, and continued on to the intersection of West Ball Road. When they turned, Disneyland was at their backs. Occasionally, they glanced back toward Cinderella's Castle, the centerpiece of *The Happiest Place on Earth* according to commercials.

144

A few minutes later, they reached a long one-storied building with a glass front. The glass was plastered with posters, most of them attesting to the imminent return of their leader in absentia. Above the entrance, a banner read:

THE DAR LUMBRE SOCIETY

Near the front door, a group of people milled around, coffee cups and breakfast snacks in hand. Conversation and laughter rippled through the growing crowd as they waited. Presently, a figure appeared inside the building, and the door swung inward. The operatives filed in, seemingly well-organized for another day of proclaiming the second coming of Dar Lumbre.

After the surge of people flowed into the building, Annie and Crane found themselves virtually alone on the sidewalk. They retreated a few paces away from the entrance and stopped next to a light pole as they pondered their next move.

"I wonder what would happen if we just walked in and asked to see Elmore Larson?" Annie said. "In spite of the fact that Dr. Cartwright told us not to."

"As a last resort, we may have to do it," Crane said, "but I think the stealth approach is best for our first attempt. If Elmore Larson is related to Dr. Lumbre and knows it, he's keeping it secret on purpose, and has no reason to tell us anything. On the other hand, if he's related and doesn't know it, we'd have a lot of explaining to do."

"There's another possibility," Annie said. "Maybe he's waiting to see if anybody can solve this mystery."

"Then, let's show him we can."

Annie swung her iTab into position and touched the screen. "Let's see where Mr. Larson is scheduled to appear next, then we can figure out the best way to trail him."

While she was googling the information, the front door of the building swung open, and two men walked out onto the sidewalk.

The man in the lead was Elmore Larson. Neither Crane nor Annie recognized Larson's companion. With no hesitation, the two men walked to the curb and got into a black robo-cab that was waiting for them. The cab pulled away immediately and merged with traffic in the street.

"We need to hurry," Crane said. Frantically, he touched the Transportation App on his iTab, and selected *Next Available Cab.*

At the signal, a robo-cab worked its way through the busy traffic and pulled to the sidewalk. By the time Crane and Annie got into the vehicle, Larson's cab was a half block away and picking up speed.

"Destination, please?" the robo-cab asked.

"Follow that black car," Crane said.

"I don't understand your command," the cab said.

"Follow that black car," Crane repeated.

"Destination, please?" the cab asked again.

"Uh…Disneyland," Crane said.

At that command, the cab pulled away from the curb.

"If we catch a red light, we'll lose him," Crane said.

"Tell this dumb robot to put the pedal to the metal."

"I don't think it would understand."

The black cab in front of them slowed and turned off Walnut Drive onto South Disneyland Drive.

"Take South Disneyland Drive to the park," Crane said. The cab slowed and turned the corner.

The black cab ahead of them coasted to a stop at the broad esplanade between Disneyland and California Adventure. Elmore Larson and his companion stepped out and joined the growing crowd of people headed toward the amusement park.

"Pull over to the curb," Crane said.

Obediently, the cab pulled over and stopped. Crane and Annie jumped out and joined the throng of people behind Elmore Larson and his companion. They kept their distance, although there was no reason to believe they'd ever crossed paths with either of the men they were following.

"What's going on here?" Annie said. "Why would two old guys be heading toward Disneyland?"

"Obviously, they're meeting someone."

"Why didn't the people they're meeting come to the office instead of here?"

"That's a good question."

Elmore Larson and his companion bypassed the ticket booths and headed straight toward the front entrance of Disneyland. The lines were short, and early-arriving visitors were pouring through the turnstiles. The two men were inside the park in less than a minute, leaving the anxious geneticists stuck outside the park without tickets.

"They already had tickets," Crane said. "Get some for us, and I'll try to see which way they go." He crowded close to the turnstiles and kept his eyes on the two men until they disappeared from view down Main Street, U.S.A.

Annie thumbed her iTab frantically for a few seconds. "Okay. I got two tickets, but there goes our dinner in a fancy restaurant."

"They're gone. I couldn't tell which way they went."

"What now?" Annie asked, as they went through the turnstiles and hurried along Main Street toward Cinderella's Castle.

Crane pondered the situation a moment. "They were hugging the left side of the street when they went out of sight. So we'll go left."

After walking past the Emporium and a dozen other stores and restaurants along Main Street, they turned left toward Adventure Land, passing the Enchanted Tiki Room which was beginning its first show of the day. They bypassed the Jungle Cruise and Tarzan's Tree House and went directly into New Orleans Square.

The Square was flanked on one end by the still-popular Pirates of the Caribbean, and on the other by the Haunted Mansion. Several restaurants were nestled between these two major attractions, and a large area of outdoor seating made it a good location to meet people. They walked up the stairs to the Disneyland Railroad, thinking the elevated vantage point would make it easy to survey the square. Dozens of people milled around--eating, drinking, shopping, and talking, but Elmore Larson was not in sight.

"We're amateur gumshoes," Crane said. "We let him slip through our fingers, and he didn't even know he was being followed."

"We're Mickey Mouse sleuths," Annie said.

"More like Goofy."

"Well, Elmore Larson didn't come here for the rides," Annie said. "He came to meet someone. I doubt that he'll stay very long."

Crane agreed. "He won't. We'd better go back and take up a station near the exit gate. We'll wait there until he leaves."

"Let's go."

They backtracked their steps to the entrance/exit area and looked around for a good place to wait. "Let's sit over there in front of the cinema," Annie said, pointing to an empty bench. "They can't come to this end of Main Street without us seeing them."

"Grab a seat, and I'll get us some coffee," Crane said. He crossed the street to a refreshment stand.

Two minutes later, he returned with coffees in hand. He gave one to Annie and sat down beside her. For the next half hour, they sipped coffee and rehashed their recent DNA adventures.

"Larson has become a well-known public figure," Crane said. "I'm surprised that he can come in here without attracting a lot of attention."

"They're used to celebrities out here. They don't pay any attention to them."

Thirty minutes later, their wait ended as both of them spotted Elmore Larson at the same time. He was walking directly toward them along Main Street. The man who entered the park with Larson was nowhere in sight.

"What's going on?" Annie asked. "I wonder what happened to the other guy."

"It doesn't matter," Crane said. "It's Larson we're after, and he's holding a coffee cup. We'll trail him until he throws it into the garbage, no matter how long it takes."

"This is looking too easy," Annie said. "I figured we'd have to follow him for several days before we could get a sample of his DNA."

"We don't have it yet," Crane said. He surveyed the situation. Almost all of the traffic was flowing into the park, with only an occasional straggler moving toward the exit. He realized  that he and Annie were an odd couple,  a string bean and a manga character--not that Larson seemed concerned that someone might be following him. Still, they had to be careful.

As Larson passed by, Annie stood and took a step in his direction. "Come on," she whispered. "We can't let him get out of sight again."

Crane caught Annie by the arm. "Stay back a bit."

Crane remained seated on the bench until Larson was about fifty feet past him, then stood casually and joined Annie. Together they followed their quarry, both trying to look like first-time sightseers casually strolling through Disneyland.

"What if he goes into a rest room?" Annie asked.

"No problem. We'll follow him."

"We?"

"They're unisex."

Annie nodded. "I know, but I'd look odd standing behind him at a urinal."

"Okay, I'll follow him."

Walking at a brisk pace, Elmore Larson exited the turnstiles and veered directly toward a trash can near the entrance/exit gates. He stopped in front of the can, and with the cup to his lips, tipped his head back to drain the last drop of coffee. When he finished, he tossed the empty cup into the trash and walked to the nearby curb where the black robo-cab awaited him.

As the cab drove away, the elated geneticists rushed through the exit and went to the trash can. Annie stood guard while Crane examined the contents of the can.

He looked inside the can. "Voila! There are only three coffee cups in here, along with some water bottles and other miscellaneous stuff. One of the cups has to be Larson's."

"I told you our luck was changing. Your serendipity is coming back."

Crane took a DNA kit out of his jacket pocket, donned surgical gloves, and retrieved the three cups one at a time. With great care, he flattened each cup and placed it in a storage envelope. As he collected the samples, several passersby hesitated, stared momentarily, and moved on. In less than two minutes, he finished packaging the three samples.

He turned to Annie and said, "This is what we came for. It's time to go. See if we can catch an evening flight back to Houston."

Annie lifted her iTab into position and tapped at the screen. A moment later, she said, "Bad news. All of the evening flights are sold out. The next available seats are on the red eye leaving at eleven o'clock."

"Book us," Crane said. "We'll go to the airport early and eat dinner there, unless you want to hang out around here for a little while."

"I'm too psyched up to putter around Disneyland. I'm ready to leave ASAP."

They started toward the Holiday Inn.

Later that evening, they left the hotel and headed for the airport. A feeling of relief came over Crane. He was certain the DNA sample on one of the cups would show a family relationship between Elmore Larson and Dar Lumbre. Nothing else made sense.

They settled into their seats as the airport shuttle swung onto West Ball Road and passed directly in front of the Dar Lumbre Society headquarters before turning onto South Euclid Street. A few minutes later, the street narrowed abruptly, and the pavement became wavy and rough as the luster of Disneyland slipped away in a few blocks. Modern stucco apartments gave way to faded commercial buildings housing small retail shops selling everything from groceries to used clothing. A crowd milled along the sidewalk. Some people went into the shops and others came out, while most wandered aimlessly about, seemingly with no specific destination in mind.

Annie jabbed her elbow into Crane's ribs. "Look at that!"

Crane's eyes followed Annie's hand gesture. Near the end of the block, a storefront had been converted into a church. A banner reading CHURCH OF THE DOUBLE HELIX stretched across the roofline of the building. Above the banner, a makeshift plastic steeple was attached to the roof with guy wires, and at the top of the steeple, a metallic caduceus glistened brightly.

"This must be a splinter group that separated from

150

the Dar Lumbre Society," Crane said.

"New religions are verboten. How did NatGov let this slip through their net?"

Crane shrugged. "Millions of people are involved in the Dar Lumbre Society. It's too late for the government to suppress the movement."

"The genie is out of the bottle," Annie said.

## Chapter 23

"How do you feel?" Crane asked, as he and Annie entered the CellTech complex.

"High as a kite--revved up on adrenalin."

A bomb threat at John Wayne Airport had delayed their return flight for three hours, turning the one-day trip to Anaheim into an endurance test, but they had no intention of calling it quits upon touching down in Houston. It was seven o'clock Thursday morning, and their colleagues were beginning to straggle into the complex. Crane and Annie exchanged a few hurried greetings, but brushed off all attempts to engage in any extended conversations. They intended to find out the connection between Elmore Larson and Dar Lumbre before the day was over, if humanly possible.

Once inside the lab, Crane handed the DNA sample kit to Annie and said, "Collect the saliva. I'll program the equipment."

Annie placed the three sample envelops in a germfree hood made of clear polycarbonate and stainless steel. After donning surgical gloves, she took out each cup and examined it carefully, first with the unaided eye, and then with a stereo microscope linked to a desktop monitor.

"This cup has lipstick on it," Annie said. "Take a look." She touched a button to enlarge the image on the monitor.

Crane studied the image briefly. "I'm sure Elmore Larson wasn't wearing makeup," he said. "Put that one in the refrigerator for the time being."

Annie placed one of the remaining cups under the microscope and repeated her methodical examination. "There's a lot of saliva on this one. I'm guessing it's Elmore Larson's cup."

"Run it first."

Annie passed a moistened cotton swab around the rim of the cup and twirled it in a small centrifuge tube containing saline solution. She capped the tube, placed it in a rack, and slid the rack along the lab bench toward Crane.

Crane ruptured the cells with a sonic disrupter, precipitated the DNA with ethanol, and centrifuged it to produce a DNA pellet. The biochemistry of the procedure was identical to that of Dar Lumbre's day, but automatic equipment sped up the process considerably.

Annie cut the purified DNA into fragments with enzymes and separated the fragments by electrophoresis. Upon scanning the results into CellTech's database, everything was set up to compare Elmore Larson's DNA to that contained in DL-666.

The two anxious geneticists left the sample preparation area and took their stools in front of the wall monitor. Annie signaled, and a 3D image of DNA appeared on the monitor. Her next flourish of sign language produced a split screen with Elmore Larson's DNA fingerprint on the left and DL-666's fingerprint on the right. They stared at the screen, transfixed for several seconds as they digested the images before them.

"What do you see?" Annie asked.

"I think we can safely say that the DNA on this cup is from Elmore Larson," Crane said, "and that Larson and Dar Lumbre are close relatives."

Annie stared at the images. "Maybe a brother or half-brother?"

Crane considered various family tree scenarios before answering, "The age difference is pretty large for them to be siblings."

"Not if you add a fertility clinic to the equation," Annie said. "Frozen ovum…surrogate mother…sperm bank father."

"You like the brother or half-brother idea?"

"Affirmative."

"Okay, let's run mitochondrial DNA to see if both of these men had the same mother," Crane said. "We could take a quick lunch break first, if you like."

"I'm not hungry. Let's just get coffee and keep on working?"

"That suits me fine. I'll make a Starbucks run while you set up the tests."

"I'll take a vanilla latte."

Crane headed toward the door, and Annie turned on the Eppendorf Thermal Cycler. After transferring a portion of the purified sample to a test tube, she added polymerase, an enzyme to catalyze the process. She placed the tube in the cycler and programmed it to go through two heating and cooling cycles, a procedure that would quadruple the amount of DNA in the test tube.

She sat before the machine, listening to the pulsating hum of its thermostat. She could visualize what was occurring inside the thermal cycler. A DNA strand was slowly turning on its axis. She thought of the molecule as a spiral ladder with thousands of rungs. As the temperature rose, every rung broke in the middle, leaving two independent half-ladders that moved away from each other. When the molecules cooled, instead of rebuilding the original ladder, each half formed a mirror image of itself, thereby doubling the amount of DNA in the sample.

Crane returned to the lab with a latte in each hand and handed one of them to Annie. They sipped while the semi-robotic equipment hummed and clicked intermittently in the background. Occasionally, Annie passed a finger over a touch screen, thereby telling the equipment to advance the sample to the next station.

"No matter how these samples turn out, we may be only half finished," Annie said. "Even if Elmore Larson's DNA is a good substitute for Dar Lumbre's, we may have to track down the source of the non-human DNA."

They continued the process of fingerprinting Elmore Larson's mitochondrial DNA, and shortly before five o'clock, Annie uploaded the data into the computer. The two tired geneticists stared at the split-screen projections for several seconds, although the first glance told the story.

"They're identical," Crane said. "No doubt about it."

"Elmore Larson and Dar Lumbre had the same mother, but a different father."

"The more we find out about this tissue, the more mysterious this saga becomes," Crane said. "We really need to find a sister to Dar Lumbre."

"Right," Annie said. "Dar Lumbre's defective X chromosome didn't get any help from the Y chromosome paired with it. If DL-666 could be made from a woman's DNA, her second X chromosome would increase the chance of the tissue remaining stable."

Crane shook his head slowly. "We can't find Dar Lumbre, and now we need to find his sister."

They continued discussing their results until they detected movement behind them. Simultaneously, they swiveled on their lab stools as Helena Cartwright approached.

"I got your text this morning, Mr. Hopkins," she said. "Nicely done."

Crane recognized Dr. Cartwright's remarks as subdued kudos, but was still wary of her. After all, the only way she could be successful at CellTech would be for DL-666 to be resurrected from the dead, and under the current scenario, it was up to the Hopkins-Lee team to call it forth from the tomb.

"Your text was somewhat brief," Dr. Cartwright said in Crane's direction. "Fill me in on the details of your California trip, and everything you've found out since returning to Houston."

As Dr. Cartwright listened intently, Crane reviewed the events of the last twenty-four hours.

"There's nothing else you can do today," she said. "Go home and get some rest. When you come in tomorrow morning, graft Mr. Larson's DNA into DL-666 and see if that corrects the problem. I want CellTech to be ready when the government is."

Both exhausted geneticists were feeling the need to press on without delay, but at Dr. Cartwright's insistence, they left the lab reluctantly.


Early the next morning, Crane and Annie returned to the lab and resumed their project with renewed vigor.

Using bacterial enzymes like scissors, they cut DL-666's X chromosome at the juncture between the long and short arms, and separated the two pieces. They performed the identical procedure on Elmore Larson's X chromosome and spliced the fragments together, thereby producing a new tissue containing Elmore Larson's DNA in place of Dar Lumbre's.

"Maybe we should call it DL-667," Annie said. "That

way we would eliminate the apocalyptic implications some zealots have attached to 666."

"I think we'll call it DL-666a for the time being," Crane said.

By the middle of the afternoon, they were ready to culture a lab batch of DL-666a. Crane was pleased with the day's progress, but still cautious about the final outcome. The section they were replacing was less than half of the X chromosome, which might not be enough to revive the tissue.

"Okay," Crane said, "it's good to go. Bring the culture medium?"

Annie took a flask of growth medium out of the refrigerator and brought it to the lab bench. Crane transferred an inoculum of the new tissue to the flask and attached sensors to measure optical density, oxygen uptake, and carbon dioxide release. When everything was ready, he placed the flask in an incubator at 37 degrees Centigrade. In about two hours, they would know if their detective work at Disneyland and gene manipulation in CellTech's laboratory had produced the hoped-for magic.

Crane went over his mental checklist one last time. When he was satisfied, he turned to Annie and said, "We may as well take a break. This equipment will run just as well without us staring at it, and we won't have any worthwhile data in less than an hour and a half, if that soon."

Annie raised her arms over her head and stretched. "I've worked up an appetite. What do you think about making a sushi run?"

"Fine by me. Maybe we'll run into your old classmate from Berkeley and see what he's up to."

They left the CellTech complex and went to the Palace of Oriental Delights.


Exactly an hour and a half later, Crane and Annie returned to the CellTech building. They hurried to the rear of the lab and stopped before the incubator. The gauges, probes, and recording devices told a quick and stark story. The improvement was significant, but not what they'd hoped for. Neither of them said a word until they double-checked the results and the instruments which produced the readings.

Finally, Annie asked, "Where do we stand now?"

Crane was long-faced. "We sped up the growth rate about fifty percent compared to the current DL-666. Significant, but still far below the average numbers exhibited by the tissue before the anomaly showed up."

"Will CellTech use it?" Annie asked.

"They might have to, as a last resort."

Annie raised her eyebrows. "Is Richard Hunter a last resort?"

"Probably," Crane said. "If we don't get the tissue back to its original condition, I think the transplant surgeons will have to use DL-666a. They can't keep Richard in the C-Unit indefinitely. He's running out of time—and so are we."

"You don't think they can find a human donor?"

"Not likely."

After a moment of silence, Annie said, "We may as well go home. There's nothing else we can do today."

"I'll probably come in tomorrow for a little while."

Annie looked directly into Crane's eyes. "You're spending too many Saturdays in the lab."

"I like lab work."

"Well, no matter how much you like it, you need to take a break before you burn out. I'll talk to Brad, and we'll come up with a daytrip the three of us can do together."

Crane was noncommittal. A daytrip hadn't entered his mind, and he doubted that he could enjoy one while Richard Hunter lay in a C-Unit waiting for resolution of the DL-666 problem.

## Chapter 24

Annie's concentration was a character trait that she took pride in, but for one of the few times in her life, outside events were distracting her. She couldn't resist the urge to check the headlines on her iTab every half hour or so, even though it was against company policy. She touched the screen, and a barrage of headlines scrolled by. They were preceded by the usual introductions, THIS JUST IN, BREAKING NEWS, or HAPPENING NOW, phrases Annie termed the *harbingers of doom* because they invariably portended bad news. A new batch was being posted now:

DOW DROPS 777 POINTS
UNEMPLOYMENT RISES
JOB CUTS IN MEDICAL INDUSTRY

The last headline stunned Annie. She touched the screen again, and the full article exploded into view:

*JOB CUTS IN HOUSTON MEDIPLEX*

*Houston--Reliable sources today report that several large medical supply companies will start layoffs in the near future, perhaps as early as today. This reduction in force looms over companies which took NatGov funding at startup, as well as those who have recently received government funding through stimulus packages. Based on the latest quarterly reports and stock performance, companies facing this crisis include CellTech Inc., Genomes Inc., V-Tek, BioLabs, and several smaller companies involved in the biotech industry. None of the companies cited would grant access to a spokesperson to confirm or deny this report.*

Annie was still transfixed by the news bulletin when Crane entered the lab and stopped behind her. Together, they stared at the news article, as if reading it over and over would alter the grim tone of the story. After a few moments, Annie swiveled around to face Crane, and they looked at each other a long time without speaking. Crane had a look in his eyes which Annie found disturbing—one of the smartest men she'd ever known was grappling with a demon known as DL-666. Maybe Dar Lumbre's numbering system made sense, after all.

Finally, Crane said, "I was afraid of this."

"One of us could get laid off."

"Possibly both."

"What would we do?" Annie asked.

"You mean about DL-666?"

Annie nodded. "Yes, that's all I'm concerned about. Not salary. With a little scrimping, I could survive on OFS's severance package for a while, or go back to California and live with my mother, now that I've mended fences with her. But the project--that's another matter. It has to be carried forward, no matter what it takes."

"DL-666 has been CellTech's bread and butter since the company started up," Crane said. "I don't see any way Dr. Cartwright would put it on the back burner."

"Not on the back burner," Annie said, "but she might bring in a new cook or two, someone who makes a lower salary than either of us."

Crane grimaced. "That would be risky on her part."

"It would, and she knows it," Annie said. "But, she won't hesitate to do it if we fail to produce positive results pretty soon. We need to have a plan in place to keep the project moving forward under any circumstances, no matter what Helena Cartwright does."

Crane nodded. "We certainly do. Richard Hunter's life depends on us, and many other lives as well. We still have time, but none to waste."

Annie's was solemn. "I'd like to propose a pact between us."

"Go ahead."

"If one of us gets laid off, and the other remains on the DL-666 project, we'll discuss it every day, just as if both of us were still working on it."

"That's the only way to operate," Crane said. "We have a pact--a blood oath."

Annie stood and put her hand on Crane's shoulder. When he turned toward her, she tiptoed and kissed him on the cheek.

"What was that for?" Crane asked.

"SWAK--*Sealed With a Kiss*. Better than a blood oath, don't you think?"

"Works for me."

Chapter 25

Crane sat on a stool in front of the fume hood preparing samples to use in searching for a molecular switch--a *ras gene*--which might be controlling the function of DL-666. He didn't know if such a gene was involved, but thought the idea was worth investigating, particularly since their X chromosome approach hadn't produced a definitive solution to the problem.

The idea of a molecular switch came with a built-in difficulty, namely the binary nature of the switch. The protein switches were either on or off, suggesting that any function they controlled would shut down catastrophically, rather than slowing to a stop over a period of time. At least three such human genes existed, and possibly others in the reptilian portion of the X chromosome. Perhaps the switches had shut down sequentially, a process which might explain DL-666's slow growth rate during the lag phase of reproduction. The idea was plausible, but just barely.

While he was mulling over the molecular switch concept, his iTab played the CellTech ringtone. He touched the screen and the words *TD's Office* appeared.

"Mr. Hopkins," the caller said, "this is Janice Smith. Dr. Cartwright would like to see you immediately, please."

"Okay, I'll be right there," Crane said, knowing from the tone of Janice's voice that something drastic was in the offing. It was not like the Technical Director's Administrative Assistant to be so formal. He'd known Janice for six or seven years, and she always called him *Crane*, not *Mr. Hopkins*. He pictured Dr. Cartwright standing over Janice's shoulder while she was making the call. A knot formed in the pit of his stomach as he walked toward the lab exit.

He took the elevator to the twelfth floor and entered the outer office of the Technical Director's suite. With a slight motion of her hand toward Dr. Cartwright's office, Janice said, "Please go in."

At Dr. Cartwright's instruction, Crane sat down in a chair across the desk from her. Even before she spoke, Crane knew what was about to take place, and couldn't have been more stunned. He was being laid off, one of the first casualties in a NatGov RIF—a *reduction in force*. The possibility of being laid off had entered his mind, but only briefly. He'd assumed that DL-666 would give him immunity. That assumption was a major miscalculation.

"This is not personal, Mr. Hopkins," Dr. Cartwright began, "but…"

"It's personal with me," Crane snapped, his cheeks flushing.

"Please allow me to continue," Dr. Cartwright said in an even voice. "It is my responsibility to return this company to profitability, and that is what I intend to do. Cutting expenses is part of the process, as distasteful as it is."

Crane glared at Dr. Cartwright. "How can you terminate me? I'm working on the most important project at CellTech." He didn't think the DL-666 problem was likely to be solved without his involvement, but obviously, she thought otherwise.

"I understand your point, Mr. Hopkins. Please try to understand mine. This is a temporary reduction in force. Hopefully, it will be of short duration. I'm following OFS's standard procedure for layoffs. Their rules require that senior staff, such as you, be laid off in proportion to layoffs at the junior level."

Crane felt cold sweat on his palms. "Are you telling me that this layoff is based strictly on some accounting formula imposed by the OFS--not on science or job performance?"

"That's correct, Mr. Hopkins."

"That doesn't make sense."

"It's standard OFS policy."

"Their polices are absurd," Crane said, his voice hot.

"I have to follow the rules laid down by NatGov."

"The rules were written by morons."

In spite of Crane's outburst, Dr. Cartwright's voice remained calm. She continued, "Let me explain OFS procedures regarding your termination package. As long as you draw OFS unemployment benefits, you remain under contract to CellTech. If you take a job with some other company, your contract with CellTech ends, as well as your OFS benefits.  When the company returns to profitability, or

NatGov increases our funding, you'll be eligible to return to your old position."

After an icy pause, Crane said, "I wouldn't give you the chance to fire me a third time."

He was beginning to accept the inevitable, and squelched the urge to say more. A smack-down with Dr. Cartwright could damage future investigative work on DL-666, and he resolved not to let such a thing happen, no matter how much tongue biting was required. Too many lives were at stake for him to burn bridges with CellTech's government-installed CEO and Technical Director.

"I won't be here long," Dr. Cartwright said. "Moreover, we're not likely to continue our career paths with the same company, here or anywhere else. The world has changed since we crossed swords over the fruit fly experiment. Today, the government controls virtually every aspect of corporate business."

Crane shook his head. "I feel like a pawn in a NatGov chess game."

To Crane's surprise, Dr. Cartwright nodded and said, "You are, Mr. Hopkins, as are we all."

Crane didn't see Dr. Cartwright as a pawn, but rather as the player moving the pawns around. In that scenario, she had him checkmated.

Dr. Cartwright leaned forward. "I'll tell you something that I seldom reveal to another person. I'd rather do the work you do than what I do, but when I saw the way the United States was changing, I decided to change with it in order to protect my own interests."

Crane wondered if Dr. Cartwright were patronizing him, or really meant what she said. For a brief moment, her façade had slipped a bit, but she reconstructed it quickly and became her old self again, stainless steel to the core.

A few minutes later, the discussion ran its course, and Crane was forced to accept the inevitable. He left Dr. Cartwright's office in a funk and took the elevator to the ground floor. He went into the lab where Annie sat in front of the monitor, which was alive with shifting images of DNA.

Crane walked to Annie's workstation and stopped beside her. She swiveled on her lab stool and faced him, a somber look in her eyes. He could tell by her expression that she already knew what he was about to say. In one breath, he blurted out the whole story.

Annie started to speak, but Crane held up his hand to stop her. Commiseration was not on his mind at the moment. He had a short speech to make, and was going to make it, even though Annie seemed primed to jump into the discussion about the layoffs and, perhaps, give Dr. Cartwright a verbal shredding.

"Dr. Cartwright will put you in charge of the DL-666 project," he said. "You'll be assigned a new lab partner, some bright young guy still wet behind the ears—probably one of those new guys from MIT. You'll be the team leader, a good one, no doubt."

"I hope I'm ready."

"Don't be ridiculous," Crane said. "You're totally ready, and this is your chance to prove it. You're a born leader, better than I ever was. Everybody around here loves you. They barely tolerate me. Dr. Rosenfield said I was the Lone Ranger, and if not for you, I would be."

"That would make me *Tonto*, which means *fool* in Spanish."

"Tonto is the masculine form, so it can't be you."

"It's hard to be politically correct in Spanish."

The light banter made Crane feel somewhat better. "Keep me up to date," he said. "I've got to hold Kim's hand on this project while her father is facing another surgery, no matter whether I'm working on DL-666 or not."

"I'll call you every day. Remember our vow."

"I'll never forget it."

He turned to go, then stopped and looked back toward Annie. Their eyes met, and they gazed at each other for a moment. Crane was galvanized by the intensity of their eye contact, and felt like Annie's dark eyes were looking into the depths of his soul.

Annie stepped closer to Crane and put her arm around his waist. "Hang in there, Protein Man."

He left the lab and went down the hallway to a side exit, a route which bypassed CellTech's main lobby and the Starbucks adjoining it. The coffee shop would be full of

CellTech employees, some of whom had just shared the same fate as him, and he didn't feel like talking about it. At the moment, he was riding off into the sunset alone.

Crane left the Mediplex. The mid-morning air was cold and damp. He took a deep breath, zipped his windbreaker, and walked south toward Holcombe Boulevard. He decided to walk home rather than take the Metro or a robo-cab. The exercise would be good for him, and since he'd just been put on a reduced income, saving the bus fare made sense.

Upon reaching Holcombe Boulevard, he turned right and walked along the sidewalk bordering the wide street. This stretch of Holcombe from the Mediplex to Kirby Drive was his pocket universe. Other than his family and Annie, everything he needed was within a locale which extended less than ten blocks in each direction. Stress usually flowed out of his mind when he entered the area, but it wasn't happening today.

Crane turned left at Kirby Street, and a moment later, entered the elevator of the Gramercy Condos, his home for the last eight years. He got off at the fifth floor and went into his studio apartment. In spite of his ordeal, he felt somewhat better upon arriving home.

The condo consisted of the standard HUD-approved one-room unit, but Crane had mechanized and automated everything possible. It was the perfect bachelor pad/man cave, and he intended to keep it, even if he had to cut expenses elsewhere.

He went to the window and looked out. The butterfly weeds on the balcony were wilted badly, but he didn't care.

## Chapter 26

At mid-morning, Annie was working alone in the lab when Helena Cartwright entered with William Sanders in tow. William was one of the new MIT graduates Annie had described as *very smart*. She realized that she was about to have the opportunity, whether she liked it or not, to find out how smart the wet-behind-the-ears geneticist really was. Dr. Cartwright's jaw was set in a firm line, and William looked a little intimidated. Clearly, they had discussed the assignment before coming to the lab.

Dr. Cartwright nodded a greeting in Annie's direction. "Miss Lee, I am assigning Mr. Sanders to work with you on the DL-666 project. He's been working on kidney tissue cultures since joining the company a couple of months ago. I briefed him and instructed him to read all of Mr. Hopkins' reports. Please bring him up to speed on recent details of the project, and utilize him to the maximum extent possible."

Annie extended her hand toward the young man.

He grasped her outstretched hand and said, "I'm looking forward to working with you."

"Miss Lee, it's unfortunate that economic conditions led to a budget cut at CellTech which forced me to lay off Mr. Hopkins," Dr. Cartwright said. "In his absence, you're in charge of this project, so it's up to you to keep it moving forward. You know how important it is."

"I certainly do."

"I've reviewed Mr. Hopkins' last report," Cartwright said, "and I have a question."

Annie made an effort to keep from cringing. "What is it?"

"Have you looked for a solution outside of the cell, such as protein markers on the surface of the cells?" she asked. "I'm thinking specifically of the study on human leukocyte antigens, the HLA complex."

Annie shook her head, dismissing the idea instantly. "That's not applicable to DL-666."

"How can you be so sure?"

"It's a replay of the early days leading up to the Genome project," Annie said, hoping she wasn't about to hear another lengthy discussion of Amish family trees and Mormon records, much less Dar Lumbre's gene pool—which didn't exist except for Elmore Larson. And Larson's relatives, if he had any, were probably Outsiders completely off the grid. They couldn't be surveyed.

Dr. Cartwright didn't give up at the first rebuff. "That study was excellent," she said. "It helped unravel the mystery of hemochromatosis."

Annie, convinced her own approach was right, was determined to hold her ground. She took a deep breath and said, "I'm totally familiar with that study. I did a scaled down version of it in graduate school. The early geneticists worked with large populations, mostly Mormons, so they were able to catalogue a huge gene pool. DL-666's gene pool consists of three members—Dar Lumbre, his half-brother, and some snake that we haven't identified yet. Furthermore, the X chromosome in this tissue has been altered until it bears no resemblance to established base lines."

Dr. Cartwright looked directly at Annie for a full five seconds and said, "Okay, Miss Lee, your point is well taken. But don't forget, the scientific method flourishes amid discourse and dialogue, even disagreement. I may come in here from time to time and challenge your thinking, just to force you to stay focused."

"I'm focused like a laser beam," Annie said evenly.

To Annie's surprise, Dr. Cartwright said, "The study Mr. Hopkins outlined looks okay to me. Continue with it."

"Affirmative."

"Let me say it again, Miss Lee. We can disagree as long as we don't clash. Disagreements can promote honest evaluation of ideas. Run the project your way, and plug Mr. Sanders into the work as quickly as possible." She turned abruptly and left the lab.

Annie thought she had a fix on the new CEO's psychological makeup. Clearly, she was trying to connect with the scientific aspect of her new assignment in order to achieve recognition as a scientist; however, her science was a little rusty after so many years away from the lab. Dr. Cartwright's HLA protein suggestion was old school, and Annie was pleased that she had successfully brushed it off. She wondered what Dr. Cartwright would suggest next.

"Good show, Annie," William said. "You got game."

"We'll see."

"Question?"

"Fire away."

"Am I going to have a fancy nickname like Crane Hopkins did?"

Annie thought a moment before answering, "The only thing I can think of is *Billy the Kid*."

"Why don't you call me Bill? That's the name I like best, even though everybody in Boston called me William."

"Okay, Bill, let's get to work."

Bill followed Annie to the computer station. "Sit," she said, indicating the lab stool to her left. "I'll bring you up to date."

Annie turned to the wall monitor and called up the reports on DL-666. She started her briefing with the extended lag phase which Crane observed initially, and went on to the problem that occurred immediately after Richard Hunter's heart transplant. Bill listened attentively, and asked an occasional question. Annie could tell that he was a quick study--young and enthusiastic, with the IQ and education to conduct a proper chromosome analysis. His only drawback--he was a novice. To be helpful on the DL-666 project, he would have to advance beyond that condition in a hurry--preferably, in a few days.

Annie ended her briefing. "Okay, that's where we stand. Crane and I had a brainstorming session at least three times a week, usually starting bright and early every Monday morning at Starbucks. We'll do the same. Any questions?"

"How often does Dr. Cartwright come into the lab with suggestions?"

"She's done it only a couple of times," Annie said. "She's mentioned the Duffy blood groups and Old Order Amish. Today, as you heard, she brought up the HLA protein complex. All of her suggestions missed the mark. Maybe she was just tossing them out to make us think."

"Isn't she a geneticist?"

Annie shrugged. "Sort of. She's a biochemist with some experience in genetics, but hasn't worked in the field

168

for years. In addition to her PhD, she has an MBA from Harvard. Apparently, she's good at turning companies around. She needs to concentrate on that aspect of the business, and leave the genetics to us."

Bill smiled easily. "Can we get some coffee before we delve into DL-666 any further?"

"Now you're talking. Caffeine is the fifth essential element."

"What...? Oh...I get it."

"That was an IQ test."

They started down the hallway. "What do you want me to do first?" Bill asked.

"I want you to do a little more work on the cups that Crane and I found at Disneyland," Annie said.

Bill looked puzzled. "I thought you said that you were satisfied with Elmore Larson's DNA sample."

Annie nodded. "I am, but there are two more cups that we didn't analyze. I want you to take a look at them."

"What are we looking for?"

"I don't have the slightest idea," Annie said. "Just check them out and let me know what you find."

## Chapter 27

Shortly before ten o'clock Saturday morning, Crane's iTab buzzed. The text was from Annie, informing him that she and Brad would arrive at the corner of Kirby and Grammercy in about two minutes. He headed for the door. After nearly a week of unemployment, much of it spent idly watching news banners scroll across his desktop monitor, he was ready for a change of pace. He was glad Annie had talked him into a trip to the Hermann Park Zoo. And, after discussing DL-666 at length the previous evening, he and Annie agreed that lab work would be a verboten topic during the daytrip.

He arrived at the corner as Brad's car pulled to the curb.

While they were exchanging greetings, Annie jumped out and climbed into the cramped rear seat, and Crane got in beside Brad.

As the car eased away from the curb, a few large raindrops splattered on the windshield. He looked up at the dark clouds, hoping rain would not spoil their plans. After living in Houston all his life, Crane knew the local weather was hard to predict, and had learned to adjust outdoor plans on the fly.

"Let's take in the zoo first, if it's not raining when we get there," Crane said. "I'd like to see the genetically modified animals and find out who's competing with CellTech for biotech stimulus money."

Fifteen minutes later, they passed through the entrance turnstile along with a trickle of early arrivals. Overhead, the clouds were breaking up and the threat of an immediate downpour seemed to have subsided.

As Crane and Brad made small talk, Annie studied her iTab for a moment and said, "Let's go see the giraffes first."

A short walk later, they came to the giraffe exhibit, a high fenced pasture resembling an African veldt. Three giraffes were lined up along the fence, watching people who were watching them. Two of them were ordinary, a male and a female known as Hi C and Hi Cecilia, two famous names which zoo officials retrieved from the previous century. The third member of the giraffe trio was a small male with markings like a zebra. His name was Hi Z. He stretched his neck and plucked a few leaves from an overhead branch, clearly unaware that he was different from his parents.

Nearby, a small groups of protesters from the American Society for the Prevention of Cruelty to Animals handed out leaflets protesting the genetic alteration of animals. According to a Supreme Court ruling, activist groups had the right to protest inside public facilities, as long as they didn't carry placards or banners blocking the view of other visitors. As a consequence of the court ruling, handout leaflets were making a comeback.

They accepted the leaflets and walked away. "I agree with ASPCA on this one," Crane said. "Although, I don't always do so."

"What company got NatGov funds for this project, anyway?" Brad asked, glancing at the leaflet as he spoke.

"The ASCPA flier claims that the company which produced these animals is owned by one of President Keynes' cousins," Annie said.

"I'll bet they made a substantial donation to Keynes' election campaign shortly thereafter," Brad said.

They reached the rhino exhibit. Several battle-ship sized gray rhinos lumbered about eating hay. A pink-skinned juvenile lay in their midst.

"Could you and Crane do this kind of genetic work?" Brad asked in Annie's direction.

"We could if we were President Keynes' cousins," Annie said.

They continued their trek through the fantasy world of genetically altered animals. The exhibit consisted of four animals, the giraffe and the rhino, plus a purple cheetah and a striped orangutan—all novelties that made little sense.

"Let's go see Crane's butterflies," Annie said. "Then, we'll eat lunch."

About ten minutes later, they entered the Cockrell Butterfly Exhibit and Entomology Hall, a three-story glass structure built around a fifty-foot waterfall. The butterfly exhibit was Crane's favorite location in the Hermann Park area. Here, as a child, he discovered the world of insects and played the interactive games and quizzes which whetted his appetite for science. At one time, he thought of becoming an entomologist, but that was before he got ensnared in the double helix.

"How do we find your offspring?" Brad asked, as they strolled through the simulated rainforest.

Crane pointed to a path that was damp with mist from the nearby waterfall. "Go around this trail until it forks, then take a left."

They wound their way along the serpentine path and stopped in front of the brass marker:

*Danaus plexippus var hopkinius*
Giant Monarch Butterfly

Crane studied the area. "See that clump of flowers over there by the rock? My relatives usually hang out there."

"We'll wait for them," Annie said.

A minute later, a gigantic orange and black butterfly appeared overhead and drifted down like a silk kite on a gentle breeze. It lit atop the flowers, flapping its wings to keep its balance. After a sip of nectar, the spectacular creature left the flower and began to circle the mesmerized trio. They stood transfixed, waiting for it to land again.

"Hold out your hand," Annie said to Crane, her voice rising with excitement. "This butterfly knows you. It wants to land on you."

Crane held out his right hand. "It doesn't know me. It's only a few weeks old, and I haven't been here in six months."

"It has your DNA," Annie said. "You're the Y-chromosomal Adam to it. Keep your hand out."

The giant Monarch circled around them three times, each lap bringing it closer to Crane's hand. The third time around, it landed in his upraised palm. Once at rest, it opened its wings and remained perfectly still for a few seconds, then flitted away in a flash of orange and black, disappearing into the jungle foliage.

"That was a good omen," Annie said. "Everything is going to be okay."

Crane appreciated Annie's never-ending optimism, but the zoo trip pointed out an enigma. Due to lack of funding, CellTech had effected a reduction in force, yet NatGov was funding a project to turn majestic animals into color cartoons. It didn't make sense.

They left the butterfly exhibit and returned to the entrance of the zoo. The fluffy clouds were beginning to turn into thunderheads again, and visitors were pouring through the exit turnstiles to head toward parking lots and passenger pickup areas.

Annie glanced at her iTab. "It's going to rain in about an hour, but we have plenty of time to grab a quick lunch before we leave. I think that's what we ought to do."

Crane and Brad agreed with Annie's plan. They ordered hot dogs and soft drinks from a food kiosk, and sat down at one of the nearby picnic tables. As they ate in near silence, Crane reflected on the events of the day. He was enjoying the daytrip with Annie and Brad, but *The Three Musketeers* relationship of nearly a year ago was lacking. Was Annie trying to recreate it? he wondered.

An hour later, Brad and Annie dropped Crane off at the corner of Kirby and Gramercy. He hurried to his condo and went inside as the first drops of rain began to fall. On an unreflective urge, he went to his desk and picked up the wrinkled copy of the *Register To Vote* leaflet which he got from Kim at Party Town. He unfolded the crumpled paper and glanced at the first page, even though he'd read it several times already.

He was stunned by what he saw.

The paper was changing before his eyes.

Crane starred at the document as words switched places like a warp-speed game of Words With Friends. The first page of the formerly-innocuous document now read:

*Fellow Americans,*
*We hold these truths to be self-evident, that all men are created equal, that they are endowed by their creator with certain unalienable rights, that among these are life, liberty, and pursuit of happiness. For the reasons stated by Thomas Jefferson and others, it is time for our country to*

*take a giant step on a journey toward a political future which will include everybody, even those of you who have never voted before. In the past, most of you have not been served well by the entities who collected taxes from you. They used your money to further their own political ambitions, and set themselves up as the ruling elite. That must change.*

*If only Democrats and Republicans have the right to vote and hold office in this great country, the bitter division between us will continue. We must claim our birthright. If we do not, the last chance to develop a genuine representative democracy may pass us by. True democracy will not come under the current system, which requires each of you to join one of the two approved parties in order to obtain your God given rights.*

*It is time to change directions. If we do not, the nebulous and fragile democracy which Washington is holding together will crumble under its own weight. We are at a crossroads. We have a choice--either a government that includes everyone, or one that will eventually lead to anarchy. The power brokers who hold the reins of this system will kill the last vestiges of democracy if they continue to deny the rights of those who disagree with them. Honest dissent cannot be squelched any longer. It is time for you to claim your birthright. Do so now before it is too late (The Double Helix Odyssey, P10).*

Crane recognized the first paragraph from the Declaration of Independence, but had never read Dar Lumbre's banned publication from which the rest of the text was taken. Dr. Lumbre's political beliefs from fifty years ago had reappeared right before his eyes. According to news reports, millions of *Register To Vote* flyers had been handed out the last few weeks. If they all were changing like the one in his hand, the political world was in for a shakeup.

He looked at his desktop monitor, which had sprung to life in a kaleidoscope of colored news banners. The news headlines, which normally scrolled along the bottom only, covered the entire screen, except for the right edge where picture-in-picture screens stacked up like a tower of ABC blocks. Every small picture showed a frantic newscaster urging viewers to turn to his/her program. Most were holding up copies of the *Register To Vote* flyer and pointing at the new message which now appeared on Page 10.

Crane switched back and forth between several channels, each reporting that all copies of the flyer had changed simultaneously by some mysterious process. Speculations regarding NatGov's response ran the gamut, with the consensus being that it was too late for them to do anything. After he heard the same comments a half-dozen times, he muted the volume and his thoughts went back to the partially-repaired DL-666.

## Chapter 28

Three days after the *Register To Vote* flyer proclaimed its Jeffersonian-style message, Crane was watching news banners on his iTab and hoping the rain would stop. He was getting cabin fever and wanted to go to the Village Antique Bookstore. Lily had texted him that someone had made an offer on *Ubik*, but she would give him the first chance to buy it, if he acted quickly. Even though he was temporarily unemployed, he didn't want to let the Philip K. Dick classic slip through his fingers. It was truly one of a kind.

The government response to the *Register To Vote* flyer had run its course. All news organizations, Republican and Democrat alike, were still trying to keep the initial frenzy alive, but their efforts were beginning to lose traction with the public. The end-around maneuver by the Dar Lumbre Society had caught NatGov completely off-guard, and they didn't know how to react.

President Keynes' initial response was a rambling discourse about declaring martial law, but he backed off quickly and said that he'd been misquoted. Congress called a special session, which fizzled in a few hours due to the lack of an actionable cause. The Attorney General made some nebulous threats and then faded into the background. Republicans and Democrats blamed each other, and finger pointing began within each party. Washington went into full chaos mode for a few hours, and as abruptly as it started, the uproar ended.

American citizens approved of the *Page 10 Incident*, as news organizations had dubbed the event. In less than twenty-four hours, millions of registered voters contacted their representatives in Washington and warned against retaliatory action. The nationwide response was too great for the government to ignore. Dar Lumbre, wherever he was and whether he was dead or alive, had won this round by a TKO.

As Crane watched idly, a new headline appeared.

CAROLINA HERRERA INTERVIEWS
THE ZODIAC PROPHET TODAY

Crane perked up when he saw the unexpected news banner. He recalled Carolina's broadcast debut five or six years earlier. Viewers loved her panache and eclectic style, and quickly claimed her as Houston's media darling. After her first show, one critic wrote, "Ms. Herrera is perfect-- feminine enough for male viewers, feminist enough for female viewers, androgynous enough for the LGBTQ community, Black enough, Hispanic enough...a perfect model for EEOC. She will surely succeed."

The critic was right about Carolina. Three months later, she had the number one show in Houston. By that time, the critic had been fired after complaints by a half-dozen minority groups.

Crane thumbed his iTab, and his desktop monitor came alive in a rainbow of lights and the sounds of a simulated rock band. As the cacophony waned, a camera panned the studio, which was at full capacity. After homing in on several oddball guests scattered throughout the audience, the camera swung around and focused on a fifteen by twenty feet stage with a single black desk and a group of matching gray chairs. At the rear of the stage, an amber curtain stretched ceiling to floor and wall to wall. The stage was set for the star of the show to enter at the top of the hour.

When the clock on the iTab showed exactly 10:00 a.m., an unseen announcer barked, "Here's Carolina."

Cymbals punctuated his proclamation.

Carolina stepped through a slit in the rear curtain and waved to the audience as she walked to center stage. Tall and svelte, she was wearing a black flight jacket, aviator sunglasses, and scarlet riding breeches tucked into boots made of ersatz leather. She was greeted by massive applause from her adoring audience.

"Thank you, Houston. Thank you, America," she said when the cheering subsided. "Welcome to the Carolina Herrera show, the number one morning program in the Bayou City. We have an interesting guest today, a man who calls himself the Zodiac Prophet. As you may recall, he made quite a splash several months ago with some unusual predictions, but he didn't reveal his identity at the time. Hopefully, he'll do so today. Houston, are you ready to meet our first guest?"

As they had been trained to do, the audience shouted, "Yes, Carolina."

Crane stared at the monitor with unblinking attention.

Carolina continued, "Without further ado, will you please give a hearty Houston welcome to our first guest... the Zodiac Prophet."

A light ripple of applause greeted the man as he came onstage via the slit in the rear curtain. The applause was followed by an audible gasp.

The man, dressed in faded jeans and sweatshirt, was wearing a Darth Vader mask covering his entire head. He was average height and average build. By his walk, Crane surmised that he must be in his late twenties or early thirties. Other than that, there was nothing to give away his identity.

Carolina shook hands with the mystery guest and ushered him to the chair nearest her desk. She moved behind the desk, took off her sunglasses, and sat down. The audience leaned forward.

Carolina looked toward her guest. "Thank you for coming on the show."

"No problem," the masked man answered in an electronically distorted voice. "Thank you for inviting me."

"Will you reveal your identity to us today?"

The mystery guest shook his head. "Sorry, Carolina, not today. I came on your show to give more details about the prediction I made a few months ago."

"Okay, we're all ears. Let's have those details."

"Remember, my prediction was based on an astrological event which will occur on September 22 of this year," the man said. "I predicted that a world-shaking event will happen when three planets align near the constellation Serpens. Do you remember that prediction?"

"Of course, I remember it," Carolina said, "and I'm sure everyone in the audience remembers it as well. It caused quite a stir, but you didn't reveal any details about the event. What can you tell us today?"

"I'm ready to tell the world exactly what will happen this September when the planetary conjunction occurs."

"The floor is yours. Go ahead."

"It will be a world-shaking event."

"You've already told us that," Carolina said. "We would like to hear more details."

The mystery guest looked directly toward the main studio camera. "Okay, here's my prediction. On September 22, 2136, less than two weeks before the election, Republican and Democrat party leaders will hold a joint conference, and concede the presidential election to a write-in candidate, who has yet to be named."

Carolina's jaw dropped, and the studio audience launched a discordant vocal uproar consisting of both cheers and boos. The cacophony lasted several minutes.

When she finally got the audience under control, Carolina asked her guest about his method of arriving at predictions, but he was evasive, and the conversation became repetitive. Surmising that her mystery guest had said all that he was going to say, Carolina began preparing to introduce her next guest.

At that point, Crane decided to go to the Village Antique Bookstore, rain or shine. He retrieved his jacket from the back of a chair, but before he could leave his condo, his iTab buzzed.

The caller was Annie. They'd talked at length less than eighteen hours ago, and he wasn't expecting her to call again this soon. Hoping that good news was in the offing, Crane touched the *Answer* button, and Annie's image formed on the screen.

"Hi," he said. "What's up?

Annie was tentative. "Something strange."

"Tell me."

"Yesterday, Dr. Cartwright assigned Bill Sanders to work with me," Annie said. "I wanted him to get his feet wet on the DL-666 project, so I had him analyze the saliva residue on the remaining two cups from Disneyland. It was pretty much a make-work project. I wasn't expecting anything unusual, but to my surprise, something popped up."

"What was it?"

"The one with lipstick on it was used by a Dar Lumbre operative named Julie Gilchrist."

"What database is she in?"

"She's in CODIS-PLUS. She used to be a police officer in California, so her DNA is on file, as required by law. She came to Houston recently when the Dar Lumbre Society got active in the Richmond-Rosenberg area…" Annie's voice trailed off.

Her hesitancy was something new to Crane. "Go ahead," he urged. "What else did you find?"

Annie cleared her throat. "I don't want to get into the Hopkins family business, but there's something else you need to know."

"Let me guess," Crane said. "The other cup had Larry's DNA on it."

Annie nodded and her image bobbed up and down on Crane's iTab. "It looks that way, but he's not in any DNA database, so I'm not one hundred percent sure."

"How do you know the composition of his DNA?"

"The sample on the cup was very similar to your DNA."

Crane was puzzled. "I'm not in any database either."

"Not in any national database, but you're in CellTech's HR files. We showed your DNA fingerprint to a group of students from Bellaire High School last year on Career Day."

"And you still remember what it looked like? I'm impressed."

Annie shrugged. "You're giving me too much credit. All I remembered was that you had genes scattered over a long polymorphic DNA fragment, sort of like DL-666. When I saw nearly the same thing on the sample from the cup, I pulled up your DNA fingerprint. It was very similar to the DNA on the coffee cup—as close as Elmore Larson and Dar Lumbre, so it has to be Larry's DNA."

"Which means he was in California with Julie Gilchrist the night before we followed Elmore Larson to Disneyland."

Annie took a deep breath. "Unfortunately, that's all it can mean."

"Thanks for telling me. I needed to know."

"Sorry I had to lay that kind of news on you."

180

After the conversation, Crane kicked himself mentally. Annie's findings seemed to verify Kim's suspicions about Larry, and Crane had not followed up as he promised Kim he would do. Although he'd been preoccupied with DL-666, he wouldn't use that as an excuse for his inaction. He had failed a friend, and must act now. The DNA evidence was forcing his hand.

He sat at his desk plotting his next move. His first impulse was to call immediately and confront Larry with Annie's findings. His brother would be home at this time of morning. The problem was, if Kim was working her usual afternoon shift, she would still be at home, too. Crane didn't want to involve her until after he talked with Larry. Maybe there was a logical explanation, although he couldn't imagine what it could possibly be. After considering the situation a few moments, he decided to wait until the afternoon when Kim would be at work.

The morning dragged by slowly. With time on his hands, Crane mentally replayed the major events of the past few weeks--the DL-666 problem, Richard Hunter's failed transplant, financial problems throughout the country, political unrest, Dr. Cartwright taking over as CEO of CellTech, and the loss of his job. Now, it seemed Larry was cheating on Kim. A melodrama of epic proportions, Crane thought, with a lanky geneticist as the lead character.

At twelve-thirty he called Larry.

Larry answered, "Hello, Crane. What's up?"

Crane plunged right in. "What were you doing in Anaheim with a woman named Julie Gilchrist."

The silence was so long that Crane thought his brother had logged off. "It's not what you think," Larry finally said. "Besides, why are you spying on me?"

"I wasn't spying," Crane said. "Annie and I were in Anaheim on company business, and by a stroke of fate, we caught you someplace you shouldn't have been."

Larry was defensive. "First of all, I'm not having an affair with Julie Gilchrist. She's an official in the Dar Lumbre Society, and she took me to their national headquarters to meet Elmore Larson."

"How can you afford to go to California? You don't

have a job."

"When you were playing with butterflies, you called it a job," Larry said. "I'm doing the same thing now, except as a computer programmer. Besides, Apple-Disney paid my way to California, and they're going to buy my program. Since I was going anyway, I decided to meet Elmore Larson while I was out there."

Larry's story sounded so innocent that Crane was taken aback. Even so, he remained skeptical. "Does Kim know about this?"

"Why are you tending to our business?"

"Does she know?" Crane repeated.

"Of course, she knows about my trip to California."

"Don't be evasive, Larry. You know what I mean. Does she know about Julie Gilchrist?"

Larry's hesitation was all the answer Crane needed. "Tell Kim the whole story," he said, "or I will.

## Chapter 29

Larry parked his car and stepped out onto the wet pavement as evening shadows engulfed the West Gray Condos. He zipped his jacket and walked along the sidewalk beside the complex. A cold damp wind blew in his face, making his cheeks tingle. Larry dreaded the task before him, but knew the time had come to face it. He was ready to tell Kim about his visit to Anaheim, as ready as he would ever be.

He pictured Kim inside the condo, anxiously awaiting his arrival. He'd called earlier to tell her there was something they needed to talk about when he got home. In a few minutes, he would spill his guts about the sociopolitical movement that had sucked him into its vortex. Larry knew he had to tell Kim everything, and he dreaded the task.

His mind replayed the vivid picture of the Dar Lumbre headquarters in Anaheim on that crisp afternoon when he witnessed the hustle and bustle of young activists at the end of a busy day. At the time, he could see himself as one of them, a computer expert writing programs for the society. Now, he realized that such an idea came from an alternate universe that he did not fit into. The people in Anaheim had motives and ideas which he did not fully understand. They were zealots. He was a computer geek. Although he was sympathetic to their cause, he now realized it was a huge mistake to envision himself as one of them. It was time to come back into his real world.

He trudged up the stairs to the condo, opened the front door, and went inside.

Kim was waiting in the kitchen. When Larry entered, she walked into the living area to meet him.

"Well," she said without preliminaries, "what do you want to tell me?" Her voice trembled and her expression was grim.

"I went to Anaheim," Larry said, "to visit the Dar Lumbre Society's office before I went to Cupertino to talk with Apple-Disney." He was ashamed, and could not bring himself to mention Julie Gilchrist in his first sentence. He knew he had to tell that part of the story eventually, but decided to wait until after Kim absorbed his first confession.

Kim's brow furrowed. "Why didn't you tell me before you went to Anaheim? I wouldn't have objected. It's a little late to tell me now."

"There's something else."

Kim's eyebrows shot up. "What else?"

"A woman picked me up at John Wayne Airport," Larry blurted out.

Kim's chin dropped. She turned away from Larry and began to sob.

"What woman?" she asked, without turning around.

"Her name is Julie Gilchrist. She's a Dar Lumbre official. She gave me a lift to Anaheim--to the society headquarters. That's all."

"How in the name of God could you get mixed up with another woman? Haven't I been a good wife?"

"Of course, you have, but please try to understand what happened," Larry pleaded. "I was a fool. I trusted her."

"I trusted you."

"I'm sorry."

"Is that all you can say?"

"I'm sorry," Larry repeated.

"Did you go to bed with her?"

"Absolutely not. I went by her condo to pick up some information."

Kim hung her head and her voice trembled. "How could you do such a dumb thing, Larry? What were you thinking?"

"It was a stupid thing to do. I was totally gullible. She pretended that I was an important recruit for the organization. She wanted to get me in a compromising situation, and I let her do it. It was entirely my fault. I should have known better." He went over to Kim and put his arm around her shoulders.

She stiffened, and pulled away. "Don't touch me." Her voice was sharp. "I can't stand it after you touched that other woman."

Larry tried to sound reassuring. "I didn't touch her. Please turn around and look at me."

Kim didn't respond, and an icy silence hung in the air between them.

The conversation reached an impasse, and Larry knew he had to do something to get past the moment.

He repeated his plea. "Please, Kim, look at me. I'm telling you the truth."

Slowly, she turned and looked up into his face.

"Nothing happened," he said.

Kim's voice trembled. "Swear to me that nothing happened."

"I swear it."

"You've broken my heart." The tears came again.

"I love you, Kim."

"You destroyed our marriage."

"You're the only woman I've ever loved."

"You certainly haven't been acting like it."

"Give me a chance to make it up to you."

Kim stared at Larry through her tears. "How can you make it up? What will you do?"

"I'll do anything you want," Larry said, realizing the gravity of his promise.

Kim hesitated before answering, "There is something I'd like for you to do."

"What is it?"

"Get us back to where we were before our world fell apart."

"How can I do that?"

"For starters, tell me that this thing's over--this Dar Lumbre obsession."

"It's over. I'm sorry I was so stupid."

"There's one other thing I need," Kim said solemnly.

"What?" Larry asked tentatively. He wondered what other concessions he would have to make.

"Promise me that we won't leave Houston."

"I promise you we won't leave."

"Not ever?"

"Not ever."

Chapter 30

It was another blue Monday. Crane sat at his desk as news banners scrolled across the bottom of the desktop monitor. He wasn't paying any attention to the headlines. No need to. Every news outlet offered the same steady diet of economic gloom and doom served up with partisan political posturing. From the news, it appeared that nothing good was happening anywhere in the known universe.

The remains of a day-old glazed donut and a half-cup of warmed-over latte sat to the left of Crane's desktop monitor. His hands rested near the keyboard below the monitor. He was trying to keep busy, even if he had nothing productive to do. Total idleness was not in his DNA. Tinkering he could tolerate, and even enjoy occasionally, but never inactivity. His make-work project for today was a review of all known cryo-preservation facilities in the world, starting with the United States.

The Dar Lumbre Society had made millions of converts since bursting onto the scene, and they believed their patriarch would make an appearance soon. For that to happen, it would be necessary for Dr. Lumbre to be in a cryo-preservation unit at some secret location. The idea made little sense because none of the commercially available cryogenic facilities used legitimate C-Unit technology. Their storage methods caused tissue damage which could never be reversed, regardless of the claims proffered. Although he questioned the logic of his search, Crane developed a list of cryonic storage facilities in the U.S. and abroad.

After eliminating several companies less than fifty years old, he was left with a list of six U.S. corporations and four foreign corporations soliciting subjects for cryonic suspension. The three longest-operating U.S. companies were the American Cryonics Society in California, the Cryonics Institute in Michigan, and Alcor in Arizona. Two companies in Australia and two in Russia also had the required longevity. Apparently, business was good. The companies claimed to have an ever-expanding client base. Customers included astronauts, actors, and athletes, as well as ordinary people with sufficient funds to bankroll an immortality long shot. In addition to facts, Crane's search turned up various urban legends, including the oft-repeated claim that Walt Disney was stored in cryonic suspension beneath one of the rides in Disneyland.

Crane planned to contact the storage facilities under the pretense of looking for a place where he could be preserved. He would ask for lists of celebrity clients, just to see what happened. Although he was certain that no cryonic suspension operation would supply a list of customers which included Dar Lumbre, he preferred to occupy his time playing this kind of game rather than video games or solitaire.

He was composing a text to Alcor when a news banner virtually jumped off the desktop monitor:

FIRST LADY SUFFERS HEART ATTACK

He touched the screen and the article appeared.

*LYDIA KEYNES SUFFERS CORONARY*

*Washington, D.C. Early this morning, the First Lady, Lydia Keynes, was carried by helicopter to the Bethesda Naval Hospital after reporting severe pains in her chest. Her personal cardiologist, Dr. Howard Rubin, reported that she is in stable condition and is resting comfortably in CCU. Mrs. Keynes has a history of cardiovascular problems, and earlier this year, it was reported that she might be a candidate for heart transplant surgery. Dr. Rubin would neither confirm nor deny this report, and the White House Press Secretary would give no further details.*

Crane thought briefly about calling Annie, but decided not to bother her at work. As per their agreement, she'd contacted him every day, and would call if Mrs. Keynes' condition triggered any news that affected CellTech. Government machinery moved slowly, but this turn of events had the potential to supercharge the engine driving the bureaucratic equipage. He couldn't visualize the First Lady lying in a C-Unit while the OFS's legal department haggled about the use of saliva retrieved from a trash can at Disneyland. Richard Hunter's plight, and the plight of fifteen hundred other ordinary citizens, had not registered with the bureaucrats, but with a high-ranking VIP on the list, the foot dragging was about to end.

He swallowed the remaining bite of stale donut and washed it down with lukewarm latte. During the next hour, he paced around his condo continuously, occasionally stopping to glance at the plants on the balcony. The butterfly weeds had died, but he didn't care.

Crane's iTab buzzed, and he touched the screen. A text popped up: CALL FROM DR. HELENA CARTWRIGHT.

He collected his thoughts before answering, "Hello."

"Mr. Hopkins, did you see the news a short time ago about Mrs. Keynes' heart attack?"

Crane's answer was resolutely minimalistic. "Yes."

"The First Lady's heart problem impacted CellTech immediately," Dr. Cartwright said. "Less than an hour after it happened, I received a call from OFS's Washington office. They are increasing our funds immediately. Basically, our budget will be restored to the original figures, and could be increased to a higher level, if necessary. They mentioned DL-666, of course, and want it to be given top priority."

She paused, but Crane did not respond.

After an awkward silence, Dr. Cartwright continued, "Mr. Hopkins, I need you back on the DL-666 project as soon as possible. Since you have not sought other employment, CellTech is still considered to be your employer under current OFS guidelines."

"I was about to make another butterfly breakthrough," Crane said sarcastically.

"Mr. Hopkins, let's not play games. I need you back in the lab immediately. Furthermore, I know this is the work you enjoy. If you hadn't planned to come back, you would have sought other employment. You didn't, so your CellTech contract is still in force. It's time for you to return to work, or be dropped from OFS's severance package."

Crane felt that he was on the horns of a dilemma, a place he always tried to avoid. He loved the work at CellTech, but hated the thought of coming back under Dr. Helena Cartwright's supervision for the third time. The first two occasions had been disasters. Ironically, if he and Annie solved the problem with DL-666, it would make Dr. Cartwright look like a miracle worker. The whole situation had NatGov politics written all over it, and he was caught in the middle.

On the other side of the equation, going back to work would reunite him with Annie. He knew he would never find another lab assistant, or a friend, like her. He couldn't picture himself working on a project without her at his side. They belonged together in the lab as the *A Team*, as they'd dubbed themselves. All of the work done so far on DL-666 had left the problem half solved, but he still believed he and Annie could piece together the rest of the puzzle. All they needed was a little more time, and Dr. Cartwright was offering that to him.

After evaluating the situation, Crane concluded that he wasn't on the horns of dilemma, as he'd first imagined. Without a choice, there was no dilemma. And in this case, there was no choice--he had to go back to CellTech.

"When do you want me to return?" he asked.

"Tomorrow morning, if you possibly can."

"I'll be there."

"Thank you, Mr. Hopkins. In spite of all that's happened between us, I knew I could depend on you. I have informed Miss Lee, and she'll be expecting you. I'll notify Security to reactivate your ID code."

"What about William Sanders?" Crane asked. "Will he keep working with us?"

"He'll return to his former assignment."

"He won't like that."

"He doesn't have a choice."

Who does? Crane wondered.

## Chapter 31

The morning after his reinstatement, Crane arrived at the lab at seven o'clock and found Annie waiting for him. She met him at the doorway and threw her arms around him. He returned the embrace, and they stood in the lab entrance a long moment, clinging to each other. When Crane released Annie, she tiptoed and kissed him on the cheek. He visualized a heart-shaped brand burned into his skin.

Annie stepped back. "Your return reminds me of an old movie," she said. "*The Return of The Pink Panther.*"

"How so?"

"In the movie, Inspector Clouseau got fired. When the Commissioner called him back to work, one of the first things that Clouseau said was, *I am unique, therefore indispensable*. That's you--unique, therefore indispensable."

"Thanks for your vote of confidence," Crane said. "We'll see if it's warranted. By the way, how did William Sanders work out?"

"I call him Bill. He's a bright kid, but needs a couple of years on the farm club before he can play in the big leagues."

"That's what I figured," Crane said. "Now, bring me up to speed on everything since we spoke last."

Annie's briefing, meticulous and thorough, was delivered at auctioneer speed. When she finished, Crane felt as if he hadn't missed a day, even though it had been two weeks.

They moved to the wall monitor. The team was ready. Annie was hyped up, and he was calm, a fire and ice combination of emotions that had worked well for them.

The rest of the week was a blur of testing and retesting.

On Friday afternoon, Crane stared at the images on the monitor until his head ached. Four additional days of lab work on DL-666 had produced no new answers, only new questions. Every day was beginning to seem like the day before. He knew Annie felt it, too, although she hadn't mentioned it.

He glanced toward Annie and said, "We're a couple

of gerbils on a treadmill going around and around, but not getting anywhere."

In a quick move, Annie swiveled on her lab stool and faced Crane. "A new idea just popped into my mind," she said, her voice rising.

"What new idea? I'm willing to try anything."

"I'll tell you as we go along," Annie said. "First, let's pull up the old images one more time."

"Which old images?" Crane asked. "We've accumulated a pretty extensive library."

"The last ones we were studying just before Dr. C showed up—Dar Lumbre's original slides."

"I thought we exhausted the possibilities with those," Crane said.

"Maybe not. Maybe we exhausted ourselves, not the possibilities."

"Where are you going with this?"

"I've spent some sleepless nights lately," Annie said. Her eyes sparkled, and a slight flush touched her cheeks. "Sleepless, but not idle. It's always the same thing when I can't sleep. Images of X chromosomes keep running through my head. Instead of counting sheep, I count genes. For some reason I can't explain, I go back to square one over and over again. I think that's what we ought to do today."

"Square one is fine by me," Crane said. "I don't have a better suggestion."

"Buckle your seat belt. Relax and leave the driving to me."

Crane sat on the stool next to Annie. He was content to let her take the lead, although she was the only person in the world to whom he would accord such status. The reunification of the Hopkins-Lee team was a magical moment for him. He felt like a new man, even though numerous problems still loomed before them.

"Let's forget about DNA bases for a while," Annie said, "and concentrate on the entire cell."

Annie flashed hand signals to the computer in rapid bursts, and presently an image stabilized onscreen. "This first slide is one you made six months ago," she said. "The X chromosome appears quite ordinary. It's a good match when compared to Dr. Lumbre's original slides. I don't think there's a geneticist in the world who would see anything unusual about the X chromosome, or its DNA fingerprint. It looks exactly like the slides that are fifty years old."

Crane rubbed his chin thoughtfully. "And yet, we know this tissue is on the verge of trouble. We started seeing anomalies in the lag phase a few days after this slide was made. Is there something here that we should have seen?"

Annie stared at the screen for a long time before answering, "Let's ignore the chromosomes for a while and concentrate on cell inclusions."

"I thought it was against the law for a geneticist to ignore chromosomes," Crane said, feeling a resurgence of confidence, maybe even serendipity. He knew that having Annie at his side was the main reason, and it was obvious she was enjoying the moment as much as he was.

"Will you humor me?" Annie asked.

Crane nodded. "Sure…go ahead."

Annie signaled again and the images moved toward each other. "I'll keep the two segments synchronized," she said. "We can look at vacuoles, mitochondria, spindle apparatuses, plasmids, or other cell inclusions. Name your poison."

Crane pointed to the lower edge of the screen. "Right there…the plasmids. Zoom in on that clump at the edge of the slide."

"Zooming," Annie said, continuing to give hand signals.

Crane leaned forward to observe the plasmids, a chain of purple dots lined up like periods at the end of a sentence. "So, what are we looking for?"

Annie increased the magnification on the image. "I'm sure Dr. Lumbre used plasmids to splice foreign DNA into his own DNA."

Crane agreed. "Nothing else makes sense."

"This next slide was prepared from DL-666 about five months ago," Annie said. "The blobs of nuclear material in the plasmid are visible, just like they are in Dar Lumbre's original slides, but several bits of the plasmid DNA appear to be in a different position when compared to earlier slides."

Crane stared intently. "I see what you mean. It looks like a different stage of mitosis."

"But, it's not," Annie said, as she adjusted the focus slightly. "The second slide shows the exact phase of mitosis as the first one. The computer has matched the samples. Time is the only variable--one month on the calendar."

"Move to the next slide. This is getting interesting."

"Tick-tock, tick-tock," Annie said. "Time marches on. I'll bring up the slide that is four months old, and we'll see how it compares to the older ones." She signaled again, and the images realigned.

"There we have it," Annie said. "Slides that are six months, five months, and four months old."

Crane examined the newest image. The position of nuclear material within the plasmid had shifted incrementally with time. "Do you have a theory?" he asked.

Annie took a deep breath. "I'm forming one. Maybe these changes in plasmid DNA precede the changes in the X chromosome, even though DNA fingerprinting shows no significant differences."

"That theory adds support to the possibility of the changes being physical, rather than chemical in nature, as we discussed earlier."

"Exactly," Annie nodded. "And here's what I think-- we're looking at some sort of early warning system, clues to lead us back to the starting point. Dr. Lumbre dropped some crumbs for us to follow, just like Hansel and Gretel."

Crane was duly impressed. "These images seem to verify your theory. Maybe this is the breakthrough we need to solve the mystery. You came up with a great idea."

"Trying to do my job."

For a few seconds, workplace protocol was replaced with sheer giddiness. Crane and Annie laughed like children, then jumped up and hugged. "You've earned your wings," Crane said. "You'll be running this place in a few years--if we ever get rid of Helena Cartwright."

"I appreciate your vote of confidence. It means a lot to me."

"Where do you think this is going to lead?" Crane asked. "Are the changes in these plasmids a preview of anomalies in the tissue? Or is this just some bizarre coincidence?"

"That's what we have to find out," Annie said. "Now, let's look at some of the latest slides—those we made within the last couple of months--and see what the plasmids were doing while the X chromosome was unraveling."

Annie motioned toward the screen and another group of plasmids swam into view. Neither geneticist spoke for several minutes as they tried to understand the significance of what they were seeing.

"This is getting weirder by the minute," Crane said. "The pattern formed by this plasmid DNA looks like a child's puzzle, the kind you solve by connecting the dots."

Annie rubbed her eyes. "Are these just random bits of nuclear material? Or did Dar Lumbre plant a clue?"

"How could he program plasmids fifty years ago?" Crane asked. "We couldn't do it today."

"True," Annie said, "but Dr. Lumbre did other things in the past which haven't been duplicated yet."

"Rotate the slide. Maybe another angle would be helpful."

The image turned slowly on its axis until Annie signaled the computer to stop the rotation. She pursed her lips and starred at the purple dots aligned in a zigzag line across the screen.

"I see a pattern forming," Crane said.

*"Eureka!"* Annie said, her voice trembling with excitement. "Look at that."

"It looks like a caduceus—or maybe a serpent."

"It's a serpent!"

"I agree," Crane said. "Could this be an accidental arrangement? Or does it relate to the DL-666 problem?"

"This has to be a clue planted by Dar Lumbre. But, what does it mean?"

"Let's play the word association game again," Crane said. "Remember the way we did on the neuron project when we were completely out of ideas? Say whatever pops into your mind. I'll do the same."

Annie closed her eyes. "D...N...A," she said slowly. "Deoxyribose...nucleic acid...phosphate ester...plasmid."

Crane continued to stare at the screen.

Annie opened her eyes. "This was your idea. Aren't you going to play?"

"I'm thinking."

"What about?"

"I'm thinking about CellTech's logo," Crane said. "It doesn't have serpents wound around the staff like a regular caduceus."

"That means something...but what?"

"Is there a connection between CellTech's caduceus and the serpent-like structure in this plasmid DNA?"

"CellTech's logo is fifty years old," Annie said. "Our plasmid serpent formed recently. How could there be a connection?"

"The connection is Dar Lumbre," Crane said. "He's the common denominator in this equation. Apparently, the caduceus is his signature...his trademark...his calling card...whatever you want to call it."

After a long pause, Annie's face lit up with a broad smile. "Hey, Protein Man, have we really found a clue? Or, are we going nuts?"

Crane shrugged. "In this profession, it's hard to tell."

"Let's summarize our findings," Annie said. "Our logo is a caduceus without any serpents, and we found a serpent in a plasmid from DL-666. Obviously, Dar Lumbre put it there. What's he trying to tell us?"

"Let's assume that Dr. Lumbre programmed the plasmid DNA to form a serpent when DL-666 began to fail," Crane said. "I don't see how that's possible, but he must have done it. This can't be an accident."

"It's no accident," Annie said. "He's trying to tell us how to solve the problem in the tissue culture."

"I wish he'd left lab notes instead."

"Notes could have been destroyed or lost," Annie said. "He didn't want to risk that possibility, particularly since NatGov had turned on him. These clues were left to be discovered only when this kind of research is legal again, as it is today. Furthermore, he planted the clues for people like us, specifically someone working on DL-666. They wouldn't mean anything to anybody else. What's he trying to tell us?"

"He's probably telling us to look outside of CellTech," Crane said." What we're looking for is not in the company's lab records—that's for sure."

"Did he plant nuclear material in this plasmid to tell us where to find the DNA needed to repair DL-666?"

"I think he did," Crane said. "And now, I'm ready to play the game with you...caduceus...snakes...DNA."

"Snakes...serpents...Serpens," Annie said.

"Stop right there. I see to see a connection."

"Talk to me."

"The serpents in CellTech's logo have been replaced by DNA strands," Crane said. "The serpents are missing from the caduceus. I think that's a key."

"Serpents...snakes," Annie said in a high-pitched voice, "or maybe *culebra*."

"Snake in Spanish."

"Dar Lumbre was of Mexican descent," Annie said, "and he transferred from UNLV to the University of Mexico. Something about that makes me believe we need to think in Spanish words, rather than in English."

Crane shook his head. "I'm not sure I can."

"We have to," Annie insisted. "Let's try our free association routine with some Spanish words."

"Okay, you start."

*"La Universidad de Mexico,"* Annie began.

Crane paused a second and said, *"La Cuidad de Mexico."*

*"Serpiente,"* Annie said quickly.

*"Culebre."*

*"La Cuidad de Culebre."*

Crane switched back to English. "The City of Culebra. I wonder if there is there such a place?"

Annie raised a fist in the air and shook it. "There has to be," she said, "and I'll bet Dar Lumbre went there to escape NatGov's clutches."

"Google it."

Annie gave a series of hand signals, and a map of Mexico appeared onscreen with a blinking arrow pointing at Culebra, a small town near Monterrey.

"Voila!" Annie shrieked.

"Are you ready to head south of the border?" Crane asked.

*"Afirmativo."*

## Chapter 32

When the airplane reached cruising altitude and leveled off, Crane ducked his head and attempted to look out of the window from his middle seat. All he could see was the back of Annie's head, so he settled back into his seat and took out his iTab. Reflexively, he pulled up an image of the X chromosome and watched it spin slowly against the black background, not looking for anything in particular. He wasn't interested in Amazon-Southwest's crossword puzzle, but needed something to occupy his time.

After a few minutes, Crane noticed the woman to his right glancing at the image on his iTab.

The woman smiled. "Pardon me for being nosey. Are you a doctor?"

"A geneticist."

Turning away from the window, Annie joined the conversation. "I see you're wearing a *We Care* pin. You must be a nurse."

"I'm an RN. My name is Sylvia Garcia. I noticed that your companion is studying chromosomes?"

Crane introduced himself and Annie, then continued, "We work for CellTech in Houston. This is the X chromosome from one of our products, DL-666, the famous tissue culture used to make artificial hearts."

"I'm familiar with DL-666," Sylvia said. "It's well known in Mexico. Dr. Dar Lumbre was of Mexican descent."

"That's why we're going to Mexico," Crane said. "We're looking for information on Dr. Lumbre's early work."

Doubt showed in Sylvia's eyes. "Many years have passed. The trail will be cold."

Crane nodded. "We know."

"Do you live in Monterrey?" Annie asked.

"I was born there," Sylvia said. "But I live in Houston now."

"Actually, we're going to Culebra, a village outside of Monterrey," Crane said. "We believe Dr. Lumbre visited it, or maybe even lived there."

"Do you know anything about Culebra?" Annie asked.

"I know it well. When I was a child, my parents took me there from time to time. It was called Guadeloupe back then, but they changed the name to Culebra."

"Why did they change it?" Crane asked, although he was certain what the answer would be.

Sylvia's expression became somber. "According to a local legend, the village was overrun by snakes."

Annie nudged Crane in the ribs with her elbow and said, "We're getting warm."

The flight attendant came down the aisle with a refreshment cart. Crane and Annie ordered lattes. Sylvia ordered Tazo passion tea, and they settled back into their seats to resume their conversation about Dar Lumbre and the snakes which overran Guadeloupe/Culebra many years ago.

Annie took a sip of latte, then turned toward Sylvia and asked, "Do you know of anyone who would have information on Dr. Lumbre's visits to Culebra? Maybe the mayor or some other city official? Or possibly one of the local priests? Anybody?"

Sylvia shook her head. "There won't be any official records of his travels in Mexico. We suffered a total loss of data during the solar flare—even worse than the United States. We never had complete data to begin with, so little *pueblos* like Culebra won't have anything at all."

"What about the local churches?" Crane asked. "Would they have any information?"

Again, Sylvia shook her head. "Not likely. There wouldn't be any cause for the church to take any special notice of Dr. Lumbre's presence in Mexico. After all, he was of Mexican descent, and probably had relatives there."

"What kind of a place is Culebra?" Annie asked.

"It's poor," Sylvia said. "Very poor. My parents said the population dropped during the depression. Many residents of Culebra moved into Monterrey to look for work. When that happened, the town slipped backwards into the last century. It's still stuck there."

"Do they have many tourists?" Annie asked.

"A lot more than you would likely expect," Sylvia said, with a nod. "It has a primitive charm that some tourists enjoy."

"As you can see, we're trying to figure out where to start searching for information on Dar Lumbre's visits," Crane said. "Any ideas?"

After a moment of silence, Sylvia answered, "I think there're still a couple of fortune tellers in Culebra, and maybe a witch doctor as well. They would know the local legends, and would be glad to share them for a small fee. That's about as close as you'll get to historical records."

"How can we find these fortune tellers?" Annie asked.

"They hang around the town square, usually along *Calle Central*--Central Street," Sylvia said. "You can't miss them. They'll start pestering you as soon as they discover that you're tourists."

Annie leaned toward Sylvia and touched her on the arm. "Thank you for your help."

*"De nada."*

The rest of the flight was smooth and uneventful, and an hour later, the aircraft trembled slightly and settled into a glide toward Monterrey International Airport. On all sides of the airport, beyond the support facilities related to the business of flying, light industry and high-tech manufacturing lined the major traffic arteries.

Almost every business in Monterrey had a counterpart in the United States, and commuter traffic filled the skies Monday through Friday. The arrangement was beneficial to both the United States and Mexico. *Hecho en Mexico* had evolved into a lifeline for several American companies locked in trade wars with China and India.

The aircraft docked, and the captain turned off the seat-belt signs. Crane stepped out and paused to allow Annie to enter the aisle directly behind Sylvia. They retrieved their carry-on bags, and followed a line of passengers moving toward the terminal.

Crane didn't know what they might find in Culebra, but they had to find something more than anecdotal evidence of Dar Lumbre's long-ago visits. They needed to find someone whose parents or grandparents knew the famous doctor personally, someone who might help pick up the spoor of the forked-tail snake. If they couldn't find such a person, they'd have to develop an alternate plan.

With his thoughts fixed doggedly on locating Dar Lumbre's old haunts in Mexico, Crane walked along the brightly lit corridor with Annie at his side.

Annie motioned with her free hand. "Look at these walls."

Crane looked at the panoramic scene stretching the length of the passageway. "Apparently painted by graffiti artists with a fixation on the trichromatic combo of red, blue, and green."

Annie sighed. "Well...I like it."

The hustle and bustle inside the terminal reminded Crane of the Mediplex, except--as Annie had pointed out-- the décor was idiosyncratic, perhaps intended to plant a suggestion that it was possible to mix business with pleasure in Mexico. People from many countries, most of them carrying brief cases and iTabs, hurried along the corridors, occasionally bumping into one another and offering apologies in polyglot.

They claimed their luggage and found a Holiday Inn robo-van waiting in the passenger pickup area. Thirty minutes later, after checking into their rooms, they returned to the hotel lobby and asked the bell captain to call a cab.

"Are you planning to go outside the city?" the man asked.

"Yes," Crane said.

"In that case, *Senor*, the cab will not have autopilot. It will have a driver."

"That's good. We need one."

After touching his iTab screen, the bell captain informed them that a vacant cab was pulling into the front driveway as they spoke.

As they exited the lobby, a rusty green Asian Autos sedan lurched into the driveway in front of the Holiday Inn, and the driver got out to open the back door. On the first attempt, the door refused to budge, but a hard pull and a threat in Spanish freed the latch. Crane and Annie got in, and the cab sped away, leaving a cloud of blue smoke in its wake.

The Houston-Monterrey connection changed a lot of things in Mexico, but cabs south of the Rio Grande hadn't changed a noticeable amount. For whatever reason, cars were still outrageously expensive in Mexico. Consequently, many cars in the country had enjoyed a former life as a family car in the United States or Canada before being reincarnated in Mexico. Crane didn't understand that part of the economic system, but suspected it was some sort of government-sponsored auto-exchange boondoggle.

"Culebra," Crane said, as they settled into the seat.

The driver flashed a friendly smile and manipulated the controls of the car. *"Si, Senor...*the village of the snakes. It's just a short ride away."

Annie leaned forward. "Do you know anything about Culebra?"

"Not much to know, *Senorita.* I drive in Monterrey most of the time. I was born and raised here. If you want to know anything about Monterrey, just ask for me. My name is Pablo. Everybody in the city knows Pablo, the cab driver."

"We're interested in Culebra, not Monterrey," Crane said.

Crane's lack of interest in Monterrey squelched Pablo's enthusiasm somewhat. He fell silent and directed his attention to driving while his passengers gazed out of the windows. Within a few minutes, they were outside of Monterrey. The city limits were conspicuous by the abrupt change in the quality of road construction.

The farther from the city they traveled, the more bumps and potholes they encountered, every jolt causing the car to squeak and rattle as it bounced along toward Culebra. The modern buildings of Monterrey interfaced with plywood and corrugated sheet metal as they entered the outskirts of the village and headed toward the town square.

"The village of the snake is pretty dilapidated," Crane said.

"Apparently, Monterrey's sister-city status ran out at the city limits," Annie said.

The cab stopped at a taxi stand adjacent to the town square, and the geneticists hopped out. The sun was bright and hot, and the smell of overripe mangoes filled the air. Siesta time had ended, and the plaza was losing its population to the market place. A few people remained in the square, lounging on concrete benches in the shade of sprawling oak trees. Empty water bottles lay against the benches. Shirtless youngsters played soccer in the streets, and teenage boys circled around on rusty bicycles. Nobody was in a hurry in Culebra.

Crane pointed to a smattering of pedestrians milling along the sidewalk on the opposite side of the street. "Let's go over there and strike up a conversation with anybody willing to talk to us."

As they stepped into the street, Annie glanced at her iTab. "The map of Culebra shows Central Street to be about half way around the square."

Crane nodded. "Good. We'll work our way toward it and see what happens."

Before they reached the curb, a blast of screechy music assailed their ears, and an elderly woman popped out of an alley intersecting the sidewalk. She was dressed in a red gypsy skirt and a white peasant blouse with puffy sleeves. She carried a street organ supported on one leg, and was cranking out an off-key version of *La Paloma Blanca*. A placard on the organ said *Una Mirada En Su Porvenir.*

Annie read the sign in English, "A look into your future."

They stopped at the curb and the woman approached them. *"Buenos dias,"* she said. "I am *Senora Adovina.* I see a happy future for a tall handsome man and the beautiful woman at his side. For five American dollars, I will tell you more."

Crane unzipped the pouch on his iPad case, removed a ten-dollar bill, and handed it to the fortune-teller. "We'll give you ten dollars if we can ask you some questions."

The woman took the money and stuffed it into a pocket hidden in the folds of her skirt. "You will get married," she said, "and have three beautiful children, two boys and a girl."

Annie and Crane looked at each other and burst out laughing.

"Hold it," Crane said. "Forget the future. We want to ask you about the past."

"What do you want to know?"

"Do you know who Dar Lumbre is?" Crane asked.

*"Si, Senor.* Everybody has heard of him."

"What have you heard?" Crane asked.

"He's a famous Mexican doctor who lived in Culebra a long time ago," the woman answered.

"Did your parents or grandparents know him?" Crane asked.

"Yes. My mother said they saw him in town on holidays. She said he was…*muy guapo…como se dice?"*

"Very handsome," Crane said. "How long ago was that?"

The fortune-teller paused before answering. "Let's see…I think my mother was a teenager. She told me that Dr. Lumbre sometimes marched in the *Dia De Los Muertos* parades…or maybe it was the *Cinco de Mayo* parades. Everyone knew who he was because they'd heard rumors that he was a snake charmer."

"Do you know where he stayed when he came here?" Crane asked.

The fortune-teller considered the question a moment before answering, "I think he stayed out near the canyons."

"Did he have family here?" Annie asked.

"I don't know."

Crane could tell that the fortune-teller knew very little about Dar Lumbre. "Do you know anyone else that might have more information about him?" he asked.

The woman shook her head. "No, *Senor."*

"Well, thanks, anyway," Crane said. He motioned to Annie, and they resumed their journey along the sidewalk.

For an hour, they went up, down, and across the streets perpendicular to Central, and talked with a dozen people. Everyone was willing to talk, but no one knew anything worthwhile. They knew that Dr. Lumbre was a famous scientist of Mexican ancestry who spent time in Culebra, but didn't know what he did or where he stayed during his visits. Most of them knew about Dr. Lumbre's sudden disappearance, and many expected him to return some day.

Other than that, *nada.*

"Did he deliberately cover his tracks?" Crane said, "Or, were they erased by the sands of time?"

Annie shrugged. "Hard to say, but geneticists never give up."

Crane didn't believe they would be going back to Houston with a report that they found nothing. They couldn't. Richard Hunter was depending on them, not to mention President Keynes' wife and hundreds of other people. They had to find something concrete, not just old stories.

Early in the afternoon on the second day, they found themselves back at the town plaza trying to regroup their efforts.

"Let's look in some of these shops," Annie said. "Maybe we'll see something that gives us a new idea. We need to come up with one *muy pronto*."

The first shop they passed specialized in pottery. The second, Mexican silver. The third, clothes styled to reflect native costumes. After a few shops, the pattern began to repeat itself with monotonous predictability. Half way around the block, they passed a shop with a small sign in English above the door: NATIVE LEATHER.

"This looks a little different," Crane said. "Let's go inside. I feel my serendipity kicking in--finally." Word puzzles danced in his head, and he struggled to put them together into a meaningful pattern.

"Leather from snake skins," Annie said. *"Piel de culebras."*

Crane responded with, *"Serpientes."*

They entered the shop and found various kinds of leather goods displayed on tables, racks, and shelves throughout the small room. Crane moved down the aisle between the display tables loaded with purses and billfolds, while Annie examined smaller items hung on the wall.

A few minutes later, Crane heard Annie's excited voice call from the other side of the room. "Hey! Come look at these snakeskin belts."

Crane went over to the display.

An elderly man appeared. "Would you like a belt, *Senor*?"

Crane shook his head. "No, but I would appreciate

some information."

"Pick out one," the shopkeeper insisted. "I'll give you a special deal--two for the price of one. Perhaps one for the *senorita?*"

"She doesn't want one."

The man wouldn't give up. "These belts have not been dyed. They are...how do you say...*de color natural?"*

"It's the same in English and Spanish," Crane said. "Natural color."

"Are there snakes like this around here?" Annie asked.

The man smiled. "*Si, Senorita.* We have very unusual snakes in this town. That's why we changed its name to Culebra."

"Did you catch these snakes yourself?" Crane said.

"Oh, no. I'd be afraid to. I bought them from a...how do you say it? A trapper. He catches the snakes outside of town, and once in a while, inside the town."

"Do you know the trapper's name?" Crane asked.

The man shook his head. "No, *Senor.* He lives out in the country near the canyons."

Crane, realizing that the shopkeeper would be of little help in finding the trapper, changed his line of questioning. "Have you heard of Dar Lumbre?"

The man's eyes lit up. *"Claro que si.* Everybody in Culebra knows about Dr. Lumbre. He's a legend around here. He used to come here a long time ago, and we believe he will come back."

"What did he do when he visited?" Crane asked.

"I don't know."

Crane came back to the question he had asked dozens of times since landing in Monterrey. "Do you know anybody around here who might have information about Dar Lumbre? Anybody at all?"

The man hesitated, as if mulling over something he was reluctant to divulge. A distant look came to his eyes and he stared at Crane for a moment before answering. "My daughter has a friend named Maria. They grew up together. When Maria was little, her grandfather told many adventure stories about hunting devil snakes in the canyons outside the city. He hunted them with a famous doctor."

"Does Maria still live in Culebra?" Crane asked.

The shopkeeper nodded. "Yes. She runs a video rental shop."

"Which way?"

The man pointed a bony finger. "That way--where *Calle Central* crosses *Cinco.*"

"Thank you," Crane said, as they turned to leave the shop. He felt confident again. This adventure was beginning to look like Anaheim redux. Hopefully, they were closing in on the answer.

Ten minutes later, they were standing in front of a small cinder-block building identical to its neighbors on both sides. A sign above the door bore a single word in block letters: VIDEOS.

They entered the dimly lit shop. A dark-haired woman about forty sat in a wooden rocking chair just inside the open door. A single light bulb hung above her head, and on the counter nearby, an oscillating fan stirred the room's musty odor.

*"Buenos dias,"* the woman said. She got up and stepped behind the counter.

"Hello," Crane said. "Are you Maria?"

"Yes, I am. Do you wish to rent a video?"

Crane shook his head. "No, we're looking for information."

Maria's eyebrows shot up, but she said nothing.

"We're geneticists from Houston," Crane said. "Do you know what a geneticist is?"

Maria smiled. "Yes, I do. Papa--my grandfather--had a good friend who was a geneticist from Houston…a very famous one."

Crane forged ahead. "Was your grandfather's friend named Dar Lumbre?"

Maria stared at Crane. "How'd you know that?"

Crane explained the circumstances that brought them to Mexico in search of information about DL-666, and added, "Tell me everything you know about Dr. Lumbre. Everything--no matter how insignificant it might seem to you."

"I know very little," she said. "I never saw him, of

course. He quit coming here before I was born. All I know is what *mi abuelo* told me. He loved to talk about his snake-hunting adventures with the famous doctor."

"What did he tell you?" Crane said.

Maria paused a moment before answering, "Dr. Lumbre came here many times when he and Papa were young. He came to do medical research, and rented a building from Papa. They became good friends."

"Do you know anything about the research?" Crane asked.

"Not really," Maria said. "Papa said the doctor kept cages of snakes in the building. He was an unusual man." She fell silent, and a faraway look crept into her eyes.

"Is the building still there?" Annie asked.

"No, a storm blew it away a long time ago."

"Is anything left?" Crane asked. "Anything?"

Maria shook her head. "No…nothing. The place is an onion field now. It has been farmed for years."

"Did this town really change its name from Guadeloupe to Culebra because of the snakes?" Annie asked.

"That's what my parents told me," Maria said. "A big storm destroyed the building where Dr. Lumbre kept the snakes, and they escaped. Something happened to the snakes. They changed and began to show up in many different colors…lots of them…fiery serpents, like that plague in the Bible."

"Were they poisonous?" Crane asked.

"I don't know, *Senor,*" Maria said, "but they were plenty scary."

"Is there anybody else around here that would have any information?" Crane said. "One of your grandparents?"

"They're all dead," Maria said, making the sign of the cross.

"Sorry," Crane said.

"Anyway," Maria said, "my family knew more about Dr. Lumbre than anyone else living here. Papa said the doctor didn't want the U.S. authorities to know when he was in Mexico. Over the years, they stopped talking about him to protect his privacy. I never understood the secrecy."

"Any chance that he left written notes?" Annie said.

"I don't know," Maria said. "I never saw any."

"Are you aware that many people think Dar Lumbre is going to return?" Annie asked.

"I've heard that many times," Maria said, "and it wouldn't surprise me at all if he's still alive." Her voice was firm with conviction.

"After so many years?" Annie said.

"Papa said he was an unusual man," Maria said. "The most brilliant person he ever met. He had a memory...uh... like a photograph...how do you say it?"

"A photographic memory," Crane said. "You said it fine."

After a brief pause, Maria asked, "Do you have any more questions?"

"I guess not, "Crane said. "You've been a great help." He knew they had found some good information, but not enough. They needed physical evidence. It looked as if the next step would be to find the snake trapper and solicit his help. No matter how long it took, they had to obtain a DNA sample from one of the local snakes. Nothing else would do.

Maria looked directly at Crane for a moment. Then, in the blink of an eye, her expression changed. She smiled mysteriously and said, "I'm going to show you something no one else knows about. No one, except me."

A chill touched Crane's spine. "What are you talking about?"

"I've got something that I've never showed anyone else," the woman said. "Wait here. I'll be back in a minute." She ducked through a small curtained doorway leading into a back room. Neither Crane nor Annie spoke while Maria was gone. When she returned moments later, she carried a small jar of hazy liquid with an object suspended in it.

Crane knew what was in the jar.

She extended it toward him. "This is the *Culebra del Diablo*, the Devil Snake."

Crane took the jar from Maria. His hands trembled as he held it up to the light. A snake the size of a pencil floated in the dingy liquid. In spite of the passage of time, the snake was still bright green. He swirled the jar slightly to make the snake turn. When the angle was right, Crane saw what he'd anticipated seeing before Maria handed him the jar.

The snake had a forked tail.

Time ran backwards fifteen years. The specimen in the jar was identical to the snake that he and Larry had discovered at Herman Park Zoo when they were teenagers. He felt sure he was holding the final piece to the DL-666 puzzle. And now, he believed the Hopkins-Lee team could put the puzzle together.

Crane licked dry lips. "Where did you get this?"

"From my mother," Maria said. "Dr. Lumbre gave it to my grandfather. After the big storm blew the buildings away, the doctor asked Papa to hide it for safekeeping. The doctor said he would come back to claim it, but he disappeared and never came back. I knew that someone would come here someday and ask about it. Since you were the first to do so, I thought that I should show it to you. This kind of snake can still be found once in a while, but this is one of Dr. Lumbre's snakes."

"Would it be possible for us to hire somebody to catch one?" Annie asked. She looked down at the floor as if expecting to see one of the exotic reptiles slither out of a crack in the cinder blocks.

Maria shrugged. "I don't think so," she said. "I've never seen a live one. They're so scary. When someone finds one, he kills it and burns it immediately. The local *campesinos* think these snakes descended from the serpent in the Garden of Eden. They burn them to destroy the curse."

"Did Dr. Lumbre discover this kind of snake here in Culebra?" Crane asked, "or did he produce it in his lab by experimentation?"

"I don't know."

"Would you sell this to us?" Crane asked.

Maria shook her head. "It's not for sale. It's all I have to remind me of Papa. When I look at it, I remember the adventure stories that he told me about hunting snakes with Dr. Lumbre."

Crane studied the small reptile. The specimen was in excellent condition after fifty years of storage in the jar of formaldehyde solution. A layer of sludge had accumulated at the bottom of the jar. Carefully, he tipped the jar to make the sludge move, and saw several scales suspended in the residue.

"Could we have a few of the scales?" Crane said. "We'd like to take a sample back to Houston and run some tests on it."

Maria was hesitant. "Okay," she finally said, "that would be fine. But be careful when you open the jar. I wouldn't want anything to happen to the snake."

"We'll be careful," Crane said. He twisted hard on the lid. At first, it wouldn't budge, but he was determined to open it or strain a muscle trying. On his second attempt, his efforts were rewarded, and the lid opened with a rasping noise. The liquid reeked of formaldehyde and rancid fat, but he was so thrilled he hardly noticed the pungent odor. The find was incredibly valuable. The team was about to chalk up another successful mission.

After donning surgical gloves, Annie took a DNA test kit out of her iTab bag and selected a green envelope from the available colors. She opened it and took out a cotton swab. Crane handed her the jar. She swirled it slightly and inserted the swab into the murky liquid. After several misses, she extracted a small clump of scales from the residue and placed them, along with the swab, in the green envelope.

"Thank you very much, Maria," Crane said. "You have helped us a great deal."

"I wish you success on your mission," Maria said. "Please let me know when Dr. Lumbre returns."

"If he returns, the whole world will find out quickly," Crane said. "Even in little towns like Culebra."

Satisfied and pleased with their discovery, they left Maria's shop. Culebra was not likely to yield any further information regarding the long-lost scientist. It was clear that Dr. Lumbre had done research in Mexico which was illegal in the United States. Evidence suggested that the doctor's work had continued over a period of years, probably right up to the point when the enigmatic doctor disappeared. After the big storm turned loose an army of devil snakes on the village, the residents withdrew their welcome, forcing

Dr. Lumbre to look for another place to carry on his work. Regardless of legalities, it was apparent that he had smuggled some of the bizarre creatures into the U.S. and continued his research at the Mediplex.

How did his illegal imports turn up in the wild at Hermann Park Zoo? A mystery for another day, Crane thought. Right now, they had what they came for. The Culebra mission was complete.

Crane was certain the non-human DNA in DL-666 would match the snake from Culebra. No other possibility existed. He hoped the formaldehyde had not denatured the snake's DNA to the point that it was no longer usable. If so, they would have to return to Mexico with a search party to find one of the creatures, regardless of how rare they were. Such a trip would require permits and a lot of time, but it could be done.

The big question was, could it be done in time to save the lives hanging in the balance, lives which included Richard Hunter, the First Lady of the United States, and many other Americans?

## Chapter 33

The day after their remarkable discovery in Mexico, Crane and Annie arrived at Bush International Airport at midafternoon and took the airport robo-shuttle to the Mediplex. They entered the CellTech complex and headed toward the labs at a brisk pace.

Six hours later, they had the answer. DNA from the devil snake was identical to its counterpart in the original DL-666. Even so, they still recognized the possibility of a *good-news-bad-news* scenario. The good news was obvious—the samples matched. Bad news would come if the sample could not be duplicated due to its lengthy stay in a formaldehyde solution. Crane and Annie had hashed and rehashed this possibility all the way home from Mexico. Discussion time was over. Now, they had to find out ASAP.

Three days later, the good news continued. After multiple failed attempts, they successfully duplicated the devil snake's DNA based on its fingerprint. A long-shot in every respect, but one which both geneticists had anticipated. They believed the pieces of the puzzle were coming together.

They were seated on their lab stools in front of the main monitor when the results were verified.

"Yes!" Annie shouted, when she saw that the images matched. She raised her left hand toward Crane to invite a high five.

He slapped his right palm against Annie's upraised hand and said, "We should have bought some Texas Lottery tickets."

Annie chuckled. "You're saying we beat the odds?"

"I believe so."

The green snake with the forked tail was a previously unreported species. Its genetic makeup was unusual, exhibiting numerous uncoiled elements and other structural anomalies. Crane realized the atypical nature of the snake's chromosomes presented a paradox, being both the characteristic which allowed it to produce functioning cardiac tissue, and the flaw which led to its downfall upon ageing.

"The snake is a family member," Annie said, "a half-

213

brother--just like Dar Lumbre and Elmore Larson."

"Let's graft the new DNA into DL-666,"

Annie checked the equipment. "We're going to start with DL-666a, rather than the original…right?"

Crane nodded. "I think that's best. We don't want to waste time, so the quickest way to proceed is by grafting the snake's DNA directly into DL-666a."

Following their plan, they transected the X chromosome of DL-666a at the juncture between the two arms, separated the two pieces, and then performed the identical procedure on the X chromosome from the devil snake. Finally, they combined the two strands, thereby producing a new tissue based on a combination of Elmore Larson's DNA and that of the specimen from Culebra, Mexico.

"Still not ready to go with DL-667?" Annie said. "Or maybe HL-667, with H and L standing for Hopkins and Lee?"

Crane shook his head. "Not yet."

"You know," Annie said, "if this works, we'll be the only people in the world, other than Dar Lumbre, to produce a viable cardiac tissue."

"I knew the Hopkins-Lee team could do it."

Annie raised an eyebrow. "You never doubted?"

"Not for a moment."

By 10:00 p.m., they were ready to culture a pilot batch of the new cardiac tissue. Both were confident the lag phase of the tissue's growth curve would be normal this time. If refurbishing both arms of the X chromosome didn't restore the tissue to the original condition, they would be completely out of ideas.

"Okay," Crane said. "Are you ready to transfer our baby to the incubator."

"Affirmative."

As per their well-established routine, Annie brought a one-liter flask of culture medium to the lab bench, and Crane removed a sample from the newly-prepared tissue. He transferred the tissue inoculum to the flask, attached sensors, and placed the flask in the incubator at 37 degrees Centigrade. In about two hours, they would know if they had successfully tied Anaheim and Culebra together.

"This kind of work makes me hungry," Annie said. "How about making a sushi run?"

"Don't you ever get tired of sushi?"

"I'm Asian."

"I don't do racial profiling," Crane said with fake solemnity. "It's against the law."

"Do you want to go to the Palace, or not?"

Crane chuckled and said, "Let's go."

With a confident spring in their step, they headed toward the exit.


After a leisurely dinner, they returned to the CellTech building and went to the lab, which was quiet and almost dark. They hurried to the incubator at the rear of the lab. At a glance, the monitoring devices told the whole story.

DL-666b was a perfect duplicate of the original DL-666.

## Chapter 34

Helena Cartwright sat in her office, contemplating the next step in the DL-666 project. Even though the tissue culture had been restored to its original condition, several government hurdles remained. OFS might drag their feet, and final approval to use DL-666b would have to be handled by legislative action or executive order. If somebody in Washington didn't get the ball rolling quickly, she would call President Keynes directly. With the First Lady as top VIP on the heart transplant waiting list, the president would have to take her call.

She relished the satisfaction of completing a difficult assignment quickly, and would add CellTech's logo to her trophy chest within a few days. Still, one aspect of the DL-666 project troubled her. She'd hoped to combine business acumen with biology in order to pave the way to the OFS Directorship, but her scientific contribution to DL-666's restoration was nil, and she knew it. She anticipated that kudos would be showered on the Hopkins-Lee team when the public heard the whole story. That was to be expected, but as she saw it, their success came under her leadership, so part of the credit belonged to her. She hoped NatGov would see it that way.

If the successful CellTech project didn't flag her as first choice to become OFS Director, she had only one card left to play. That card was the ace up her sleeve. As a last resort, she would ask her estranged husband to pull a few strings in Washington. Ahab was a politico par excellence, and throughout their lengthy separation, they remained in contact. In the early years of their marriage, she thought his charisma was potent enough to propel both of them to any office they desired, and that might have been the case, except for Ahab's multiple scandals which diminished his political prowess.

Ahab Cartwright was the last card she had left in the OFS Directorship gambit, and she would play it, if necessary. If that card got trumped, she was out of the game.

Her introspection was interrupted by her desktop iMessenger's ringtone, *Mona Lisa.*

As per standing orders, her Administrative Assistant, Janice Smith, answered in the outer office. Reflexively, Dr. Cartwright glanced at the monitor on her desk and saw 714-000-0000 on the display, but no pic. She recognized the California area code, and wondered why neither the entire number nor the caller's image appeared. She normally requested a callback number when someone tried to make an *Image Not Available* contact with her.

"Dr. Cartwright," Janice whispered through the open door, "Elmore Larson is on the line. He wants to speak to you."

"Are you sure it's Mr. Larson?" Dr. Cartwright asked. "His image is not on my monitor."

"It's on mine," Janice said, "and I've heard him speak several times recently. I'm sure it's Elmore Larson."

"I'll take the call," Dr. Cartwright said, wondering if he was calling about the saliva issue. If so, he was calling the wrong person, and was calling too late. Nobody short of the Chief Justice of the Supreme Court could stop this project from going forward, probably not even her.

"Hello," she said toward the iMessenger. "Dr. Helena Cartwright speaking."

"Good morning, Doctor. This is Elmore Larson with the Dar Lumbre Society."

"What can I do for you, Mr. Larson?" Dr. Cartwright asked warily.

"Before we go any further with this conversation, I need to tell you something about the Dar Lumbre Society," Larson said. "We've been monitoring CellTech's activities since it incorporated fifty years ago."

"Why such scrutiny?"

"We were anticipating the deterioration of DL-666. Its failure signaled the society to go into action."

Dr. Cartwright was stunned to silence, an event that rarely happened.

"CellTech's geneticists did a remarkable job," Larson continued, "but, this double helix odyssey is not over yet."

"What do you mean?"

"Another chapter in the Dar Lumbre chronicles is about to unfold—an extraordinary event will occur soon."

"What event?"

"The resuscitation of Dar Lumbre, my brother," Larson said evenly.

"Are you serious?"

"Absolutely."

"If he's alive, why didn't the society resuscitate him to solve the DL-666 problem?"

"An obvious question," Larson said. "Before he went into the C-Unit, my brother established two signals to be met before his resuscitation. The failure of DL-666 was the first signal. After that occurred, the Dar Lumbre Society came out of hiding and began to operate openly. When the geneticists solved the DL-666 problem, that fulfilled the second signal, indicating it was time for him to be revived."

"It seems odd that the society would wait until after the problem was solved before resuscitating Dr. Lumbre," Dr. Cartwright said. "CellTech could have used his help."

"The fact that NatGov allowed scientists to work on DL-666 indicated the dark age of science was over. That was very important to Dar."

Doubt still laced Dr. Cartwright's voice. "How could he survive so long in a C-Unit?"

"In addition to DL-666, my brother developed a preservation fluid making it possible to survive for decades in a C-Unit."

"Why didn't he release it to the medical community?"

"He was a fugitive from NatGov," Larson said. "He completed the new fluid shortly before going into hiding. After President Garwood lost his bid for a second term, NatGov banned most genetic research. A number of scientists got into trouble, and some were sentenced to prison. Dar didn't want to suffer that fate, and chose to go into a C-Unit instead. He knew DL-666 would eventually fail and believed that, by the time it did, scientists could correct the problem without being persecuted by the government."

"How did he disappear so abruptly?"

"For several years, Dar knew the government would block his efforts and brand him as a criminal," Larson said. "NatGov opposition wasn't due to his science. It was due to his politics, which didn't mesh with their rigid two-party system. He formed the Dar Lumbre Society and disappeared. The organization went underground after the solar flare and remained in hiding for fifty years, growing in numbers, while waiting for the right time to come out of hiding and resuscitate their leader."

Dr. Cartwright was skeptical of the timing of events related to Dar Lumbre's disappearance. "It seems like the solar flare occurred just in the nick of time," she said.

"Dar believed it was an act of God so he could continue his work at some future time," Larson said. "And now, I have a favor to ask of CellTech."

"What do you want, Mr. Larson?" The conversation had taken an unusual turn. Dr. Cartwright, who was accustomed to being in control, realized that Elmore Larson had seized the lead.

"The society would like for the Hopkins-Lee team to be present when we resuscitate my brother," Larson said. "We believe they've earned the right to observe this event."

"When is the resuscitation scheduled?"

"We haven't set the exact date, but it will be soon— no more than two weeks. Would that fit the schedule of the Hopkins-Lee team?"

After a brief pause, Dr. Cartwright said, "That timing is not good for CellTech. We're about to ramp up production on the new version of DL-666. As you know, the First Lady is on the waiting list for a heart transplant. I believe President Keynes would be unhappy with any delays."

"I spoke to the President a few days ago," Larson said, "and he's decided to wait until after the resuscitation before authorizing surgery on the First Lady. He feels that the inventor of the original DL-666 might have information pertinent to the new version."

"This is an unusual situation," Dr. Cartwright said. "I'd like to discuss it with the OFS Director. I'll be transferred soon, and want to assure a successful conclusion to this project at CellTech before I move on."

"Dr. Cartwright," Larson said evenly, "a successful conclusion to the DL-666 project is assured already. What objection could the director have to a short delay which might result in an even better outcome?"

"I'm a *chain of command* manager, Mr. Larson. That's the way I like to operate."

"Well…this chain of command is simple. The OFS Director reports to the President, who has made his wishes clear. I can ask Mr. Keynes to speak to the director, if you like."

Dr. Cartwright realized that further objections were futile, and could hamper her chances of being appointed the next OFS Director. She assumed that President Keynes would be elected to a second term, and she had to be in his good graces to have a chance at the directorship. Even though it was obvious that Elmore Larson had stacked the deck against her before calling, his argument was irrefutable. It was time to concede gracefully

"There's no need to involve the director, Mr. Larson. Let me know when you want the geneticists to come to California."

"Thank you for your help, Dr. Cartwright. I'll call you in a few days."

Shortly thereafter, the conversation ended with Dr. Cartwright sorely aware that she had not been invited to the resuscitation of Dar Lumbre.

While pondering Elmore Larson's failure to recognize her contribution to the DL-666 project, she heard noises in the street below. She looked out of her office window, realizing that Peaceful Protest Day had rolled around again. People were beginning to mill about in the streets and on the sidewalk. Some of the early arrivals were jockeying for prime positions along the curb of Main Street. Police officers on Hover-Harleys eased along the street, keeping a watchful eye on the proceedings. The gathering was orderly, and the stage was set for the parade to start momentarily.

Today's parade had received considerably more advanced publicity than usual. One of the marching groups was starting a movement to change the U.S. flag from Old Glory to a rainbow-colored banner. Several senators and representatives were onboard with the idea, but most polls showed it had little chance to pass, except in California and New York.

Although she was busy, Dr. Cartwright continued to

stare out of the window for a few minutes. When she was at the point of turning away, Houston's broadcast diva, Carolina Herrera, appeared on the sidewalk. Ms. Herrera, dressed in black leotards and a red waistcoat, began to mill about and mingle with the early arrivals, stopping occasionally to elicit comments from an onlooker.

An idea struck Dr. Cartwright—a brilliant one, in her opinion.

After informing Janice that she would return in about thirty minutes, she donned her white lab coat, left the office, and walked down the hallway at a rapid pace. She took the elevator to the first floor and walked past the cytogenetics lab without a glance it its direction.

Dr. Cartwright left the building via the security exit nearest the intersection of Dryden and Main Street. The sidewalk was filling with people and polyphonic noise, both nearly constant features in the streets of the MediPlex any time day or night.

She looked around and saw Carolina Herrera walking directly toward her with a cameraman at her side. It's my turn now, she thought.

After a split-second glance at Dr. Cartwright's nametag, Carolina said, "Good morning, Doctor. Could I have a moment of your time?"

"Yes, I suppose so," Dr. Cartwright said into Carolina's hand-held microphone, trying not to appear overly eager.

"What's your name?" Carolina asked.

"Dr. Helena R. Cartwright."

"Dr. Cartwright," Carolina said, "I believe I recognize your name. Aren't you associated with CellTech, the famous tissue culture company here in the MediPlex?"

"Yes, that's right. I'm the Technical Director and CEO."

"Both the Technical Director and CEO?"

"That is correct."

"I remember when Dr. Rosenberg was CellTech's Technical Director," Carolina said. "Is he still with the company?"

Dr. Cartwright nodded. "Yes, he reports to me."

"Everyone is acquainted with CellTech's flagship creation, DL-666," Carolina said. "Did you come here due to the failure of that product?"

"Yes, I did," Dr. Cartwright said. "I'm a business turnaround specialist with the OFS. NatGov sent me here to resolve CellTech's financial problems, which were caused by the failure of DL-666. We have solved the technical problem with the tissue culture, so CellTech's financial problems will cease to exist in a short period of time."

Carolina motioned toward Dr. Cartwright's lab coat. "I see that you're dressed for lab work," she said. "Did you actually work on DL-666 with other scientists?"

"Occasionally," Dr. Cartwright said. "But, primarily, I offered suggestions from time to time to keep the scientists focused."

"How many scientists worked on DL-666?" Carolina asked. "And what is their background?"

"Two experienced cytogeneticists worked on this project for several months. We have a unique relationship in that they report directly to me, rather than to a laboratory manager, as would be the case in most similar situations."

"What are their names?"

Without batting an eye, Dr. Cartwright answered, "It is against my policy to release the names of company employees who are working on sensitive projects under my supervision."

Carolina leaned forward and asked a follow-up question, but the Peaceful Protest cacophony drowned out her words.

Dr. Cartwright was glad. She had made her point.

## Chapter 35

A black limo, complete with chauffeur, met Crane and Annie at John Wayne Airport. Accompanied by four police officers on Hover-Harleys, the limo whisked them northwest along the Santa Ana Freeway. Their driver was a taciturn youth with a blond ponytail protruding beneath his chauffeur's cap. Either he knew very little about Dar Lumbre, or had instructions to keep quiet. They left him in peace to interact with the car's autopilot as they sped along the freeway at a rapid clip.

The geneticists were surprised to find paparazzi waiting in front of the Dar Lumbre Society headquarters in Anaheim. Crane wondered if they were there to see Elmore Larson, or the geneticists who had purloined his spittle. Maybe they were expecting Dr. Dar Lumbre himself. That possibility was being whispered about in the streets of Anaheim. Whatever the case, the celebrity-seekers were making quite a fuss, and the air was supercharged with excitement.

"Stay in the car, please. I'll let Mr. Larson know we're here," the driver said, as he touched the screen of his iTab.

A swarm of paparazzi ran toward the car, but a squadron of police officers foiled their advance by quickly and precisely splitting the crowd into two distinct groups. Under the direction of the officers, the groups moved apart, forming a corridor from the building to the waiting car. The paparazzi resisted a little, but pulled back as ordered.

The black-uniformed chauffeur got out of the limo, came around to the passenger door, and stood at parade rest. He kept his eyes fixed on the front door of the office building.

"This police protection we're seeing is surprising," Annie said.

"How so?"

"Law enforcement officials harassed the people attending those early rallies around Houston," Annie said. "They were probably following instructions from NatGov. Now, they're helping."

"Things have changed since those early days of this

movement," Crane said. "The reappearance of Dar Lumbre is of vital interest to everyone."

They kept their eyes fixed on the front door of the office building. Like the paparazzi, they wanted to get the first glimpse of Elmore Larson when he appeared. Their wait was short. Moments later, the office door opened, and Elmore Larson emerged. He walked briskly toward the waiting limo. The driver opened the car door and waited at attention.

Neither Crane nor Annie uttered a word as Elmore Larson entered the car, and the silence remained unbroken as he sat down in the seat facing them while the car eased into traffic. He looked directly at the awestruck geneticists for a brief moment before speaking.

"Mr. Hopkins and Miss Lee," he said, with a nod of his head. "I'm pleased to meet you."

"We have a million questions," Crane said.

"I imagine so," Larson said, "and I will answer all I can. But first, let me start by telling you something about our family history--which is unusual, to say the least."

Crane and Annie leaned forward in anticipation of having some long-standing questions answered.

Larson continued, "As you know, Dar Lumbre is my half-brother. He was born and educated within the NatGov system before the solar flare. When he was a teenager, his father was killed in a car accident under mysterious circumstances. Dar believed NatGov staged the accident-- he was always something of a conspiracy theorist. After the solar flare, our mother changed her name and became an Outsider by letting her party affiliation lapse."

Larson paused and Annie said, "I have a question."

"Go ahead."

"Chronologically, Dr. Lumbre is much older than you, and yet, you're half-brothers," Annie said. "What can you tell us about that part of your family history?"

"When Dar was a child, our mother realized that he was a genius," Larson said, "so she arranged to collect several of her ova in order to have another child in the future. Dar's father was already dead when she formulated this plan. Many years later, a surrogate mother gave birth to me using my biological mother's frozen ovum and a sperm bank donor."

"Is Lumbre a real name, or an alias?" Annie asked.

"It's a real Spanish name," Larson said. "Not a common one, but real, nevertheless. My name, Larson, is my mother's maiden name, so she gave it to me."

The limo turned south onto Harbor Boulevard and moved slowly past the perimeter fence of Disneyland, stopping at the main entrance where a shuttle bus waited near the curb. The limo driver touched a button to open the door for his passengers.

Crane stepped out and turned to offer Annie his hand. She caught it and squeezed. Their eyes met, silently acknowledging the special bond which had formed between them during the past few months.

"This is our transportation into the park," Larson said. He got out of the limo and moved toward the waiting shuttle with Crane and Annie at his heels.

The plaza was packed with throngs of people, many of them waving hand-lettered signs heralding the return of Dar Lumbre. The content of the signs and banners covered the gambit, but far the most popular two were:

WELCOME BACK, DR. LUMBRE
and
DAR LUMBRE FOR PRESIDENT

Crane was awed by the demeanor of the crowd. There were no obvious dissenters, no negative signs, and no shouts of protest. A unifying event was unfolding. The activity swirled around one man, the enigmatic Dar Lumbre who had not been seen in fifty years.

Obviously, the crowd believed he was alive in a C-Unit in Disneyland, just as the urban legends proclaimed for decades. The Hopkins-Lee team finally believed it, too--not because of the legends, but because they'd seen Dr. Lumbre's fingerprints along a million DNA bases.

The police escort opened a wide corridor through the crowd, thereby allowing the shuttle bus to pass. Even as they were shoved back, the throng of people remained good-natured, many of them fixing their attention on the passengers in the shuttle creeping toward the front entrance of Disneyland. Several people waved at Elmore Larson and shouted greetings in his direction. The charismatic Larson smiled and waved back.

"We're witnessing something you don't see often," Annie said. "A peaceful mob."

As they neared the entrance of the park, some of the onlookers recognized Crane and Annie and began to chant their names. Although their stories had been told on national television, this spontaneous demonstration of affection still shocked the two geneticists. Ten years of working in a secluded lab did not prepare them for this type of public notoriety, but they were adapting to it.

At President Keynes' request, Disneyland was closed for the day, with the Disney organization giving full support to the monumental event about to occur on their iconic property. As Crane evaluated the situation, he surmised that only a handful of Disney officials knew the full magnitude of what was going on. If all went well, magic far beyond anything the Magic Kingdom had produced in its entire history would unfold soon.

Still under police protection, the shuttle eased down Main Street USA, swung left into Frontier Land and stopped near the Pirates of the Caribbean ride. The amusement park, devoid of visitors, looked forlorn and lonely, like a scene from an old science fiction movie.

The irony of the situation struck Crane. Many people had spent decades trying to find the whereabouts of Dar Lumbre. Those who thought him to be dead searched cemeteries all over the world. Others who believed he was in a C-Unit contacted every cryo-preservation company in existence. Still others searched millions of terabytes of digital data for clues. All attempts to find him failed, yet here he was, having been at rest for decades in one of the most crowded locations in the United States.

Those who picked this spot did so with utmost care, and were able to hide the legendary figure virtually in plain sight. Crane believed Dar Lumbre must have anticipated the exact situation which was taking place at this moment. Otherwise, he wouldn't have risked a Rip Van Winkle gambit.

"We'll go underground the rest of the way," Larson said, as they stepped off the shuttle. With the geneticists trailing behind him, he went to the entrance of the Pirates of the Caribbean ride, stepped inside, and stopped before a steel door in the side wall of the tunnel. Using an old-fashioned brass key, he unlocked the door and led them into a tunnel.

"You've probably passed by this door several times and never noticed it," Larson said. "It's one of the portals built by Disney so cast members and other personnel can utilize a network of tunnels beneath the park."

The main tunnel connected to the Pirates attraction was broad and well lit, but smelled of dust and mold. Larson went ahead, and like foot soldiers, Crane and Annie fell in step behind him and marched along briskly, looking back occasionally. Every few yards, side tunnels branched out along the main hallway in maze-like fashion, and doors appeared at regular intervals along the corridors. Most doors were unlocked and labeled with the name of one of the Disneyland attractions, but a few were unmarked and locked. The whole complex suggested dungeons and dragons, even though much of it was used daily by Disney employees.

Elmore Larson stopped near a door labeled PIRATES OF THE CARRIBEAN and tapped on the screen of his iTab as Crane and Annie waited in silence. He studied the screen briefly and said, "All security cameras show that we are alone in the tunnel. We can proceed."

Larson touched the iTab screen again, and a section of the wall near the door slid back to reveal a hallway. They stepped through the secret opening. Once inside, Larson touched a thumbprint actuated screen beside the door, and the wall slid back in place behind them, triggering a soft glow of light from fixtures recessed in the ceiling. A short hall led into an alcove furnished with a sofa, chairs, and tables in Amish craftsman style. The room had two doors on the wall opposite the entry. One of them was cracked open slightly and had a brass plaque with the name DAR LUMBRE attached to it. The other door bore no sign, but sported two locks, one a sturdy mechanical Amazon-Yale, and the other a thumbprint variety.

"Medical professionals have been on site since yesterday," Larson said. "They're people you know--Dr. Sean Tanner and his surgical team."

Crane was surprised. "Is he working with CellTech again?"

"No one would turn down the opportunity to participate in this event," Larson said. "It transcends the rift between Dr. Tanner and CellTech."

They followed Elmore Larson into the room where three men and a woman in green scrubs were carrying on an animated discussion. The medical team turned to face the incoming group, and Dr. Tanner dipped his head in a slight nod. "Mr. Hopkins and Miss Lee, the genetic sleuths from CellTech--congratulations on a job well done."

Crane and Annie acknowledged Dr. Tanner's gracious comments and greeted the other members of his group, all of whom expressed congratulatory comments as well. With pleasantries exchanged, they directed their attention to the area behind the medical team where a familiar sight greeted them.

The room was a fully equipped intensive care unit. Life support monitors sat on shelves around the room, their dully-glowing screens an ever-changing pattern of lines and dots. A bundle of thin multicolored tubes ran along rails attached to the walls. Relays clicked on and off in rhythmic fashion, and circuits hummed periodically.

A C-Unit stood against the far wall.

"Dr. Lumbre!" Crane and Annie said together.

Elmore Larson nodded. "Yes, go look at him."

The eager geneticists rushed to the C-Unit and looked at the comatose man beneath the frosty glass. He lay like a corpse with arms folded in an X across his chest. Fog swirled in front of Dr. Lumbre's face, momentarily obscuring his features. When it cleared, a further surprise was in store.

He looked about sixty years old.

Elmore Larson read the astonished geneticists' faces. "Although my brother has been in the unit fifty years, he did not age. Chronologically, he's a hundred and ten years old. Physically, he's only sixty."

"We started the revival process three hours ago,"

Dr. Tanner said. "All seems to be going well. His body is responding to the gradual temperature increase of the preservation fluid."

Annie shook her head in amazement. "DL-666 was functioning well when Dr. Lumbre went into this C-Unit. He took a terrible chance by basing his wakeup call on the failure of the tissue."

"Dar was not afraid to take chances," Larson said. "When it became obvious NatGov would not allow him to finish his work, he opted to go into a C-Unit in order to have a chance to survive until the laws changed. His revival was contingent upon geneticists solving the clues he left behind, an event that would prove the arcane genetic laws were no longer in effect."

"Who had the authority to revive him?" Annie asked.

"As current leader of the society, I was the only one authorized," Larson said. "But, we have always utilized a chain of command system in case something happened to the society's leader. Before I inherited this position, one of our uncles headed the organization for twenty-five years."

"Why Disneyland?" Annie asked.

"Dar was able to forge some useful relationships with the Disney organization," Larson said. "They funded a lot of his work under the table, much of which was probably illegal."

Dr. Tanner turned back to the C-Unit and studied the monitors attached to the comatose Dar Lumbre. "The next hour will be critical," he said. "Vital signs are beginning to strengthen, and the instruments have detected a faint heartbeat. The C-Unit will not revive him faster than his body can tolerate, so all we can do is wait."

Crane stepped closer and studied the corpse-like figure of Dar Lumbre. He marveled at the man's long-term survival in the C-Unit. He believed Dr. Lumbre's will power had been instrumental in the process. Even while in suspended animation, he had a subtle emanation about him that permeated the room, an aura which was inexplicable, yet tangible. Maybe he will be deified as some sort of medical messiah, Crane thought. Just like his followers have proclaimed for years.

Sean Tanner studied the battery of monitors on the

C-unit and said, "The revival process is accelerating rapidly. His cardiac rhythm should normalize within a few minutes. When it does, he'll wake up."

He touched a button, and the glass top slid away from the unit, exposing Dar Lumbre to natural atmosphere for the first time in fifty years.

"Start the IV," Dr. Tanner said to the nurse.

Crane leaned over the C-Unit and studied Dr. Lumbre's pale bony face, which was beginning to show signs of life. One eyelid twitched, although both remained closed. He inhaled, and seconds later, he let the breath out slowly. After several shallow breaths, the breathing process became rhythmic. Progress over the last few minutes had moved at a remarkable pace. Crane felt like he was watching a marble statue come to life.

Dr. Lumbre's eyelids fluttered open, and he looked vacantly at the faces above him without focusing on anyone in particular. His expression was calm. After fifty years of deep sleep, the corpse-like figure was easing back into the conscious world as if waking from a Sunday afternoon nap.

Annie leaned toward Crane and whispered, "I wonder what his first words will be?"

"Something extraordinary, I'm sure."

"Dr. Tanner has awakened the greatest geneticist who ever lived," Annie said. "Even greater than Gregor Mendel, the father of genetics."

Will he remember everything? Crane wondered. Can he tell us how to improve DL-666? Is the secret of a Methuselah gene really locked inside his brain? The questions linked together like DNA bases on a chromosome.

Dr. Lumbre's parchment-like lips moved for the first time. "I've seen God in the double helix," he said in a barely-audible voice.

Crane glanced at Annie and tried to read her expression. She, like everyone else in the room, seemed shocked at Dar Lumbre's cryptic pronouncement. The onlookers waited breathlessly to see what the newly-wakened legend's next words would be.

"I had a dream," Dr. Lumbre said in a creaky voice. "I was in a city called Luz, and saw a ladder ascending into heaven, just like Jacob in the Bible. The ladder was a DNA double helix. God stood at the top, and spoke to me in a loud voice."

Elmore Larson turned to the astonished group crowded around the C-Unit and said, "History is repeating itself. Dar had this recurring dream years before he went into the C-Unit. He told me about it when I was eight or nine years old. He believes that God wants him to change the world."

"He already has," Crane said.

"He had plans to do more, but NatGov forced him to disappear," Larson said.

Dar Lumbre struggled and tried to sit up.

"Please lie still, Dr. Lumbre," Sean Tanner said. "You're very weak."

"I have an appointment with President Garwood. I can't keep him waiting."

"Mr. Garwood died a long time ago," Dr. Tanner said. "You have been in suspended animation for fifty years."

"Fifty years?" Lumbre echoed. For the first time since waking, he looked directly at the people standing over him. "Then my gamble worked."

Larson stepped forward. "Dar, look at me--I'm Elmore."

Dar Lumbre focused his eyes on Elmore Larson, as everyone waited with bated breath to see if he had retained his cognitive powers while in suspended animation. After a moment, recognition crept into his eyes, and a faint smile touched his pale lips as he said, "Elmore, you were a child the last time I saw you. Now, you're an old man."

Everyone breathed a sigh of relief, and Larson said, "Physically, I'm about the same age as you, thanks to the fifty-year nap you just took."

"Can I raise my head?" Dr. Lumbre asked.

Dr. Tanner checked the vital sign monitors, and touched a button that raised the head of the bed to a forty-five-degree angle. "It will be okay for you to sit up for a few minutes?"

"Who are those people behind you?" Dr. Lumbre asked in the direction of his brother.

Elmore Larson stepped to the head of the C-Unit to

make the introductions. "Dar, let me introduce Crane Hopkins and Annie Lee, the team of geneticists who broke the code you programmed into DL-666."

Dr. Lumbre gazed at the two scientists. "Good work. Apparently, the dark age of science has passed."

"When you feel well enough, we have many questions we'd like to ask you," Annie said.

"I feel fine," Dr. Lumbre said. "Ask anything you like."

Dr. Tanner cast a cautionary glance toward Crane and Annie. "Just a couple of questions, then we have to get him ready to be moved."

Annie deferred to Crane. "Go ahead."

"My first question is not scientific," Crane said, "but is one that has given us a lot of grief. Why did you use 666 as the designation for the cardiac tissue?"

"It was the next number in my series," Dr. Lumbre said. "I failed 665 times before success came. Since 666 is a hot-button number with some religious groups, I thought about skipping it. After a lot of consideration, I decided it would be a sell-out to do so. Why should I change my numbering system to pacify those who opposed me?"

"It added significant irony," Annie said, "especially since part of DL-666's X chromosome is from a snake."

Dr. Tanner checked the monitors again and held up his right hand like a traffic cop. "That's all he needs to talk now. He's exerting himself too much. We have to move him to the hospital right away. We'll transfer him to Houston in a few days, and you can see him there."

Dr. Larson waggled a bony finger in the direction of Crane and Annie. "Come to see me as soon as they let me have visitors. I was working on a new project shortly before I went into hibernation to escape NatGov's clutches. Now that things have changed, you can help me with it."

"We have to move him now," Dr. Tanner insisted.

Dar Lumbre attempted to protest the moratorium on conversation, but was not strong enough to make an issue of it, finally giving up with a long sigh.

With great reluctance, the group began to make preparations to go their separate ways.

"I hate to let Dar Lumbre out of our sight," Annie

said, as they walked ahead of the group leaving the underground medical complex. "We spent a lot of time trying to figure out where he was."

"He was at the epicenter of a *chronosynclastic infundibulum*," Crane said.

Annie flashed an amused smile. "A Kurt Vonnegut novel?"

Crane chuckled. "Right. According to *The Sirens of Titan*, a *chronosynclastic infundibulum* is a place where all kinds of truths fit together."

"You mean like religion, politics, and science?"

Crane nodded. "Exactly, and the revival of Dar Lumbre has merged all three."

## Chapter 36

A nurse clad in green scrubs led Crane and Annie down a dim hallway to Dar Lumbre's hospital suite. A uniformed guard sat at each side of the door. As the trio approached, both guards stood and one of them said, "Hello, Nurse Madison."

"Hello again, Officer."

The officer looked at Crane and Annie. "I know who you are," he said. "I've seen your pics on TV, but I'm still required to scan your ID's."

The geneticists held out their iTabs, and the officer passed a small scanner over each screen. "You can go in," he said. "Enjoy your visit."

Gingerly, they stepped inside the door and found Dr. Lumbre seated in a wheelchair beside his bed. He was nibbling on an oatmeal-raisin cookie, and a glass of milk set on a tray beside his chair. He had gained a few pounds since arriving in Houston, and looked stronger, but was still pale.

Dr. Lumbre beckoned. "Come on in. You don't have to tiptoe around like that. Sit on the sofa."

"How are you feeling?" Crane asked, as he and Annie sat down on the sofa next to the wheelchair.

"Great," Dr. Lumbre said. "I've been asking to see you for two days, but Dr. Tanner has kept me in solitary confinement, except for a bevy of doctors he sends in to poke and prod me two or three times a day."

"Do you feel like answering some questions?" Crane asked.

"Of course. Ask anything you like."

"Why didn't the Dar Lumbre Society resuscitate you when DL-666 failed?" Crane said. "You could have corrected the problem without a big rigmarole."

"Except for me, that's how the original founders of the society wanted to operate," Dr. Lumbre said. "We had some heated arguments about the *wakeup protocol*, as we referred to the event. They wanted the failure of the tissue to trigger the event, but I wouldn't allow it."

"Why not?" Crane asked.

"I wanted to avoid being awakened amid continuing

NatGov oppression, so I insisted on waiting until DL-666 was repaired. To me, that would prove the dark age of science had ended."

"We suspected as much," Crane said

"Next question," Dr. Lumbre said with a faint smile.

"How did you program a plasmid to give a preview of what was about to occur in the X chromosome?" Annie asked. "That's been one of our main questions since we discovered the serpent-shaped structure in the plasmid."

"The unusual structure showed up in a plasmid I was using as a splicing tool," Dr. Lumbre said. "I realized the serpent would make a great clue for an astute observer. It mirrored the region of the X chromosome where my DNA joins that of the garter snake from Mexico. I assume you found the forked tail reptile without too much trouble?"

Annie shook her head. "Not exactly. We eventually found it, but had plenty of trouble before we did."

"The *Culebra del Diablo*," Crane said. "The final piece of the puzzle, and the hardest one to find."

"A snake invasion caused the village to change its name," Annie said.

"I know," Dr. Lumbre said. "And they unfriended me at that point. As odd as it seems, reptiles were the only creatures I ever found which contained genetic material compatible with my own, and complementary to it as well. The garter snake with the forked tail showed amazing power to regenerate tissue, which was the main characteristic required to produce DL-666."

"It was, indeed, an unusual snake," Annie said.

"As you've undoubtedly discovered," Dr. Lumbre said, "my chromosomes are loosely coiled. This condition caused a weak point near the Xp21 location--the site where I spliced DNA from the snake in order to make a workable cardiac tissue." He paused, as if inviting a follow-up query.

"I have another question about devil snakes," Crane said. "Why did they show up near the Hermann Park Zoo?"

Dr. Lumbre's licked his thin lips. "I was transporting some snakes from one lab building to another in a small pickup. An animal rights group was following me, one called SPCR, *Society for Prevention of Cruelty to Reptiles*. When

I stopped at a traffic light near the zoo, they grabbed one of the cages and threw it into the street. It broke apart, and the snakes escaped down a storm drain. I wasn't able to recapture them, and they reproduced."

Neither Crane nor Annie responded, and Dr. Lumbre continued, "Early in my research, I discovered the aging process in DL-666, and calculated that it would fail in around fifty years."

"How did you calculate it?" Annie asked.

"By computer simulation," Dr. Lumbre said. "As you know, since DL-666 cannot be stock cultured by freezing, it ages in real time. When I noticed that it aged at a constant rate, I set up a computer program to study the process. I projected the aging process fifty years into the future, and a dramatic visual change took place in the X chromosome. The DNA began to resemble a serpent, so I took a clone of that fragment and inserted it into the accompanying plasmid as an early warning system."

Crane nodded in appreciation. "The DNA fragment in the plasmid was relatively free of clutter, so it was much easier to observe than the corresponding fragment in the X chromosome."

"Exactly," Dr. Lumbre said, "but I believe the fact that the fragment looked like a serpent was a message from God. I told you about seeing God in the double helix, didn't I?"

Crane shot a quick glance at Annie, then turned back toward Dr. Lumbre and said, "Those were your first words when you woke up, and who are we to question what you've seen?"

Crane wondered if Dr. Lumbre would equate his resuscitation from the C-Unit to a resurrection, thus lending support to the religious implications associated with DL-666. The enigmatic doctor was a messiah-like figure who, at least in the minds of some, rose from the dead. Splinter groups of zealots were forming churches like the one near Disneyland. NatGov restrictions showed no ability to stop the Dar Lumbre juggernaut, especially after the *Register To Vote* flyer turned into a red hot political message.

"NatGov shut me down fifty years ago," Dr. Lumbre said, "because they opposed my politics. I couldn't finish my work, so there's still one major step left--something you can help me with."

"Are you talking about a Methuselah gene?" Annie asked.

"No, not a Methuselah gene. I never used that term," Dr. Lumbre said, disgust evident in his voice. "That's a media invention. However, I have plans to make an improvement in the cardiac tissue, apart from any M-gene considerations."

"What improvement?" Annie asked.

"Rebuilding it from female tissue," Dr. Lumbre replied. "With DL-666 having only one X chromosome, there's no backup when it fails--no second X chromosome to serve as insurance."

Annie looked toward Crane and her eyes sparkled. "I told you so."

"Where are we going to find female DNA compatible with the devil snake?" Crane asked, suspecting that he already knew the answer. The legendary Dar Lumbre was always one step ahead of everyone, friend and foe alike.

"My mother's DNA is compatible, and I stored a sample in the C-Unit with me."

"Why didn't you make this improvement yourself?" Annie asked.

"I didn't have time," Dr. Lumbre said. "My arrest was imminent. If I hadn't planned my disappearing act well in advance, we wouldn't be having this conversation right now. I'd be some reference in a genetics textbook--probably a footnote--and DL-666 wouldn't exist."

Annie shook her head in amazement. "How did you know the new cryonic suspension fluid would work?"

"I worked on it for many years," Dr. Lumbre said, "and achieved perfect results with laboratory mice shortly before incorporating the fluid into the C-Unit I was preparing for my own use. I was certain it would work."

"How can we help with this project?" Crane asked.

"I would like the Hopkins-Lee team to develop a new cardiac tissue based on my mother's DNA."

"Aren't you going to lead the work?" Crane asked. He couldn't imagine the legendary scientist stepping aside and leaving the project to others.

Dr. Lumbre shook his head. "I have another project in mind which requires my attention."

Annie's eyes widened. "Another genetics project?"

"No," Dr. Lumbre said. "Our country needs to make some changes in the sociopolitical area, and I'm in a unique position to expedite those changes. However, I can't give up genetics unless you agree to develop a replacement for DL-666 based on my mother's DNA. It wouldn't seem right to trust this work to anyone else."

"We wouldn't want anyone else to do it," Crane said. "We'll start the project immediately."

"And work 24/7 until it's finished," Annie added.

"After the riddle you've solved, this project should be easy," Dr. Lumbre said.

"Now…" Crane said. "Can you answer a non-science question for us?"

"Possibly."

"What can you tell us about Disney's involvement in your work?"

"They were one of my most generous sponsors," Dr. Lumbre said. "When I could no longer get NatGov funding, they provided financial assistance that allowed me to continue my work."

When Crane didn't follow up quickly, Annie asked, "What about that locked room beneath the Pirates of the Caribbean? What's in there?"

"I have an agreement with the Disney organization that prevents me from discussing certain aspects of our relationship," Dr. Lumbre said. "Even my top lieutenants don't know all the details."

Annie leaned forward. "Is Walt Disney in that room?"

Dr. Lumbre remained stoic. "I must respect my agreement with Disney. Let's talk genetics."

Crane glanced toward Annie and she rolled her eyes. At this point, he knew the legendary doctor well enough to realize that no one could change his mind. If NatGov hadn't been able to do it fifty years ago, he and Annie didn't stand a chance today. For the time being, they would have to toss in the towel on the Disney question and concentrate on Dar Lumbre's work.

"Okay," Crane said. "We'll get back to science."

Thirty minutes later, Dr. Lumbre began to tire, so Crane and Annie ended the visit and went to the lab to draw up plans for the upcoming project.

During the following month, the geneticists lived out Annie's 24/7 promise to Dr. Lumbre. After the first few days, they brought clothes and other necessities from their condos and stored them in a vacant supply closet. Often, they worked all night, catching only an occasional nap on sofas in the break room. Crane loved the work, and knew Annie did as well; still, he was glad to see light at the end of the tunnel.

As for the project, everything went right.

DNA from Dar Lumbre's mother was compatible with genetic material from the devil snake, and the new tissue exhibited outstanding results as it progressed through the resting phase, lag phase, and logarithmic growth phase. Crane named the new tissue DL-667, and released it to CellTech's Production Department, which began to produce artificial hearts at a record pace. Numerous backorders for the new hearts had piled up, and CellTech's stock price was rising exponentially.

Five weeks after the revival of Dar Lumbre, CellTech's Production Department fabricated the first heart from DL-667. The heart was flawless, and amid much fanfare, Lydia Keynes received the new heart. The surgery was performed at the Houston Mediplex, rather than the Bethesda Naval Hospital, where presidents and their families generally had medical treatment. Many believed the President changed locations in order to bring his personal cardiologist into the venue which included Dr. Lumbre.

Dr. Sean Tanner led the surgical team. He had mended his rift with CellTech, a situation that pleased all concerned. Crane and Annie watched the operation from CellTech's VIP booth. This time, they sat in a reserved box, along with Dr. Lumbre and Dr. Rosenberg. When Dr. Tanner entered the operating theater, he nodded in the direction of the reserved box.

Crane glanced at Annie.

She winked. "Now, we have credentials, too."

"Yeah, I guess."

Richard Hunter's surgery took place a week later. He showed no ill effects from the Code Blue emergency, or his time in a C-Unit. Again, results were perfect. Three days after his surgery, Kim and Larry took him to their newly acquired condo to convalesce.

Dar Lumbre, still technically a patient at Methodist Hospital, made regular tours of the CellTech facility, visiting often with Crane and Annie in the cytogenetics lab. He came mostly to talk, and relayed many stories of the 665 failures he encountered before producing DL-666. Surprisingly, the legendary doctor no longer showed any interest in hands-on genetics work, and began to concentrate on social and political ideas tangential to medical issues. The developer of DL-666 had passed his mantle to the Hopkins-Lee team and walked away.

One question was buzzing around the Mediplex constantly--would Dr. Lumbre settle in Houston, or go back to California to become more involved in the society that bore his name? The world waited for his answer.

When the time came, he answered the question in a decisive way. The day he was released from the hospital, Dr. Lumbre returned to Anaheim and joined Elmore Larson as the society prepared for their first nationwide rally. The event was scheduled to take place at the Anaheim Convention Center. The return of Dr. Lumbre raised the status of the society in dramatic fashion. In less than six months, they moved from rundown strip centers at the edge of cities to high-rent venues in prime locations.

Media pundits no longer doubted the viability of the movement. It was apparent to everyone that NatGov couldn't check the Dar Lumbre juggernaut, and they were no longer trying. Washington politicos on both sides of the aisle saw the handwriting on the wall, and the message was plain.

*Dar Lumbre couldn't be squelched a second time.*

## Chapter 37

Crane sat idly before the wall monitor, giving an occasional signal to rotate the holographic image in front of him. He glanced at the clock at the upper right of the screen, an act he'd repeated a dozen times since noon. Annie had not returned from lunch, and he wondered why. Being late was not in her DNA.

Annie had gone to lunch with Brad, saying that she might get back a little late. It was two o'clock now, and Crane knew she would have told him if she anticipated staying so long. He wondered if she and Brad were having an argument, although it didn't seem likely. They were never contentious with one another, at least not around him. But, something was wrong, and she hadn't called or texted. He was worried.

While he was pondering the situation, Annie burst into the lab. At first glance, Crane knew his suspicions were right. Annie looked flustered. Her eyes were red and her mascara smeared. Clearly, she'd been crying.

Crane jumped up. "Annie! What's wrong?"

Annie looked at Crane, and he could see a slight tremor in her lower lip. He'd never seen his uber-confident lab partner rattled about anything before.

"Brad and I broke up," she said in a low voice. Tears formed in her eyes and trickled down her cheeks.

"I'm sorry. What happened?"

Annie struggled to compose herself. "It's nothing. I'll be okay."

Crane put his hand on Annie's shoulder. "You can tell me anything."

A tear trickled slowly down Annie's cheek, and she didn't answer.

Crane caught Annie by the hand and led her to the adjoining lab stools where they'd spent countless hours working beside each other on CellTech projects. They sat down facing each other in the area which was a comfort zone for them, a place so familiar it was like a second home. But the scenario was different now. The scene had shifted from artificial hearts to affairs of the heart.

241

"Tell me what happened," Crane said. "I'm not going to let you evade the issue."

Annie daubed her eyes with a tissue. "Brad asked me to marry him."

"You're not crying because you're happy."

"I said *no*."

Crane's heart skipped a beat. "You said *no*?"

Annie nodded.

"Why?"

"You're the smartest guy I know. You figure it out."

They looked at each other, neither speaking for a long time. Crane stood and put his arms around Annie as she sat on the stool. He held her close, and felt her body tremble. She looked up at him and started to speak, but he touched her lips with one finger to silence her.

"There's something I want to say," Crane said.

Annie reached up and pushed Crane's hand away. "Well, what are you waiting for? Talk to me."

"I love you, Annie."

"I love you, too, Crane. But if we're so smart, why did it take us so long to figure it out?"

Chapter 38

On the first day of spring, Crane and Annie were sharing a beef teriyaki bowl at the Palace of Oriental Delights. They sat elbow-to-elbow with the usual array of eclectic patrons, some of whom were in Hollywood retro mode. Two Elvis impersonators sat at a nearby table, each proclaiming loudly that he looked exactly like the original. One of them leaned toward Annie. In a fake Southern drawl, he said, "Howdy, ma'am. Which one of us is the best Elvis?"

Annie mimicked the drawl. "I reckon I'd call it a draw. Ya'll both look fantastic."

"Thank you very much," the impersonator said. He turned back to his companion, and the friendly argument resumed.

Crane was totally relaxed for the first time since the DL-666 anomaly cropped up last October. Since then, he and Annie had eaten numerous meals at the Palace, not a single one without an accompanying problem to deliberate. Today, it was different. They were enjoying a major reversal of fortune.

Helena Cartwright had moved to her next OFS project, and Dr. Rosenfield had been reinstated as CEO and Technical Director of CellTech. To Crane, that was the first step toward normalcy.

He saw a bit of poetic justice in Dr. Cartwright's new assignment. Upon leaving CellTech, she had taken over as CEO of a large waste management company that recovered methane gas from garbage dumps containing excessive amounts of diapers. Not quite as glamorous as her CellTech assignment, to be sure.

Jerry Legrand had provided the biggest surprise of all. A month ago, he revealed that he was the Zodiac Prophet, and had made his predictions in order to publicize the Dar Lumbre Society. Upon finding out about Jerry's involvement in the scam, the society had revoked his membership, and Elmore Larson publically stated that Jerry no longer spoke for them. Undaunted, by this rejection, Jerry went back to Anaheim and became the leader of The Church of the Double Helix.

In Crane's opinion, the genetic odyssey had come to a near-perfect denouement.

As they were finishing their meal, the monitor over the bar exploded in a kaleidoscope of digitized fireworks. In unison, Crane and Annie fixed their eyes on the live broadcast. The much-anticipated convention of the Dar Lumbre Society was about to begin. Dr. Lumbre had told them to expect something big when he returned to California, but was still holding the details close to his vest when he left Houston.

The society's rally in the Anaheim Convention Center was receiving worldwide press coverage, and everyone was waiting to find out what the society planned to do. Rumors were running rampant.

The monitor showed a round-faced, middle-aged blond reporter on the verge of hyperventilating as he stood near the stage in the Anaheim Convention Center. "People from all over the country have turned out tonight to see Dar Lumbre," the reporter said. "They seem especially excited that he has been reunited with his brother, Elmore Larson. This is a monumental occasion in the history of political movements."

Behind the reporter, a throng of people milled about in aimless fashion. They cheered constantly, and waved banners. Many attendees with assigned seats were already in their places waiting for the convention to come to order. A band played onstage, but could barely be heard above the crowd noise. The whole scene was chaos—happy chaos.

A camera swept back and forth over the crowd for a few seconds, giving the announcer time to take a deep breath.

Annie looked at Crane. "Are you thinking what I'm thinking?" she asked.

Crane met her gaze and nodded knowingly. "Dar Lumbre is going to declare himself as a candidate for the presidency."

"Exactly," Annie said. "And he's going to do it in a way which is completely legal--as a write-in on both party's tickets. I don't see any way he could lose. President Keynes' approval rating has dropped below thirty percent. His hope and change rhetoric sounded good during the campaign, but he never delivered on any of it."

"The Republicans don't have an inspiring candidate either," Crane said. "They're considering the *white-haired-white-guy* routine again, and that hasn't worked well in a long time. This country is tired of slogans and excuses. We're ready for real change."

Annie started to speak, but stopped when the excited TV reporter announced, "Elmore Larson is coming to the podium."

Amid thunderous applause, and accompanied by the squawking of various novelty shop noisemakers, Elmore Larson marched confidentially to the podium. He looked over the crowd and waved. After three minutes of cheering, Larson held up his hands for silence.

Instantly, the crowd obeyed the charismatic Larson. A hush, abrupt and complete, fell over the hall.

"Thank you very much for that warm welcome," Larson said. "This is special night for the Dar Lumbre Society. It is our first national convention. Our great nation has already begun the presidential election process. As you know, President Keynes will be the Democrat candidate. The Republican Party will hold Super Tuesday activities in twenty states this month. Both the Democrat and Republican slates for all offices will be set after these primaries. We need to be ready as well. At this point, I'm going to dispense with the usual preliminaries which make political conventions terribly boring. I'm going to turn the podium over to our keynote speaker immediately. Without further ado, please welcome my brother, Dr. Dar Lumbre."

The crowd went wild again as Dar Lumbre appeared onstage and walked up to Elmore Larson. The two brothers embraced and patted each other on the back, after which Larson retreated behind the band and left the stage.

Dr. Lumbre turned to face the crowd, most of whom were in a near-ecstatic frenzy. After five minutes, he walked away from the podium and approached the rail near the edge of the stage. People in the front row came to the rail and stood with uplifted faces. Some reached up and tried to touch him. The stage lights shifted, making Dr. Lumbre's face appear to glow. The applause grew more tumultuous, giving no signs of waning.

Crane studied the crowd in the hall. Some had waited fifty years for this moment, while others had heard of the Dar Lumbre Society only months ago. Still, in spite of age differences and past sociopolitical leanings, this moment had united them into a formidable force. Dar Lumbre was a legendary figure in the world of medicine, even after his fifty-year interlude. Now, he was stepping into the political world to even greater acclaim.

Dr. Lumbre held up his hands for silence. The crowd did not stop cheering abruptly as they had done at his brother's signal, but over the next few minutes, the noise level abated slowly a few decibels at a time. Eventually, the hall was silent again.

"Good evening, my fellow Americans," Dar Lumbre said. "Thank you for that extraordinary welcome. Tonight, we take the next step on our journey toward a political future which will include everybody, even those of you known as Outsiders. In the past, you have not been served well by the entities who collected taxes from you. They used your money to further their own political ambitions, and set themselves up as the ruling elite. That must change..."

Another roar of applause swept through the crowd, completely drowning out Dar Lumbre's words. He waited patiently, with a faint smile on his thin lips.

Annie looked at Crane. "NatGov persecuted him fifty years ago. Now, he's going to get even."

Crane nodded. "His first few words are based on Page 10 of *The Double Helix Odyssey*. We should have seen that coming."

"That publication caused NatGov to turn against him fifty years ago. Now, he's waving it under their noses."

When the applause declined sufficiently, Dr. Lumbre continued, "If only Democrats and Republicans have the right to vote and hold office in this great country of ours, the bitter division between us will continue. We must claim our birthright. If we do not, the last chance to develop a genuine representative democracy may soon pass us by. True democracy will not come under the current system, which requires each of you to join one of the two approved parties in order to obtain your God given rights. We must change directions, or the nebulous and fragile democracy which Washington is holding together will crumble under its own weight. We are at a crossroads. We have a choice--either a government that includes everyone, or one that will eventually lead to anarchy. The power brokers who hold the reins of this system will kill the last vestiges of democracy if they deny the rights of those who disagree with them. Honest dissent cannot be squelched any longer. It is time for you to claim your birthright. Do so now--before it is too late."

Thunderous applause echoed through the chamber, completely drowning out the speaker again.

Eventually, the cheering waned, and Dr. Lumbre continued, "I've come here tonight for one purpose, and I will tell you right now what that purpose is. After meeting with high-level organizers in all fifty-two states, I have agreed to run as a write-in candidate for the office of President of the United States..."

Everyone in the audience stood in unison, and deafening applause resumed. Hundreds of red, white, and blue balloons appeared from secret locations throughout the hall and floated lazily above the heads of the frenzied crowd, coming to rest against the ceiling.

The ovation roared on and on in the background as news banners scrolled across the screen:

INSTANT POLLS
DR. LUMBRE'S APPROVAL RATING AT 90%
ELECTION ASSURED

Annie's dark eyes twinkled. "It'll be good to know the President of the United States. Do you think he'll invite us to his inauguration?"

Crane put his arm around Annie and drew her close. "Of course he will, and we'll ask President Lumbre to arrange for us to sit next to Walt Disney."

THE END

---

247

## ABOUT THE AUTHOR

I was born in rural East Texas a long time ago, and grew up with a sister and a brother. Upon completing high school, I joined the U.S. Air Force and served three years as a jungle survival instructor in Panama. Following my military service, I enrolled in Stephen F. Austin State University and got married. After getting my degree in biology and chemistry, we moved to Houston where our only child, a son, was born. I worked fifteen years as a chemist for companies in the Houston area, then started my own business.

I have been a member of Sugar Land Baptist Church for over 20 years, and have led Bible study classes throughout that time. Many of my best friends are in Bible study together. My wife of 53 years died of cancer in 2014, leaving me the patriarch of a small family--a son, a daughter-in-law, and three grandchildren. In 2018, a new family member was born, a great granddaughter. My family is my pride and joy.

I wrote numerous technical articles and reports during the early years of my career, but no fiction until recently. Upon retirement, I began to study fiction writing, especially concentrating on science fiction, the genre I love. *The Dar Lumbre Chronicles* is my first venture into the world of self-published paperbacks; hopefully, it will not be my last as another work is in progress, *The Mirror Image Conspiracy*. Look for it in a year or so.